Also by Lucy Bexley

No Strings

Must Love Silence

The Bright Side

Checking It Twice

Just My Type

Flying First

First Day: A Flying First Short

HOWL

Home of the Wayward Lovers

Lucy Bexley

Edited by: Em Schreiber

Synopsis

Lou McCallister owns HOWL, the only surviving queer bar in Boston. When an investment opportunity to save the floundering bar is inadvertently sabotaged by Clementine Darby, Howl's newest employee, Lou is ready to give up. Now Clem will do anything she can to make it right and keep Howl alive, but will she be able to save the bar in time? This sapphic Coyote Ugly reimagining brings the funny and the feels.

)O(

This book is part of the I Heart SapphFic Pride Collection, which contains eight standalone books from some of the top authors in sapphic fiction today. Each one promises a Pride theme and a happy ending. The collection was organized by I Heart SapphFic, which is a website for authors and readers of sapphic fiction to stay up to date on all the latest sapphic fiction news.

Em, you deserve credit for every comma and many of the words in between those little teardrops, too.

Acknowledgments

A heartfelt thank you to T.B. Markinson, Miranda MacLeod, and I Heart SapphFic for creating this project. Thanks also to the other authors in this project—Haley Cass, Cara Malone, Lily Seabrooke, Nicole Pyland, Erica Lee, and Bryce Oakley—it was fun to work with so many people I admire.

Thanks to everyone who supported this project and preordered books in this series for charity. I'll be donating to The Trevor Project, which focuses on suicide prevention efforts among lesbian, gay, bisexual, transgender, queer, and questioning youth.

To my amazing editor, Em. You are an actual angel. There are not enough synonyms in the English language for how much I appreciate you, but I'm sure you could help me find a few.

Susie and Steph Shea—you read the earliest, messiest versions of these chapters and encouraged me all the same. Thanks for helping these characters take shape.

Monica, Haley, and Mila the group chat saved me. Love you all.

Thanks to Bryce Oakley for supporting the idea for Howl early on and watching Coyote Ugly with me (she had no complaints)!

To Meryl Wilsner and the awesome members of the productivity zoom for helping me get back to writing after a very difficult time.

We all have Christi Lincoln to thank for the bartop dance song selection, you are a visionary.

G, thanks for all you do to keep us afloat so I can write jokes on the internet and also in word documents. It's a dream come true.

Thank you to my gram for letting me write some of this book at her bedside before she passed away in March. Thanks for hand-selling my books to your hospice nurse and for always making me feel like the most cherished person in the world. You will forever be my favorite person.

And most of all, thank you to anyone who has read one of my books. None of this would be possible without your support.

Chapter One
Clementine

W ho the fuck steals a Toyota?"

The voice of Clementine Darby's best friend buzzed against the Formica table in front of her. A nasty look from a woman and child in the booth next to her had Clem scrambling to take her phone off speaker. "Sam," she whispered harshly. "Can you appreciate how that is absolutely not the point of this story?"

It was a tale as old as time: a woman decides to bravely change her life but stops for a snack on the way. The universe punishes her for the rest of eternity. Probably. When she'd emerged with sour watermelon gummies, her *third-choice* candy, her car was not where she'd left it, which meant neither were her clothes or computer or... her life.

"I'm just saying if I was at a gas station and I had my choice between your grandma's old Corolla and literally any other car I would—"

"Sam! I'm stranded in a very depressing McDonald's that smells vaguely of gasoline and I'm trying to figure out a new life plan. Can you maybe not insult my car right now?"

"Fine, fine. So, your big move to the city was a bust. That's okay. You can come back to Hart's Hollow and regroup. Mi sofa es su sofa."

"I just—"

"Hold on a sec."

Clem heard a muffled sound and knew she had been summarily tucked into Sam's cleavage as her friend carried things to her car. She was mostly used to it by now except for that one time where they had been on a video call and well, nothing against Sam, but Clem wasn't looking to repeat that anytime soon. The whole experience had reminded her of Mrs. Frizzle and the Magic School Bus boldly going where a school bus full of children should never be.

She patiently listened to the click of her friend's heels against the flagstone steps in front of the Hart's Hollow Library, Sam's laugh as she said goodbye to her colleagues, all the sounds of her best friend on the move that she knew so well, and Clementine felt just the tiniest twinge of missing home. Which was absurd, she hadn't even been gone for half a day. The perky chirp of Sam's jeep unlocking pulled her attention back. The car started, and a loud blast of Bonnie Raitt cut off abruptly.

"Okay," Sam said, a little breathless. "Are you safe where you are? Look, I know you're disappointed, but coming back to Hart's Hollow isn't the worst thing in the world. Boston will still be there next year."

Next *year*? The mention of delaying her move again sent a queasy feeling through Clem. She'd spent months saving and planning and one very unpleasant night breaking her father's heart when she'd told him she was leaving. If she went back, she'd never make it out again. She couldn't explain how she knew that, but she felt it like her own heartbeat. Clem in Hart's Hollow took over the diner for her dad and maintained the garden her mom had started twenty years ago and lived with a deep, aching sense of loneliness. She didn't want to be that Clementine. She couldn't.

"Did I lose you?" Concern clouded Sam's voice. "I just got off work so I can be there in like five hours. Three if I don't stop for snacks."

"What kind of snacks are you getting? A buffet? A three-course meal?"

"It's not my fault the lines are long at the new Starbucks now that Betty's Brew went out of business. Momma needs her macchiato. Though I will say I've learned a lot of new ways to spell 'Sam'."

Clem rolled her eyes. "I am begging you not to refer to yourself as 'momma' or in the third person."

"Look baby, momma's gotta do what she's gotta do."

Clem stifled a laugh. "I hate you."

"I hate you more. Now drop me a pin and if you're taking orders, I'll have a vanilla milkshake and fries."

"No, Sam, I—" Clem took a deep, calming breath.

Sam sighed. "Fine, no fries. Though I'm not sure this is a time to be stingy with your knight-in-shining-armored-vehicle."

"No, Sam, as in I can't come back to Hart's Hollow. I have to do this. I'm supposed to meet my new roommate in like an hour and my stuff is gone and my car and my life. *Shit.*" Clementine winced and shot an apologetic look to the mother and child next to her, then focused on her heartbeat to keep the tears at bay. She'd called Sam because she knew her friend wouldn't feel sorry for her. When she was sad, the absolute last thing Clem could handle was someone being kind to her. She'd take Sam's sarcasm to stave off tears any day. "I can't believe I've already messed this up."

"Clem, I know that car was your grandma's, but it was also a deathtrap. I'm not even sure it had airbags. I just think maybe this isn't the worst thing. I mean, obviously, it's not a good problem to have, like all your clothes are gone or whatever, but we can fix this. Hell, maybe it's even a sign from the universe."

"What kind of sign?" Clem's body went still. She'd never been as into omens as Sam, but over the years her friend had been right more often than she was wrong. The thought of another regular night with her best friend washed over Clementine like a warm bath, the kind of thing you crave at the end of a long day. Sam was the comfort she'd clung to these past few years.

"A sign that you belong back home with meeee?" Sam dragged out the word, and Clementine could picture the grin on her best friend's face. How her hair would be falling out of its bun after a day at the library. How her inappropriately sexy vintage dress would somehow still look great. She glanced down at her own cutoff jean shorts and diner t-shirt. Her boat had sunk, and now she had to do her damndest to swim to shore.

Clementine grit her teeth. "Sam, I have to do this."

"Okay." Sam sobered like she sensed the determination renewed in her friend. "But hear me out—do you?" She asked gently.

"Yes." Clem closed her eyes and nodded. Something in her life had to change. She'd felt suffocated in Hart's Hollow, as though each day there pulled the strings of the perpetual diner apron she wore a bit tighter.

"Okay, hold on, I'm pulling over." Tires squealed, punctuating Sam's statement.

A few minutes of rumpled silence followed while Sam seemed to be getting herself situated.

"Okay, all set. Your Uber will be there in seventeen minutes."

"Wait, how? I never told you where I was and there's no way you googled McDonald's and interstate because there's one every five miles."

"You never turned off location sharing after you went hiking last month."

"Oh." Clem swallowed the lump forming in her throat. Just like that, Sam had solved her immediate problem. Her friend was hours away, and still she felt surrounded by her love.

"Look, Clemmy, if you're going to go through with this, promise me you'll live a little.

Clem blinked at the sudden change in topic. "I am living."

"I mean really live. You've spent years holding everything together for your family. This is your chance to have an adventure, kiss a stranger, make some big mistakes. Those are the things that make life worthwhile."

"Mistakes?"

"Lots of mistakes," Sam said. "I'll send you the info for this car and then I'm going to hop on this coffee line. I have so much Grey's Anatomy to catch up on."

"Hey, Sam?" Clem brushed at the tears in her eyes with a napkin the consistency of sandpaper.

"Mm-hmm."

"I love you."

"If you don't text me when you get there, I will show up at your door and murder you."

CLEMENTINE SAT in the backseat of a black suburban, dipping fries into her vanilla milkshake because Sam had made one or two good points.

Outside the tinted window, she watched the city lurch by in fits and starts. Little slices of life passed by at every red light: a man who was not an athlete dressed head-to-toe in professional Red Sox gear, glove on hand as though he expected a foul ball to fall from the sky, a woman drinking an iced coffee the size of her head, way too many Goldendoodles.

Maybe if she'd gotten an iced coffee instead of her candy, she'd be driving herself through the city right now and not wondering where her next clean pair of underwear would come from. Oh god, where *would* they come from?

The driver came to a screeching halt as a flock of extremely large, prehistoric-looking birds approached their SUV.

"Ugh, these wise guys don't have anything better to do?"

"You mean the turkeys?" The birds were unbelievably big, the size of garbage cans, with cold, dead eyes and seemingly no fucks to give. They *were* giving her new life goals. It occurred to Clementine that she'd never properly seen a turkey before. They looked... not at all like an outline of a child's hand. And she certainly hadn't been expecting them in the city. "Does this happen a lot?"

"Yeah, forget the mob. The little gang out there runs this town."

They sat in silence for a few moments while the offending birds pecked at the road like it was covered in grain. Assuming that's what turkeys ate. Did she actually not know anything about them? "Can't you just honk?"

"Nah, it only emboldens them." He unbuckled his seatbelt and opened the door. As he shooed the birds across the road, she thought for a moment that she might be about to witness a murder. *A murder most fowl.* Clementine laughed to herself. It was the kind of dumb joke her father would love, and as soon as he started taking her calls again, she'd tell it to him. Probably.

"Sorry about that," the driver said as he slid back into his seat and put the car into drive. "Not much longer now. Is this your first time here?"

"Why do you ask?"

"You seemed surprised by the turkeys."

"Oh, right. No, I'm just moving here. Or trying to, except

6

that my car got stolen from the parking lot, which is why I called you, and now I feel a little defeated."

"Oh yeah, that'll happen. What kind of car was it?"

The response struck her as odd, but she was grateful for the conversation. Anything that kept her too busy to check on what was happening at home. "It was, um, a Corolla, older than me. It was my grandma's, actually."

"That's messed up. I didn't realize people stole old cars."

Clem's mind went to the laundry basket in the trunk full of her favorite clothes. The perfectly worn-in jeans she'd never see again and, oh god, her boots. "I know. It had sentimental value, but also all my stuff was in it—"

Before she could finish, the SUV came to a halt along the curb and the door locks popped open.

"You all set with your bags?"

Clem looked down at her purse and the crumpled fast food paper bag. "It'll be a struggle, but I think I can handle it."

As the car pulled away, she gazed up at the building.

There must have been a hundred steps to get to the front door, and all of them seemed to be crumbling. Maybe it was a blessing in disguise that she wasn't trying to carry her belongings up.

She huffed her way to the front door as she texted her new roommate. She'd met Alyssa once, over Skype, and she got the feeling she might have sublet the room to anyone.

Alyssa: *The front door lock doesn't work, just come up to the fifth floor.*

The lock doesn't work? That didn't seem like a good sign. She shouldered open the door and peered up the winding staircase. Bits of dust danced in the light streaming through the windows. It was very close to beautiful. The boards gave a little as she

7

climbed the stairs, pausing to catch her breath halfway up when it turned out the fifth floor was actually the sixth.

BEFORE SHE COULD KNOCK on 5A, the door flew open and Alyssa stood in the entryway, looking breathless. She was in a crop top that said 'e-turtle peace' and in extremely tiny bright yellow spandex shorts, her cheeks still flushed with whatever exercise she'd been doing.

Clementine had to pull her eyes away from Alyssa's abs. She wasn't usually one to stare. Maybe she was so tired from her trip that her brain was short-circuiting. Or maybe no one in her hometown greeted her half-naked.

"Don't mind me, I was sweating to the oldies."

"I don't know what that means."

"It means I was doing a spin class with songs from, like, the 80s." Alyssa made a sweeping gesture and Clem stepped into the apartment. The door creaked behind them and shut with a thunk that indicated broken hardware.

"I don't think the 80s are oldies."

"Sure they are! Anything older than me is an oldie and anything younger than me is a baby. I don't make the rules."

Clementine laughed. Listening to Alyssa was like watching a cartoon, confusing but not unpleasant. "I'm pretty sure you just made up that rule."

"Okay, Miss *I'm determined to take everything seriously*. I'll show you to your room. Franklin left all the furniture like we talked about. Well, bed, dresser, and a rug you will almost definitely want to throw out."

Alyssa pushed open the door to a narrow space. The light from the solitary window on the far wall seemed to be doing a much more efficient job at turning the bedroom into a sauna rather than providing a light source.

"Welcome home!" Alyssa pushed past her and launched onto the bare mattress. "Where's your stuff?"

"Hopefully still in my car with the person who stole it."

"Oh shit. Did they steal it with you in it?" Alyssa's blue eyes were so wide and full of wonder that Clementine was reminded of those pictures of the earth from space. Alyssa sat up as she appeared to wait for an answer.

Clementine paused while she tried to decide if she should take the question seriously. "No?"

"Well, that's good. Stuff is just stuff. You can always get more. I have extra sheets and things you can borrow, too."

"Let's hope I can figure out a way to get more money first."

Alyssa's eyes lit up as she squeezed Clem's bicep. "You should come to Howl later."

"What's that?"

"How do you not know Howl? It's only like, the best sapphic bar in Boston. I mean, it's also the *only* one, but it is the best. And it's even better since I started working there. You'll love it, very queer but in a laid-back way."

"What makes you think I'm queer? I mean, you're not wrong, but I'm curious." Not once in all her years in Hart's Hollow had anyone aside from Sam read her as sapphic.

"Honestly?" Alyssa tilted her head and tapped her chin. "Yup, it's the length of your cut-offs."

Clem couldn't hold in her incredulous laugh. "What?"

"Put your arms at your sides. I bet the hem reaches your fingertips."

Clem did as she was told, fighting back a blush as her fingertips fell several inches short of the ragged edge of the denim.

Alyssa laughed, but it sounded delighted, not judgmental. "That length is adhering to a high school dress code, my love. I've got my scissors around here somewhere if you fancy a little trim," she said, raising her eyebrows.

"At this point, I'm not willing to part with any of my clothes, even if it is just a few inches of them."

Alyssa shrugged. "Suit yourself." She paused for a moment, then laughed. "I just got the joke. Anyway, don't stress about it. Your shorts will be accepted and so will you. Like I said, it's a very chill space."

"What does that mean?" Only an hour in the city and already Clementine felt like she couldn't keep up.

"It means glitter optional but encouraged, by me mostly. I'm pretty sure Lou is fundamentally opposed to glitter."

"Who's Lou?"

"You'll see." The wink she gave was exaggerated, her unbelievably long eyelashes fluttering likc they were too heavy for the gesture.

"Were you wearing fake eyelashes to exercise?"

"One thing you need to know about me is that I'm always wearing fake eyelashes." Alyssa stood, flipping her hair dramatically over her shoulder. "I need to get ready, but I'll text you the address. Come around nine." She looked Clementine slowly up and down. "And feel free to borrow something cute from my closet."

Clementine half expected her to evaporate in a cloud of pink smoke, but instead, she just walked down the hall and closed the bathroom door.

Chapter Two
Lou

Lou turned her key in the lock and eased open the door to the old, cape-style house. Before she stepped inside, she bent to scoop up the mail from the front mat as she went: animal shelter fundraising, meal service, credit card offer, credit card offer, credit card offer, student loan scam, and oh, wouldn't you know it, yet another credit card offer. If people took their mail seriously, it could ruin their life.

The final envelope was lavender and stopped Lou in her tracks. Though she hadn't seen it in years, she'd know the soft loops of her mother's handwriting anywhere. She knew Grandma and her mom talked. Even after how her mom had treated Lou and their subsequent falling out, seeing evidence of it still knocked Lou for a loop every time.

"Hey Gram, it's me." Her voice sounded choked, and she cleared her throat. The card was none of her business.

The silence she was met with was as loud as a siren. Chances were, her grandma was just watching one of her shows. Or had taken out her hearing aids. Again. But those rationalizations didn't stop Lou's heart from shifting up a gear or two. There was always that worry in the back of her mind, that 'what if?'

What if today was the day she lost the only person who truly mattered to her? The very best part of herself.

With her disastrous trip to the bank to beg for a loan to stop the implosion of her bar, she hadn't gotten over to Dorchester in a few days, as evidenced by the pile of junk mail she was currently clutching to her chest. But what good was saving Howl from eviction if she let down the only family she still had? The thought of losing her business—the last queer bar in Boston—made Lou feel like her heart had been shucked clean out of her chest.

Lou made her way through the house toward the back bedroom. A pitiful yip and the clatter of paws on hardwood drew her attention a moment before Canoodle, her grandma's toy poodle, crashed into her leg with the force of a falling leaf. She ripped up scams and pyramid schemes, all targeting Eleanor McCallister, then dumped the entire pile into the full recycling bin, making a note to take it outside before she headed back to work. She clutched the pale purple envelope in her hand, wishing and not wishing that it could go into the bin, too.

"Gram?" she called again.

Still, no response greeted her as she wandered into the bedroom with Canoodle at her heels. She pushed open the door to find her grandma lying on her bed beneath an afghan she'd made herself before Lou was even born. It was one of the most beautiful things Lou had ever seen, even though she suspected its bright orange and blue yarn might be a little garish to someone else. Probably to anyone not too blinded by love for the woman who had made it, to see that it was, in fact, a little ugly. So often beauty had absolutely nothing to do with the way something looked and everything to do with how it made you feel. And this blanket made Lou feel warm, even from across the room.

"Gram, are you asleep?"

"Just resting my eyes, dear."

"It's almost three in the afternoon. Are you cold? Is something wrong?"

The dog scrambled up onto the bed like a free climber on Denali fighting for his life.

It was a warm day for May, well into the 70s, but the space was cool with the curtains drawn against the bright sun.

"No, I'm perfect. I tried to read my book, but I think they made the font smaller again."

Lou barked out a laugh. "This would stop being an issue if you'd use the e-reader I got you."

"That thing's too fiddly. Besides, then you'd be able to see all the steamy books I'm reading." A smile cracked across her gram's dry lips.

"As opposed to now, when I pick them up from the library for you and can clearly see the shirtless young Lothario on the cover there."

"He's a duke, thank you very much."

"Of course, my mistake. Here, I brought in your mail." Lou set the card on the nightstand and made her way over to the window. She walked slowly. She didn't need to run from the card. And besides, she wasn't the one who had anything to be sorry for.

Lou parted the curtains an inch as a test balloon, pausing to see if her grandma would protest. When she didn't, Lou committed and pulled them open all the way, watching as the dust particles in the room danced in the stream of sunlight. She really needed to find some time to come over and do a deep clean. Her life falling apart was severely hampering her ability to keep her grandma's life on track.

"Ah," her grandma said. "I suppose you saw who this is from."

"Yeah, my mom." Lou nodded, the word *mom* stinging her

13

mouth like bottom shelf vodka. She hadn't seen her family in years. Why was she feeling anything at all?

"I can read this later." Her grandma shoved the envelope under her pillow.

Lou bristled. She didn't need to be babied, definitely not with this. "It's fine, Gram. I've gotten over losing her love a long time ago."

Eleanor frowned. "Oh honey, you never get over that."

Lou swallowed hard, turning back to the window so she could blink her tears away in private. Her parents had been the first to teach her that if you belonged to someone, you gave them the power to cast you out. That was a mistake she didn't make anymore, her gram being the only exception, grandfathered in because she predated the lesson.

"Agree to disagree," Lou said, turning back around and smiling. "How about you get up and give me a hug, and then I'll make you some food?"

"You know I can cook for myself, Louise."

"Yes, Gram, I know that. But it makes me feel good to do it for you."

"Fine, as long as we can both acknowledge that I'm saying *yes* for you." Eleanor's blue eyes twinkled as she slid on her jaunty, bright pink glasses.

"So generous, I know where I get it from." Lou rolled her eyes, but smiled as she offered her hand to help her grandma out of bed.

The 'something smells good in here' perfume of garlic and onion permeated the air as Lou dumped a cutting board's worth of potatoes into the pot while she carefully avoided stepping on Canoodle, who was camped out at her feet. When she cooked for her gram—which was the only time she cooked if she was being honest—she tried to make hearty meals that would last a few days.

Usually, her grandma was a good sport about eating left-overs, though Lou found takeout bags stuffed into the trash a little more often than she'd like. A cursory glance at the fridge indicated that the lasagna Lou had made a few days ago was mostly untouched, the noodles and cheese now nearly petrified beneath the foil. Lou held the Pyrex dish up accusingly in front of her grandma. She debated turning it over like a Dairy Queen Blizzard for the drama of it, but she wasn't sure about the adhesion properties of cold mozzarella.

Eleanor's eyes widened as she assumed a face of innocence and wrongful accusal. "I had bridge yesterday and I ate at Carol's."

Lou raised an eyebrow. "Did you eat more than just chips there? Because last time—"

"There were vegetables involved. Scout's honor." Her grandma smiled, a dimple revealing itself beneath the laugh lines around her mouth. Her pink lipstick was smudged, but still mostly on point.

"Is there any particular reason you were wearing lipstick to nap?"

"I told you I wasn't napping. I was—"

"Yeah, yeah," Lou said, waving her off. "You were resting your eyes. That doesn't answer the question, Gram."

"I had coffee with Joseph earlier."

"Remind me who Joseph is?" Lou turned her attention back to the pot, adding in the carrots.

"Louise," Eleanor drew out her name, sounding exasperated. "You know Joseph. Father Joe from church."

Lou bit back a smile. "Can't he be disbarred or something? For fraternizing with parishioners?"

"He's not a lawyer and it was just coffee."

"Gram, coffee is never just coffee." Lou didn't trust this guy, even if he was a priest. A literal prince could try to take her grandma out for coffee, and she'd feel uneasy about it. That was the trouble with someone being so good to you. No one else was ever quite good enough for them.

"You're right." Eleanor put up her hands in mock defeat. "I had a cookie too. One of those Mint Milanos."

Lou narrowed her eyes. "So you had coffee earlier, and that's it?"

"That's it. Isn't it kind of the dream scenario? Someone who just wants to chat, will never expect me to take care of them, and won't be moving into my house?"

Lou laughed. It did sound kind of dreamy. Lou had never been one for relationships, and her work interactions were limited. As the boss, she had to keep everyone at arm's length. Even more so now that the future of the bar was uncertain at best come the end of summer. "Fine, fair points. But if this guy crosses a line, I'll be showing up at his place of business."

"Well, that would be a first, since his place of business is the church I can never seem to drag you to."

"I work really late, Gram. It's hard to get up early. Plus, you know, I don't like going there with the threat of bursting into flames and all."

Lou put the finishing touches on the pot of soup. "Okay, now this just needs to simmer for about an hour. Do you want me to stay and watch it or are you okay to turn it off? I guess I can call to remind you—I'll set an alarm on my phone."

"Louise." She could tell her grandma was biting back a smile, her expression so much like Lou's own that it was like looking into a mirror. "I'm eighty, not an invalid. I can turn off the soup."

Okay, a time travel mirror, but still.

"Fine. I do have some things I want to take care of before the bar opens tonight."

"Oh, like maybe finding a nice girl to bring home to meet me?"

"Sure, that. Or like, you know, washing my dishes."

Eleanor sighed dramatically. "I suppose washing your dishes is an important step on the path to meeting a nice girl."

Lou rolled her eyes. "I hope you mean 'a nice woman.'" Setting aside the fact that anyone younger than forty was considered basically a teen by Eleanor, she knew she was lucky to have the kind of relationship where her grandma teased her about needing a girlfriend instead of idly wondering if she'd ever change her mind and marry a nice boy from the neighborhood. But some days, the pressure to settle down with a woman was still pressure that made Lou squirm.

And that pressure combined with the stress of the situation with the bar was kicking up Lou's desire to do something drastic and meaningless to blow off some steam. It was something she'd been trying to be better about ever since her last one-night stand had come back to the bar and thrown a $400 dollar bottle of scotch at her head. This time she'd go for someone who looked nice, and also like they couldn't throw. She'd learned her lesson about softball players.

She put the lid on the pot and lowered the heat until the flame was just a flicker. Lou gathered up the bag of recycling before heading back through the house, avoiding Canoodle like the tripwire he was, her grandma hot on her heels. She paused in the living room and turned to face her. "I guess you could always set a timer for the soup. Do you want me to go back and set one?"

"Louise, I will turn off the stove, I promise."

"Okay then." Lou brushed her hands down the front of her jeans, glancing around the living room to see if there was anything she'd missed that she could take care of quickly. "I'll come back tomorrow. Sunday's my day off this week. Just leave your laundry and stuff until then. I'll clean out the fridge tomorrow, too. I'd tell you not to have the old lasagna, but you eating it really wasn't the problem."

"Very funny." Eleanor rolled her eyes. "If you come by in the morning, you can go to the 10:00 a.m. service with me. I was telling Father Joe all about your bar, and I'm sure he would love to see you, ask you some questions about it."

"Fat chance," Lou whispered under her breath.

"What was that?"

"I'll do my best, but I have to work pretty late tonight. And you know the bar's in trouble, Gram. I'm not sure I can find a way to save it this time." Lou gave her a sad smile and pecked her on the cheek. "And please, for the love of god, eat the soup."

"Language, Lulu," Eleanor said, holding open the door for Lou to exit. "I'll see you tomorrow, my love. Remember, if you ask, the Lord will provide."

Chapter Three
Clementine

owl didn't exist. After wandering around the South End for twenty minutes, searching for street addresses like she was playing one of those hidden image games, Clementine was now sure that Alyssa had been messing with her. An incredible underground sapphic bar, the oldest and last in the city, seemed to be as much of a unicorn as it sounded.

Clementine paused to watch two women approach a scarred, red metal door. It blended in so well with the brick exterior of the building that she hadn't seen it at first glance. One of the women had an undercut, a promising sign that sent a little flutter of anticipation through Clem's chest. Maybe she *was* in the right place, even if nothing else about the location—from the industrial buildings to the sparse streetlights—indicated that. The street overall had a murder-y vibe, like at any moment a detective would discover a body between two of the buildings.

A few blocks over, she'd passed restaurants with outdoor seating filled with laughing men in enough gingham plaid to suggest a run on J. Crew. But this section of Machine St. was so deserted, she'd even seen a rat just walking down the sidewalk like he was on his way home from work. It was an established fact that all rats were guys who spoke with a thick New York accent. Would they have Boston accents here? Another mystery she'd need to uncover.

She'd been ready to text Alyssa that she'd just see her at home, but something had stopped her, pushing her to circle one more time. This was her first night in the city after all, and it wasn't like she had anything better—or anything at all —to do.

Sure, she'd had a long, shitty day that had culminated with the police basically laughing off her complaint about her stolen car. But still, this was why she'd left Maine. She wanted adventures and opportunities. After years of surviving, she was ready to live.

Clementine approached the nondescript door just as a group of women in satin sashes and tiaras spilled out. Curious. The only indication that it was a place where people might be welcomed was the wrought iron sign above the door showcasing the cutout of a wolf with its head thrown back. In the top right corner of the sign, was a sliver of moon.

She raised her hand to knock and then thought better of it. This wasn't some speakeasy—though it might have been one once. Now it was just a grungy bar hiding in plain sight. Maybe it was a safety tactic—like those butterflies who looked like moss to hide from predators. The thought sent a shiver down her spine. *Get it together, oh my darlin' Clementine.* She could practically hear her best friend's voice in her head. *You're the butterfly. This place is for you.*

The door nearly collided with the bouncer's knee when she pushed it open with renewed confidence. They were in a small vestibule lit by a purple neon light that approximated the sign she'd seen outside, only the glow made the wolf look other-worldly. The person sitting on the stool reminded Clementine of someone from the 50s just getting off work from the assembly line. They ran a hand through their dark, slicked-back hair and looked up at her. James Dean, eat your heart out. Arms sheathed in tattoos were showcased by the rolled-up sleeves of their white t-shirt. Rounding out the outfit was a pair of suspenders that ran down to the waist of black pants tucked into scuffed leather work boots. The vibe was quite... effective. There weren't a lot of people that looked like *that* back home.

"ID?"

"Oh, right, sorry." Clementine dug into her back pocket and flipped through cards until she found her license. It had been years since she'd been carded, probably not since her twenty-first birthday when her dad had made a big show of it at the Dirty's—Hart's Hollow's beloved dive bar—as a formality before he bought everyone a round of Natty. That's what happened when the town you grew up in topped out at 300 people.

She handed the card over and tried not to think of the unfortunate Sam-inflicted bangs the picture displayed. We were all young and heartbroken once.

"Okay, Clementine Darby. You're almost all set. I think you know what you have to do."

Clementine did not know what she had to do. Was there some rule about being gay in the city? A secret handshake or code word she didn't know about? She was about to say as much when the bouncer pointed to the sign. "Full moon tonight. The rules are the rules."

"And what rules would those be?" Clementine forced a smile as she shoved her hands into the pockets of her denim cutoffs. She had a guess and she hated it.

"Well, they don't call 'er 'Howl' for nothing. Let's see what you've got."

"No way. That can't be a requirement." She looked back at

the door to the exit. She could still return to the apartment like none of this had ever happened.

"It is, but just for pretty women." The bouncer winked, tucking back a strand of dark hair that had fallen across their forehead.

"Isn't it usually the opposite? Like pretty women get drinks free, and not that they're subjected to public humiliation."

"Trust me," the bouncer's eyes made a slow appraisal over Clementine's body in a way that felt much more flattering than it did gross. A talent. "You'll get plenty of free drinks. And everyone who's ever been drunk knows that it almost always comes with a side of public humiliation. You've gotta loosen up. Here, I'll go first."

And then, without further ado, the bouncer braced their hands on their knees, head thrown back, and howled, holding the baleful note for a surprisingly long time. When it was over, they caught Clem's eye and smiled.

Clementine froze, too stunned for several moments to move, simply gawking at the bouncer bathed in purple light who had transformed something horrifying into a sound that was almost beautiful. Her thoughts were interrupted when the door pushed open behind her, hitting Clem in the back and propelling her forward.

The bouncer shot out their hand to hold the door and stop it from opening. "Just a minute," they called before returning their attention back to Clementine. "It's now or never if you want to do it without an audience."

"Fine." Clementine squeezed her eyes closed as she threw back her head and let out a sound that sounded an alarming amount like an injured cat.

Mercifully, a raspy chuckle cut her off. "Yeah, okay. I can see why you didn't want to do that." They pushed open the interior door and held it for Clem. "You can head on in."

)(

THE INSIDE of the bar was vampire dark, with a soft purple glow as the main source of illumination. Clementine felt like she was stepping into a frat party at Halloween rather than a sapphic bar in May. Even in the dim light, the place looked a bit run down, like a shrine to years past. She half expected to see plastic slipcovers on the barstools. Clem waited for her eyes to adjust a bit more before scanning the space for Alyssa, who appeared to be... nowhere. Great. No problem. Clem could be alone at a bar. Not that she'd ever done it before, but that's what self-possessed, sophisticated adults did, right? Or at least that's what they did in the movies. Clem was supposed to be having an adventure. But maybe she should call Sam, just to be sure.

She pulled out a battered stool and smiled at the bartender, who scowled back behind a curtain of dark brown hair. Clem smiled harder. Sam always said that Clem met adversity with adorableness, and she wasn't wrong. Kill 'em with kindness. As long as they end up dead you might as well be nice about it.

The woman walked over slowly, crossing her arms over her chest when she reached Clementine. Her posture was the picture-book example of closed-off and grumpy. Hot in the meanest way possible. "What can I get you?"

"Just a water to start."

"Water, water, everywhere."

"And not a drop to drink?" Clem furrowed her brow. Were they playing some kind of poetry Jeopardy?

"Look at that," the woman said with mock astonishment. "She's smarter than she looks."

23

Clem tried not to bristle. If this was the welcome she was getting, maybe alcohol would be better after all. Not that she liked to use drinking to solve her discomfort, but when in Rome... "Um, what kind of Merlot would you recommend?"

"None, next question."

Was there a next question? She paused, trying to come up with one. It seemed better to just order with authority. She could see why Alyssa had said the bar needed help. "Okay, I'll take the house red then."

"Look, hon," the woman sneered, bracing her hands on the bar top and leaning forward. Clementine wasn't sure she'd ever heard "hon" leveled as an insult before—it was a masterclass in tone versus content. "Can I let you in on a little something?"

Clem swallowed and nodded. Was she doing this all wrong? She wanted to bolt, but she absolutely would not let herself do that. So instead she curled her fingers around the edges of her seat, letting the splintering wood bite into her palms.

"Howl is not a bar for tourists."

Okay, she could deal with regular city-mean, an insular mindset. But she *was* a Bostonian now, technically only for a few hours, but still. It counted. She'd already had her car stolen, for god's sake. The city owed her a freaking glass of shitty red wine. Maybe even on the house! Instead of saying any of this, she smiled again, tamping down a mild concern that her teeth were likely glowing in the violet light. "Oh no, I'm not a tourist, I just moved here."

And that jerk behind the bar rolled her eyes. Clementine had served her fair share of not particularly kind customers at her family's diner over the years. Sure, she'd dreamt of 'accidentally' dropping chili cheese fries on rowdy guys many a night, but never once had she rolled her eyes directly at one of them.

"Not that kind of tourist. We actually just asked a bunch of you to leave. I'm guessing that was your party?"

"My *party*?" Clem glanced around the bar, but it was still early enough that it was fairly empty. She definitely didn't see anything that would be confused for a party.

"Yeah, the sorority bachelorette whatever. We don't do that here. This isn't the zoo. We're not here to be ogled by straight people."

Clem pushed back from the counter forcefully, leaving her stool wobbling. She stood up straight, hands fisted at her sides. She no longer wanted to flee, she wanted to flip the entire bar if it wasn't bolted down. "That's really offensive."

The woman scoffed. "Really? You feel offended when you and your friends come in here like we're some kind of oddit—"

Clementine was aware other people were starting to notice their interaction. *Good*. This wasn't the first time she'd been read as straight and dismissed for it, but no one else got to decide her identity or if she was queer enough. A blonde, slightly rugged-looking woman behind the bar was watching her with such intensity that Clem's mind stuttered. She looked away and raised her voice a bit. If people were interested, then school was in session.

"No, it's offensive to think you know someone's identity by looking at them. Or think you can make them disclose it. There's not a litmus test for being sapphic, and this kind of gatekeeping is absurd."

"Oh." The woman's eyes flicked down and then back up. Clem felt them tracing over her. "So you're..."

"None of your business. Who I fuck will never have anything to do with you. That's a promise." Clem smiled sweetly.

The other woman behind the bar let out a wolf whistle, and Clementine spun toward her. If there wasn't a counter between them, she'd be tempted to kiss her right on the mouth. Partly for her support and partly because it was suddenly all Clementine wanted to do. The woman's blonde hair was in a messy bob, and her sleeveless black t-shirt showcased some pretty impressive muscles. Hopefully she hadn't just embarrassed herself in front of the other, hotter bartender? And how could she go about getting her number?

Alyssa wandered out from wherever she'd been hiding and sidled up to the woman. Clementine tried to catch her eye.

"Okay. I like this one." The blonde woman turned to Alyssa. "This is your friend, right?"

"Yeah! Clem, this is Lou. She owns this fine establishment."

'Fine' felt like a bit of a stretch, but the bar was comfortable in a way Clementine couldn't quite put her finger on. It actually reminded her a bit of Maine Course, her family's diner. "No one really calls me Clem, except my dad and best friend. Clementine is fine."

Lou narrowed her eyes in a way that shouldn't have been a turn-on to Clem, even though her body was making it very clear that it was. "Well, here you're Clem. Unless you prefer Lemon? Lemontine?"

"I do not." Was this teasing? Clem wondered.

"Tangerine?" If words could wink, Lou's just had. It did something wicked to Clem's insides.

"Mmmm... nope." Okay, definitely teasing. For a split second she thought of Sam saying, "people who like you don't call you by your full name, Clemmy. I don't make the rules."

"Okay then, glad we could agree on Clem." Lou clapped her hands and turned to the scowling bartender. "Rachel, get this beautiful woman a drink."

Rachel. So her nemesis had a name.

Rachel nodded, flicking her long, dark hair over her shoulder, a small, shit-eating smile pulling at her lips, almost as though she'd learned nothing from their interaction.

Lou tapped her chin. "What do you think, Lyss? A Supermarket?"

"Definitely A Supermarket." Alyssa nodded.

A Supermarket? Clementine mouthed the words to Alyssa.

"It's like our version of Long Island Iced Tea, but think more tropical. Kind of like if a Capri Sun had a vengeance."

Clem hoped she'd never find out what that juice box's villain origin story was. But maybe Boston Clementine's motto shouldn't be why, but *why not*? For once, maybe she didn't have to be the responsible one, making sure her father's bills were paid and he ate things resembling meals. Boston Clementine could get decimated by angry fruit drinks. "Okay, that sounds... interesting, I guess. But why is it called A Supermarket?"

"You know, like A Supermarket in California."

"Like 'what peaches and what penumbras?'" Clementine tilted her head.

"Oh, would you rather have that one instead?"

"Is everything here a poetic riddle? I think I might need to lay eyes on the drinks list."

The paper Alyssa handed to her was incredible, like something out of her college poetry class. The connection suddenly seemed both obvious and unexpectedly inspired based on the rather lackluster atmosphere of the rest of the space. A bar called Howl, with a menu full of Ginsberg references, *was* the perfect fit. Even the shabbiness of the atmosphere seemed a bit more intentional next to the offering of Stale Beer Afternoon.

"Are all of these drinks pretty much straight liquor?"

"You're damn right." Alyssa winked. "Welcome to Howl, baby. And don't leave without me. After a few of these, I don't want you navigating public transportation alone. I'll be done around two."

Clementine checked the time on her phone. 10:22 p.m. Welcome to Howl, indeed. It had been an impossibly long day with Boston trying to slam the door in her face before she'd even reached it. But sitting in this bar, surrounded by other sapphics, Clem didn't feel so alone. She felt like just maybe she'd found the spot she'd been looking for all along. And the people, too.

She thought about what Sam would do if she found herself unattached and in a new place, though she didn't have to think too hard. Clementine threw back another swallow of her drink and scanned the bar until she found Lou. One was enough if she wanted her wits about her, and for what she had in mind, she definitely did. Live a little, indeed.

CLEMENTINE WAS BEING OBVIOUS, and she did not care. All night she'd been watching Lou, trying to catch her eye, and every time she did, she attempted to telegraph *you are the hottest woman I've ever seen, let's do this.* Boston Clem was a new, sexually liberated person. And she wanted to do something drastic to cement this new version of herself, to prove to herself this was the life she was destined to have, away from Hart's Hollow. She wanted to be the version who could get robbed and still go out and have a good time. No longer was she doing the same monotonous things day in and day out. Here, away from her dad and the obligations of the diner, she was someone who would find comfort in the unfamiliar. She'd thrive on the unexpected. She'd sleep with a woman she *hadn't* known since kindergarten.

If the loaded glances worked, like the little cupids Clem wanted them to be, she'd have to admit to Sam that just maybe sometimes the universe *was* listening. Not as well as her phone hanging onto her every word to then show her ads of those exact things, but still.

A smoky voice very close drew her attention. "Hey, can you help me with something? Everyone else is pretty busy."

Clem blinked out of her thought spiral to find Lou looking at her. She stood just on the other side of the bar, her forearms resting on its scarred wooden surface. God, her arms looked strong—strong enough to inspire fantasies about rolled-up shirtsleeves at the end of a long day. Delicious. Lou had a little tattoo of a wolf on her wrist that had Clem wondering if they could go somewhere a little more private.

"Sure!" As Clem hopped down off her seat, her shoe snagged on the leg of the barstool, causing her to stumble a bit. Lou looked like she intended to jump over the bar with the way she swiftly reached across to steady Clem. Her hand was warm on Clem's arm. She hadn't realized she'd been chilled in the air conditioning of the bar.

"How many of those have you had?" Lou nodded to her half-full drink on the coaster.

Clementine debated lying, but that was never a good way to start off what could be the beginning of something good. No, not the beginning of anything, Clem chided herself. This is supposed to be the opposite of a beginning. It's supposed to be a whole experience. Her best friend's voice echoed in her head. *Kiss a stranger, Clementine Darby. Live a little.*

"That's still my first drink, actually. It's really good, so no offense intended—I'm just not a big drinker."

"Well then," Lou said with a throaty laugh, "you've definitely come to the right place." She looked pleased with Clementine's answer, not annoyed that Clem wasn't drinking more. "Come with me?"

She sure hoped so. Clementine nodded in response and suppressed the joy surging through her. She needed to be cool and calm and sophisticated. Basically the exact opposite of Hart's Hollow Clementine.

)○(

LOU LED her down a dark hallway that Clem was seriously hoping ended at a secluded office with a big desk that Lou would clear with one sweep of her strong arm before lifting Clem—

"Just to be sure, you don't play softball, do you?" Lou asked.

Clem frowned. This better not be an actual favor about sports. "Um, not since I was seven or so. Why?"

"Okay, good. That's great. And no reason, just curious. Are you having a good time in Boston?" Lou's smile was mischievous, and Clementine's face heated immediately.

Could Lou hear her thoughts? Or was her miserable poker face showing her hand again? She coughed, trying to ensure her voice was steady before she attempted an answer. "It's good so far. Well, good-ish. Better now."

"You should be sure to see the North End while you're here."

She was so busy watching Lou's lips move as she talked that she barely processed the suggestion. "Oh, um, right, I'm planning to see it all."

"Boston's bigger than you think. Anyway, here we are." Lou stopped in front of a closed door and unlocked it quickly.

Clem ran her hands over her top in a last-minute effort to make her t-shirt sexy. Lou flipped a switch and a light flickered on, illuminating metal shelves full of boxes and bottles. Not an office, but Clem could work with this. There were still plenty of... surfaces.

"So did you need help with something?" she asked, taking a

step closer to Lou. "I should warn you, I'm not as strong as I look."

Lou turned to her, her sapphire eyes searching. "People usually say the opposite."

"Well, I'm from Maine. I've seen my friend Sam lift a Christmas tree over her head while wearing heels, but I know my limits." Why was she talking about Sam at a time like this? She loved her friend, but for years Sam had had pretty much whomever she wanted while Clem had had... dinner alone in front of Top Chef reruns. She'd considered getting a cat on several occasions.

"Okay, well, if you didn't come to help carry things, what did you come for?" Lou raised an eyebrow, closing the door behind her. Skepticism should not be that sexy, but Clem's body was reacting like Lou's lips were on her neck.

Clem drew on all her courage, her inner Sam. If she wanted her life to be different, *she* needed to be different.

"For this." She took a step closer. She had had the worst fucking day, but City Clem didn't care about that—she rolled with the punches and made the first move. After getting consent, of course.

Clementine was fully in Lou's space now, and Lou hadn't stepped back. Actually, she seemed to lean closer, so close that Clem could smell the sweet mint of Lou's lip balm and lord help her, Clem's mouth watered.

She paused as Lou's breath ghosted her lips. "Is this okay?"

In response, Lou closed the gap between them, her body crashing into Clem's hard enough to take her breath away. Though any amount of Lou's body against hers would have rendered Clem breathless. Lou walked Clementine backward until her shoulder made contact with the door of the stockroom. Clem tried to turn them, to regain control, but Lou's hands were on her hips pushing her more firmly into the door, the coolness of the metal seeping through her t-shirt, countered by the warmth of Lou's body, like climbing into cool sheets on a warm night.

"You really only had one drink?" Lou asked, pulling back a fraction to look Clem in the eye.

Clem's throat was desert dry, and she wished she had that drink now, even if she appreciated her clear head. "Not even."

"Good girl." Lou's hands moved from Clem's hips to her wrists, raising them above her head.

And Clem... made it easy. She wanted this. She wanted to be a new person who pursued hot women without worrying about the whole town being in her business, or finding out that person had already been with her best friend or one of her best friend's many exes.

When Lou pinned Clem's wrists to the door with one hand, she groaned. Clementine Darby was absolutely sure she'd never been kissed like this.

Lou pulled away with a soft moan. "When's the last time you were tested?"

"I went to Planned Parenthood in Portland before I moved. All negative. You?"

"Same. I try to go about once a month, so I think about five days ago. No one since then."

"No one since then, really?" Clem hesitated, feeling a little out of her league. But she was here for the experience, right?"

"Hey, don't shame me." Lou smiled.

"Oh, I would never." Clem was doing it, having sex with a stranger in a semi-public space, and in mere moments, she would literally be doing it. Carefree Clementine had arrived.

"Is this what you wanted my help with?" Clementine gasped as Lou's lips moved to her neck and then lower to her collarbone.

"It is. You've been very helpful." Lou's lips brushed Clem's cleavage and her voice reverberated in Clem's chest. "Now, you should probably be quiet for this next part."

Lou's free hand traced along Clementine's waist, dipping beneath the hem of her shirt. Clem let her head drop back against the door with a soft thud, her eyes trained on the ceiling as Lou's hand slipped beneath her bra and cupped her left breast.

God, she wanted this. Her body felt ready to combust. Clem pushed her hips forward, seeking any kind of friction that might anchor her to this earthly plane. And Lou, bless her, slipped a leg between her thighs. The denim of Lou's jeans created delicious friction against Clem's bare legs. She tried not to worry about the fact that she was currently ruining her only pair of underwear. Maybe City Clem went commando. Nope. Strike that. She forced away an image of the kind of chafing that would ensue from denim. But underwear was a problem for the future.

Each roll of Lou's hips against hers sent Clem higher, until her own movements were uncoordinated, ruled by the rhythm of pure need. She wasn't sure she'd ever wanted to be touched so badly. Lou took one of Clem's nipples between her fingers, and a new rush of heat made itself known between Clem's thighs.

All she wanted was to clear her mind and enjoy being fucked by this beautiful stranger. And then she planned to fuck her in return. Clementine didn't mean to be selfish, but she needed Lou to make her come like five minutes ago.

She struggled against Lou's grip on her wrists, freeing one of her hands as Lou chuckled against her lips. "Sorry, did you need that for something?"

"Well, if you're not going to touch me, I am."

Lou licked her lips and her eyes flashed what Clem thought was hunger teetering on recklessness. Clem shivered.

"I like a woman who knows what she wants, but I intend to finish what I started." Lou grabbed Clem's hand and led it beneath her shirt, her own skin feeling silky beneath her fingertips. Lou was watching her like she wanted to devour Clem, so she made a show of slowly sliding her hand over her breast, and the pressure of her grip felt so much better than it ever had before, when Clem had done this alone, getting herself off. Again, regrettably, in front of Top Chef.

"See, I knew you'd be able to help me with this errand," Lou said before leaning in and gently biting Clementine's lower lip.

Clem's breath staggered as Lou slid down the zipper of her shorts in one swift motion and dipped two strong, sure fingers into her wetness.

She needed to find a way to compose herself if she didn't want to come the second Lou touched her again. She needed to be calm and collected and oh god, her own whimper surprised her as Lou's fingers traced gently over Clem's clit. Her grip on her own breast tightened as Lou drew circles exactly where Clementine needed her.

Above her head, Lou's grip remained firm on Clem's wrist and she focused on that steadying presence as she lifted her right leg and wrapped it around Lou's hip, pulling her closer.

Lou groaned like Clem's closeness was fulfilling a basic need. It was the sexiest sound Clem had ever heard. This sure beat Top Chef reruns and morning diner shifts. Here, in this storeroom, Clementine Darby was living.

"I want to fuck you," Lou said against her neck. All Clementine could do was nod as Lou entered her deftly with two fingers, curling them slightly as she pulled out. She caught Clem's gaze and entered her again. Even as she struggled to stay standing, her orgasm rushing through her, Clementine couldn't look away from those deep blue eyes.

Lou released the wrist pinned above Clem's head gently as she regained her senses. Her mass of red curls was a sweat-slicked mess, she knew that much without even looking. Clem's hair tended to telegraph her general state of being, and right now that state was half-crazed with her need to touch Lou, to make her come.

With her now-freed hands, she grabbed Lou's hips and spun them. "I need to touch you."

Lou laughed as her back hit the door. "Oh, it's like that, is it? And I thought you might let me go for round two."

"Don't count that out," Clem whispered as her fingers made their first brush against the soft, warm skin of Lou's stomach. "I just have something I need to take care of first."

Chapter Four
Lou

This was reckless and she fucking knew it. But what harm could it really cause to hook up with this pretty woman who was only in town for a few days? Hadn't Alyssa and Rachel been telling her she needed to stop seducing customers that they had to see all the time? She'd gotten into a few rough spots with one-night stands coming in night after night, looking for more. Lou was not the kind of person who could offer more. Which made this quick fuck with Clem absolutely perfect.

She'd get off and get back to work, happy and sated with absolutely no complications. Plus it would take her mind off everything going on with the bar. It was a flawless plan, she thought to herself, as she lifted her hips to meet Clem's hand. So what if this didn't bring her any closer to permanent happiness? Who needed forever when they had now?

As soon as Clementine worked open the button of Lou's jeans, she surprised herself by losing her balance and slumping forward into Clem. Against Lou's back, the door moved slightly as someone tried to open it from the outside. The knob rattled again in the sudden silence of the room.

Clem jumped away from her like a bomb had gone off between them. Her eyes shot wide in panic, like she'd never been caught fucking someone in a stockroom before.

Everything stopped. Lou's pounding heartbeat rushed in her ears. She took a few stumbling steps forward as she redid her button quickly, not hazarding a look over her shoulder to see who had interrupted them.

"Hey, there you two are!" The bright voice could only be Alyssa's. Sunshine and rainbows and puppies having ice cream cones, with none of the complications that came after. Of course, Alyssa would come looking for her friend, Lou should have thought of that. No matter, though. She could play this off.

She ran a hand through her hair, hoping it looked her usual, intentional carefree messy rather than wrecked.

"You found us!" Okay, that was too enthusiastic. Lou didn't speak in exclamations, she needed to sound like herself, and she was not cheerful. "I was just um..." Lou scanned the shelf in front of her and reached for the first bottle her eyes landed on, "...looking for this for Clementine to try."

Lou held up the bottle triumphantly as she turned toward Alyssa, careful not to make eye contact with Clementine.

Alyssa squinted. "You wanted Clementine to try Wild Turkey? That's available at, like, every liquor store."

"Yeah, well," Clem's voice came out rocky. "I told you about the turkeys I saw earlier. Lou said we'd do a special toast."

Alyssa tilted her head before flipping her long blonde hair over one shoulder. "Okay, that makes sense, I guess. So, should we go do shots?"

"Actually," Clem shifted from foot to foot and Lou suppressed a satisfied grin, knowing they were both too turned on to function properly. "I should let you and Lou get back to

37

work. See you at home, Alyssa? I'll get a rideshare. I'm too exhausted to take the subway anyway."

Home? Lou paused. Did people call their friend's apartment home? She felt like she was missing some piece of critical information. It could be worse, and Lou hadn't technically done anything out of line. So she'd fucked Alyssa's friend, which meant Alyssa would probably know all about it before the night was over. As long as Clementine was gone in a few days, who cared if things were a little awkward? "Oh, you're staying with Alyssa for the weekend?" Lou tried to sound casual.

Clem's brow furrowed. "I moved in today, so I'm staying there this weekend and many weekends in the future, assuming I can find a job and get back on my feet here in Boston."

Okay, that was much, much worse.

Fuck. Sleeping with her employee's roommate was the opposite of casual. But it was an honest misunderstanding. Lou tried to ignore the ache between her thighs. When she'd take care of it later, she would think of absolutely anyone except Clementine.

"Clemmy, you are brilliant!" Alyssa reached out and draped one arm over each of their shoulders. "Lou, you have to give her a job. How great would that be? All of us working here together?"

So far this day was a complete waste of ironing a shirt—a task Lou usually relegated to critical occasions: weddings, funerals, divorce parties.

She had gotten up before noon *on a Monday,* only to be rejected by some loan officer named Todd before her second cup of coffee. To make things worse, she kept thinking about Clementine, wishing they hadn't been interrupted. It seemed like nothing was going her way lately. Now she was left with an aching head, a scorch mark on her pinkie, and quickly dwindling hope that anyone would loan her the money to save Howl. The window Lou had to make an offer to buy the building would close at the end of June.

She ran her thumb lightly over the angry red skin, wishing she'd been able to find a Band-Aid, though something about the little kick of pain felt appropriate, like an extra shot of espresso she was craving.

Even though she'd tried her best to shove herself into the box society wanted for a business owner, the man in the green cardigan who held her entire dream in his hands had looked her right in the eye and said no. He'd called her a risk. Nothing she did mattered enough to change the outcome, which was starting to feel more and more like a foregone conclusion. It seemed no semblance of respectability would convince a bank that queer people deserve joyful spaces. That community is essential.

There weren't enough spreadsheets in the world to make this okay. Howl was about to go under and drag the rest of Lou McCallister's life down with it. If she wasn't able to get the loan she needed to buy the building, her landlord would sell it to someone who could. And whoever that person was would not give a damn about keeping the bar open. Lou could admit that Howl wasn't the most profitable. It was never going to make her rich, but she didn't need it to. It was home to her, and she wasn't ready to lose another one of those.

It's not that she'd had much hope of getting the money

when she'd walked in to meet with the loan officer, not after all the other rejections she'd gotten lately, but that didn't stop the bitter well of disappointment in her gut. What if just once things had broken her way? If she could only make this guy with his gold name tag and expensive pen understand how important Howl was, make him see why it mattered so much to her to keep it open. The bar was practically a historical site, and everyone knows how Boston just loves its history. But for as good as Lou was at serving drinks, it seemed she was miserable at presenting her case.

Three years ago, Howl had become the last sapphic bar in the city. Even though it started as a lesbian bar before Lou was born, Howl had evolved—it became a place that welcomed all sapphic people who needed a place to land. Money wasn't the only reason Lou hadn't renovated the bar. Queer history was so often overwritten or actively destroyed. She liked being able to see the initials of brave women who'd risked everything to be together written on the very walls (and bathroom stalls) of Howl. That legacy of being a safe communal space *had* to mean something. And yet, somehow it didn't. Outside of Pride month, companies didn't seem to care much at all.

TWENTY MINUTES LATER, Lou was overheating from her walk as she unlocked the battered front door of the building that had been her home for years. So long, that she could barely remember ever feeling at home anywhere else. It was still hours before the place would open for the Friday-night crowd ready to blow off their workweek steam. She made her way through the bar to the back hallway, allowing herself one moment to remember the things she'd done to Clementine in the storeroom before she climbed the metal stairs to the second floor and let herself into her apartment.

The desire to crawl back into bed was nearly overwhelming, but because of the useless meeting, she was behind schedule. She needed to do a quick inventory to see what liquors they had an abundance of, but even thinking of that space brought her thoughts back to Clem. Again. Lou hadn't stopped thinking about her for the rest of that night. She'd started stripping off her clothes the second her apartment door clicked shut behind her. She'd been ready to fall apart the instant Clementine had touched her, and the time since they'd been interrupted hadn't done anything to resolve her desire. When she'd come a few minutes later, her forehead pressed against the cool wall of the shower, hot water steaming around her, it was with Clem's name on her lips.

Lou didn't have time for thoughts like that. Distractions were a luxury and there was nothing more distracting than a broken heart. She'd had her time with Clementine, and now she needed to move on like she always did. No mess, no complications. Right now, Lou still had a bar to run, and that included determining the drink special for the night. It needed to be easy and quick enough to make that the bartenders stood a chance, which meant What Price Bananas, Howl's take on a Piña Colada, was off the table, even though she'd gotten a good deal on banana liqueur and there wasn't much call for it otherwise.

Rachel kept pushing for a special on Stale Beer Afternoon, which was her invention—essentially just pitchers of Natty that she liked to draft in advance, but it fit the Ginsberg vibe, so they went with it. For some reason, that was an unexpected hit with the Monday regulars; just a few old-timers who liked to come in and play cards for money while Lou looked the other way.

Fridays tended to be Howl's busiest night, and they still were, even with the recent decline in revenue. People were eager to leave their standard nine-to-five jobs behind them with two full days ahead to recover from any bad decisions made in the liminal hours between week and weekend. Lou wondered what that would be like—whole weekends off to spend catching up on laundry and grocery shopping, Saturday nights cuddled up with a girlfriend, watching a cheesy movie or doing some hobby. For some reason Clem's face flashed across her mind—what kind of movies would she pick? She probably liked to put on old romcoms and then fall asleep halfway through, leaving her girlfriend to carry her to bed. Nope, not appealing at all.

If Lou had a hobby, it was being busy. She liked tucking into bed just before sunrise, her body aching and her mind numb after working a long shift. And Howl—with its faulty plumbing and ancient ice machine—kept her very, very busy. She couldn't imagine what she'd do without it, but if things continued on like they were, she might have to find out.

Her current lease ended September first, but she needed to make her landlord, Helena, an offer by the end of June. If it were up to her, she'd buy the building for just over market value and be done with it. Hell, if money wasn't so impossible to come by, Lou would buy the whole block and put in a queer bookstore and a decent sandwich place. She would continue to put off making that call to Helena for as long as she could, but she'd run out of banks to ask for a loan, and barring some miracle, it was starting to feel like the writing was on the wall. And when it came to miracles, Lou had about as much of a chance at winning the lottery as she did with having a successful relationship. Which is to say absolutely no chance at all.

Well, the writing was actually on her fridge in the form of a letter from one of Helena Smee's lawyers, outlining the right of first refusal clause from her original lease and the fast-approaching date for Lou to make her offer before the building would go on the market. Helena was being generous, she'd stressed. By only asking for market value, she was practically *losing* money.

As Lou scanned the dates on her calendar next to the letter, Lou realized Howl's annual Pride bash might turn into an impromptu goodbye party. Would it be better to cancel it altogether rather than face that uncomfortable situation? All those people feeling sad. Lou shuddered at the thought of letting everyone down. All she could do was focus on making tonight and the next night and the night after that a success. Bankruptcy: one day at a time.

After weeks of searching for solutions, including calculating the income she could make from selling her plasma, Lou was crashing face-first into the reality of the situation. She couldn't afford to buy the building from Mrs. Smee, not with property values soaring with a velocity not seen since the great Beanie Baby run of 1997. Even for a gambler like Lou, it was simply too risky to stay on in the building and take a chance with a new owner. If Lou was going to close Howl, she wanted it to be on her own terms, even if those terms were bitter. It wasn't that she blamed her landlord. Helena hadn't been shy about disclosing her failing health, which had taken a turn for the worse in the past year. The sale of the building might not even pay off her medical bills, depending on how human the person reviewing her insurance claims was feeling on a given day.

Lou knew Helena was trying to give her a fair deal. She'd done her research on what a few other buildings and retail spaces in the neighborhood were going for, and the offer on her fridge *was* on the generous side of outlandish. Lou scanned the property value estimate on the letter from Helena. Much to her chagrin, it had not suddenly become reasonable overnight. She'd been using it as a coaster for weeks because if she ruined it, she might feel less bad about not being able to sign it and save what she loved. But to sign it would be to set herself up for failure, and Lou never much liked failing. She'd expected a rent hike was coming ever since the condos in the neighborhood stopped being barely-converted warehouses and started being billed as luxury. The main differences seemed to be granite countertops and HOA fees.

Lou grabbed a glass from the cabinet and filled it with orange juice she'd liberated from the bar yesterday, before wandering to the window. She gazed out over the street below. Every other building seemed to be in some state of construction.

Over the last few years, the nearby restaurants had slowly switched from pie and drip coffee to gourmet donuts and matcha lattes. It was almost amusing, the way gentrification tried so hard to cling to humble trappings: the chalkboard signs, vintage bicycles as the primary form of transportation, outdated facial hair configurations. Right now, Lou's eyes burned and she felt about a decade too old for all of it.

She hadn't had the heart to change Howl. She'd intended to preserve its legacy rather than water it down with, well, watered-down anything, really. She knew one thing for sure: Home of the Wayward Lovers would never, ever serve brunch or happy hour specials with truffle fries. She would not be caught dead putting a mini cheeseburger on top of a Bloody Mary like a fancy little hat. That was her sacred oath.

Howl was rowdy and delightful and a little maddening, like your family's house on its most chaotic holiday. It was a bar for those who didn't owe anyone anything but owed their community everything. Community. That was the word Lou kept coming back to. The weight she felt on her shoulders. The H of HOWL stood for 'home' for a reason. Who was she to give up on that? To take that away from people who might need it? To take it away from herself?

. . .

As Lou emerged from the back hall to open the bar, she caught sight of Rachel standing out front, flicking her lighter open and closed with a flourish. The lights were still dimmed in their pre-open glow, like a sun slowly rising. It was nearly five p.m., time to start her day. She grabbed a pint glass from the stack and filled it with water, trying to ease her tension headache. She had a month to get everything figured out. So thirty days to win the lottery or marry a millionaire, or get the wizard to give corporations a heart. Simple.

Rachel tossed the rag onto the counter. "Water, really? In this bar? You look like shit, by the way."

"Yes, hence the water. Lovely to see you working hard as always, Rach."

"Well, you're lucky it's just us. Otherwise I'd be going for the ice. The mean boss has this rule about dumping a bucket of the stuff on anyone who dares to order water in her bar."

"What can I say?" Lou shot back. "I contain multitudes. And if I can't get this pain under control I might murder someone."

"If you'd been out here five minutes ago, you could have taken your pick of five punk kids who wandered in early. Where the hell is the bouncer, anyway? We need to open soon."

Lou frowned. "The bouncer has a name, you know that. And Dana's shift doesn't start until we open. You're supposed to lock the door behind you after you come in."

"Don't use logic on me, Lou. I'm too fucking tired." Rachel groaned as she reached for a glass. As her head tilted up, the bruise on her cheekbone caught the light, looking gruesome.

"I think boxing has been a really good thing for you. Did you have another fight last night? I guess that would explain your shiner. I hope you won this time." Lou smirked, then ducked seconds before Rachel sprayed the water gun in her direction.

"This time? I always fucking win, especially with how hard I've been training. Actually, that reminds me, I've got to cut out early tonight for a sparring match. With things being a bit slower lately, I'm sure Alyssa and whoever else can cover."

She hadn't realized that Rachel noticed the downturn in business. Then again, how could she not? It must be written all over the place, from the decrease in their tips to the number of times they had to run to the storeroom for new bottles. Ugh, now she was thinking of the damn *incident* again, her body reacting as though Clementine's hands were still on her like a promise.

Lou couldn't quite figure out why women swooned over Rachel. She was often covered in bruises and she was almost never kind—two things that were bafflingly a huge turn-on to the sapphic women of Boston. It was an odd night when she didn't have one or two hanging out around closing, nursing their drinks and hoping for a chance to check her for other injuries.

"I love Alyssa, but there's no way she can cover the entire bar. Maybe I could call Megan in?" Lou sighed. Having to work the bar tonight would only put her behind with everything else, though it wasn't like she had a better option. "I'll help her. Just promise you'll try not to sustain any major injuries."

"Nothing worse than I dish out." Rachel flicked her braid over her shoulder with authority, causing her bicep to bulge around the gold snake cuff constricting it.

As if conjured, Alyssa breezed through the door. When she reached them, she squinted at Rachel. "You should really let me put glitter on your eye. It will distract from the bruise." Alyssa dug in her purse until her hand emerged, triumphantly clutching a makeup pallet.

"Alyssa, if you come near me with that makeup, you'll have your own bruise to cover up."

"Lou! Did you hear that?" Alyssa gaped.

"Rachel, we do not threaten other employees."

"Or customers," Alyssa input helpfully.

"Right, or customers." Lou nodded, although in her heart of hearts she knew the customer was not always right. A lot of times, they were belligerent. "Well, not unless they give you a good reason to anyway. I can't afford a lawsuit."

"Maybe if I save you money on lawsuits, you could use it to spruce up the place. I think that dingy paint is older than I am." Rachel squinted at a patch of plaster behind the bar not covered with shelves.

Lou crossed her arms, trying to hold in the wave of defensiveness she felt rising. *Did no one value history anymore?* There was nothing wrong with her bar. And even if it could use some improvements, there was hardly any point if she might be out of the space by the end of the summer. Let alone the fact that she shouldn't spend money on so much as new paint right now if she wanted to buy the building. She'd just have to be happy with what she had for as long as she got to keep it. "It has character."

"Mm, no." Alyssa studied her reflection in her compact before snapping it shut. "That's not character, that's nicotine residue."

"Fine, I'll consider new paint, but no promises. Now please go watch the door until Dana gets here. I have a few orders to finish, then I'll be out to help."

The night was not a success. By eight p.m., Howl was down another bartender after Megan hurt her hand trying to fix the ice machine—which Lou had specifically told her *not* to reach into. She'd even made a sign and stuck it right next to the machine. TREAT THIS MACHINE LIKE AN ALLIGATOR, IT WILL EAT YOUR FINGERS. Megan was from Florida, so Lou had tried to use language that would be meaningful to her. Her hand had looked only slightly masticated, not fatal, but you could never be too careful. A workplace injury was not something to mess around with. Lou shoved her in a cab to urgent care and planned to cover the bar herself.

Alyssa might as well be out of commission with all the time she was spending talking to Clem, who apparently just lived here now, both in Boston and at the bar. Not that Lou could blame Alyssa, really, with the way her own mind had been wandering to her time with Clementine all night. The way Clem ran her fingers through her hair as she talked, just like she'd done to Lou's in the storeroom, tugging it just a little. She seemed to give whatever she was doing her full attention, and Lou knew first-hand how good having Clementine's attention felt. What she wouldn't give to be that napkin that woman had been ripping to shreds for the past five minutes.

And then it hit her; maybe Clementine could work at Howl, and Lou could get back to saving it. That must be why Lou couldn't stop watching Clem—it was just her brain trying to solve her current staffing shortage. Plus, when Lou had seen her in action the other night, shutting Rachel down, she'd shown she had the mettle to be one of them. Putting Rachel in her place was the Howl equivalent of one of Hercules' labors.

Lou set down the tray of glasses she'd just pulled from the dishwasher and dried her hands on the bar rag that was nearly a permanent fixture in her back pocket.

"Hey Alyssa, are you planning on serving any drinks tonight?"

"Yes! Sorry, I was just filling Clemmy in on our plans for tomorrow. Did I mention she's *still* looking for a job?"

Clementine leaned across the bar to smack Alyssa but missed. "Geez, it's only been a few days."

"Your subtlety is truly astounding, Alyssa. I'm not sure we can bring you on permanently, Lemontine, but we're short-staffed tonight. How about an audition and Alyssa will split her tips?"

"Hey!" Alyssa spun toward Lou.

She held up a hand. "Would you rather she get *all* your tips?"

Alyssa narrowed her eyes in response.

"Right." She turned her attention back to Clementine. "Have you ever bartended before?"

"No, not exactly. But I waited tables in my family restaurant, so I have experience in the industry."

Lou held back a laugh. "If we use 'industry' to just mean food, then sure. What kind of restaurant was it?"

"It's more of a small diner really, up in Hart's Hollow, Maine. But we're kind of famous for our lobster mac-n-cheese and we draw a decent summer crowd, so I know how to handle a rush with a smile."

She gave Lou a dazzling one then, a dimple appearing on her cheek that damn near stopped Lou's heart. This woman was dangerous.

Lou blinked, trying to assemble a response. "You served lobster at a diner?"

A glowing blush spread across Clementine's fair cheeks until it matched the flames of her red hair. "Well, when in Maine..."

"Of course, how silly of me." Lou took a step back, waiting for Clementine to get off her stool. "Well, are you coming?" Lou extended her arm with a flourish, gesturing behind the bar. "We've got thirsty customers in need of assistance."

Clementine set down her drink and nodded. Her grin sent

Lou's insides swooping. This wouldn't do at all. No one got to have that kind of power over her. Not anymore.

"Oh, and Lemon?" Lou's tone was clipped.

The woman rolled her eyes. There, that was better.

"Yeah?"

"Lose the smile or you're fired."

Chapter Five
Clementine

S horts too short, shirt too tight: the official Howl uniform. Clementine snuck into the bar for her first shift mostly unnoticed, feeling self-conscious looking at the neon purple moon. The door was unlocked, but Dana, the bouncer from the other night, was nowhere in sight. She tugged down the edges of the cutoff shorts Alyssa had loaned to her as she made her way around the bar. Her roommate had what she was calling "a sabbatical night" to teach a Sweatin' to the Moonlight Jazzercise class in the courtyard of a local retirement home. Which left Clem working with... Rachel, who was currently a scowling sentinel behind the bar. Perfect.

"I didn't think you'd come back here." Rachel eyed her up and down, and Clementine fought the urge to turn on her heel and walk back out.

Clementine knew that sometimes running was almost indistinguishable from freedom. Both left things behind. She couldn't fight the thought that she didn't belong here, even if the drinks did have fun names. A lingering feeling that she'd made a mistake by acting like someone else the other night when she'd seduced Lou had been following her around the apartment for days. Maybe her dad was right and she should just go back home and be happy with what she had. Somehow, that thought made facing off with Rachel moderately more appealing.

Clem drew in a fortifying breath. "I heard showing up to work is a big part of getting paid."

"*You're* going to work here? Aren't you a little too... nice?" Rachel sneered as she said the word like there was something distasteful about it.

"Is that a bad thing?"

"If you're friendly, you have no one to blame but yourself when people walk all over you. Cute shirt, by the way. Did you just get done with summer camp?"

Clementine looked down nervously. If she'd been at summer camp, her ass would not be threatening to fall out of her cutoffs. Also, she probably would have made a friendship bracelet or something. "Am I wearing the wrong thing?"

"You could say that." Rachel flashed a grin that was all malice.

Clem shivered at the chill in the air. She couldn't let Rachel get in her head.

"Hey, Lou!" Rachel called over her shoulder. "New girl didn't get the dress code memo."

Rachel tapped a sign behind the bar that said, "No shirt, no shoes, that's service."

"Clever." Clem frowned. "But I'm pretty sure that's a health code violation."

"I wouldn't let Lou hear you say that," Rachel shot back.

Lou emerged from the back carrying a large, transparent blue jug of ice balanced on one shoulder. It made her white t-shirt ride up just enough that Clem could see the line of her hip bone peeking out. If only she'd had more time with those hip bones.

She'd been satisfied after her orgasm, but something about their encounter had also left her wanting more of Lou. Much, much more. Which her brain helpfully pointed out was the opposite of a one-night stand. Or closer to a one-hour stand in their case. In theory, she should want less now. Or nothing at all.

Lou paused, taking in Clem's outfit. She felt the heat of her gaze everywhere. Suddenly even her feet were hot, which was a potential medical issue.

"This is worse than I thought." Lou dropped the ice on the floor, the container landed upright with a loud clatter. She stepped into Clem's space.

Clem swallowed hard. "What's worse than you thought?" *Shit.* She should have known better than to listen to Alyssa. She was underdressed in more ways than one. Her borrowed Derby Dykes t-shirt looked absurd next to Rachel's corset and her shorts were literally smaller than her underwear. She felt like a yard sale disaster from top to bottom.

One of Lou's hands came to anchor on Clementine's hip. Clem's mind went blank as Lou's fingers dug in slightly to the soft skin of her stomach. Lou's grip tightened as she leaned back to take Clementine in. "Alyssa has clearly done you a disservice here. I mean, the shorts are fine."

"I'm sorry, I—wait, did you say the shorts are *fine*? They're barely covering me. I'm not sure I'd even wear these to the beach. One wrong move and you could have me arrested for indecent exposure."

"Well, that's not a problem so much as a positive. They're called tips, baby. But if you're worried, I can fix that." Lou winked. "Rachel! Toss me the tape."

Rachel grunted, then rummaged beneath the bar and pulled out a roll of tan-colored tape that she tossed to Lou.

Lou knelt in front of Clem. "Is this okay?" She asked.

Clem's knees were weak with their proximity, but she nodded anyway. She wanted Lou's touch.

Lou slid her fingertips beneath the hem of her shorts and holy shit Clem couldn't breathe. She looked down and Lou's blue eyes were sparkling.

"Spread your legs." Lou wasn't asking now. She was telling.

Clementine's throat went dry and she choked out a cough. She was in serious danger of swallowing her tongue if—Lou nudged the inside of Clem's thigh with her forearm. How was she supposed to stop lusting after Lou when she did things like *that*?

Lou quirked an eyebrow. "Do you want your shorts secure or not? This is like boob tape. It can hold down anything."

Well, Clementine was the master of misreading whatever the hell this was. Not that she'd really had a read on what Lou was doing. She nodded again.

Lou pulled a strip of tape and then she leaned in and tore it with her teeth before placing it under the edge of Clementine's shorts. Clem imagined Lou's teeth ripping her bra in the same fashion, and suddenly the only thing keeping Clem from passing out with want, was the firm pressure of Lou's hand on her thigh, securing the tape. Clementine was in some hybrid of heaven and hell, where she was simultaneously having the best and worst experience of her life. Lou's shampoo smelled almost smoky, like she'd just built a fire. And if the heat between Clementine's legs counted, then she technically had.

After a very long moment, about a month in dog years, Lou stood slowly. She placed her hands on her hips and tilted her head to one side. And god, Clementine knew she should be scared of Lou or at least have a healthy apprehension, but that head tilt reminded her of a pit bull she was desperate to adopt. She shivered under Lou's gaze.

"Okay, I've taken care of your ass," Lou said, making a beckoning motion. "Now your shirt. Take it off."

Clem choked, dissolving into coughs that only made her throat drier. Out of the corner of her eye, she saw Rachel reach for a glass. Was she getting Clem water? Wonders today would never cease. A moment later, that glass slid down the bar with two fingers of amber whiskey in it. Clem downed it in one and immediately started coughing again. Smooth.

When she looked up, Lou's eyes were still on her.

"I don't think I can do that," Clem whispered, her voice raspy. She tilted her head toward Rachel by way of explanation.

Lou smirked but didn't press. "Fine, have it your way."

Oh, thank god. Clem let her shoulders drop just as Lou stepped forward and grabbed the bottom of her shirt with both hands. And then she ripped. The fabric split and Lou pulled the bottom half off as effortlessly as if she was peeling an orange, spinning Clem in the process. By the time she was done, the shirt ended just above her navel. Goosebumps rose on Clem's skin as the air and Lou's gaze hit it, like every atom in her body was standing at attention, waiting for what happened next. Because really, where could the night go from here that would be more exciting? Well, she supposed there was *one* direction.

"That'll do," Lou nodded. "Now, get to work. We open in ten."

Clementine searched for her voice and finally found it. "Why did you do that?"

"Because you looked like you came from soccer camp, we needed to make you a little... hotter."

Clem valiantly attempted to blink away the pure wave of *stunned* that washed over her. "I need to be hotter? Can I remind you that I came here to be myself, which I thought was the entire point of this bar..."

"On that side of the counter, sure. But on this side, it's

about the tips, baby. You can thank me later. And you do look really good by the way." Lou's eyes trailed over her, and Clem's swallow echoed in her own ears.

The other night that look had *not* been about business. Clem lowered her voice to a whisper. "Do you think we could talk about what happened between us? We left things unresolved."

Lou smiled tightly. "There's nothing to say. We had our fun, right?" She spun to leave but then turned back, giving Clem a smile that was half kindness, half mischief. "Don't touch anything unless Rachel tells you to. And Rachel, she can prepare garnishes and run drinks, nothing else. You're the boss."

"I've always wanted to be a boss," Rachel said, her eyes glinting.

LEAVE it to limes to let you know just how many cuts you have on your hands. Clem went to put her finger in her mouth, then thought better of it and reached for a bar rag instead.

"Rachel, are there any rubber gloves I could use? My hands are stinging from the lime juice."

"Huh. I thought you'd be one with the citrus."

"Funny." It was not funny, and Clem hadn't worn the right shoes to be standing for this many hours. "Gloves?"

"Not that I've ever seen. Sorry you're finding the simplest task too taxing. I'll tell Lou you weren't up to the job. You can give up and go home now."

Clem sighed, looking over her shoulder at the crowd that was lined up three deep at the bar, waving and winking and whistling for Rachel's attention. She wasn't sure she'd ever seen so many sapphic people in one place. Though sometimes it was hard to tell, with flannel being the official Maine uniform and all. Even when she went to Portland, there wasn't really a sapphic bar, just places that were queer-friendly, which really wasn't the same.

The pace had picked up consistently all evening until it reached a kind of fever pitch around nine p.m. Even as barback, Clem was struggling to keep up. It would seem the summer rush in Hart's Hollow had nothing on a Howl Friday night.

Rachel's ability to take orders, serve drinks, and manage the crowd, all while slipping in snide comments that made Clem question her entire life, was impressive if unsettling. She wasn't just tending bar, she was performing. Would Clem be capable of doing all that if she ever got promoted off garnish duty? She doubted it as she snuck awestruck glances at Rachel spinning a bottle in one hand while lighting shots on fire with the other. Clementine continued watching as Rachel did a shot with a customer, chasing it with a beer.

She was so engrossed that she sliced her own thumb open with the knife she was using to quarter limes. In unrelated news, she wondered why they called it 'salt in the wound' instead of 'citrus in the wound', because holy hell did it hurt. She blinked back a tear with the aim of composing herself, but thought better of it. Rachel seemed like the kind of person who could smell weakness, like one of those dogs finding a body in the woods. It would be impressive if it wasn't also a little terrifying.

Clem swiped a bar towel from the cutting board at the scene of the crime and wrapped it around her finger before shoving her now gigantic hand into her very tiny front pocket because... women's jeans.

"I'm going to run to the restroom."

Rachel barely glanced up, but her face clouded for the briefest moment when they locked eyes. Maybe Clem hadn't done quite the bang-up job of seeming fine that she'd thought. She rushed toward the back hall without waiting for an answer.

There were a lot of wonderful things about Howl, but

right at the top were the two gender-neutral restrooms. She waltzed right into the one with urinals, blissfully empty. Clem unwrapped her hand and watched the ruby-red blood pool on the pad of her thumb before running it under the tap. It stung, but soon enough she couldn't feel anything at all. Was there a way to run her entire life under cold water for the same effect?

She wanted more than anything to splash her face, but Alyssa had talked her into some sort of elaborate contouring and glitter eyeshadow situation. Each day of living with Alyssa led to a new, elevated sleepover makeover. Instead, Clem went with her second grounding element of choice and drew in a deep breath. When she still felt shaky, she retreated to one of the stalls and did the only sure thing she knew: she pulled out her phone and called Sam.

Sam answered as though they were mid-conversation. "If you're already on the road, you can make it in time to split a frozen pizza and listen to me bitch about Phyllis accusing me of stealing her sticky notes."

"God, again? Doesn't the library buy those?" Clem felt something in her chest unclench at the prospect of having an utterly unremarkable night with her best friend. *Frozen pizza! Phyllis!*

"Yes and Yes. I've explained to her that we have the same Post-its because that's what's in the supply closet. Anyway, what's your ETA?"

Clem swallowed, tears pooling in her eyes again. Damn. Hearing Sam's voice was having the opposite effect of what she'd intended.

"Okay, Miss Deep Breaths. What's wrong?" Sam's voice softened. "I was just joking about the frozen pizza; you know I love you more than that. We can order in."

Clem swallowed hard, trying to pull herself together. "I'm

working at Howl tonight, and it all just feels like too much. My clothes were wrong, so then Lou had to rip them. And—

"Wait, she *had* to what?"

"That's not the point," Clem mumbled.

"Clementine, babe, there's simply no way that isn't the point of this call. Your hot boss ripping your clothes off of you, I assume, is headline news."

"Sam, focus. Wait, how do you even know she's hot?" Clementine stopped talking when she heard the break in her own voice.

"She owns a bar and is named Lou, no way she's not hot." Sam sighed. "But, in my infinite wisdom, I have decided to table the clothing incident. Tell me what's going on."

"I don't think I can do this. I keep messing up. And Rachel, who I'm working with, is so *mean*. What am I doing? I came to Boston for a change, but what if I just traded one place that made me feel frustrated for another?" Tears stung Clementine's eyes again. Her makeup was fucked.

"First of all, what you're doing is surviving. You got an unlucky break. Serving drinks a few nights a week until you get back on your feet and buy some underwear is not the same thing as being trapped in your dad's diner. And everything is new and hard before it isn't. Give yourself grace."

"I guess I just haven't ever had to do so many new things at once before." As she said it, Clem realized it was true. Her whole life in Hart's Hollow had been familiar, like a house she could make her way through without turning on the lights.

"Mmm. I'm afraid that's the adventure part of your new life, my love," Sam said.

"Okay, you're right." Clem's breathing had evened out as the familiarity of talking to her best friend worked its magic. "Now tell me what else Phyllis did this week."

"I hope you're ready to be grossed out because this next

episode of the Phyllis saga is the one where she put her fish stew in the break room microwave and a library patron called the fire department. Not to mention that microwaving lobster is an actual crime."

"No," Clem gasped through a laugh. "Did Bill show up?"

"Oh yeah, him and a full engine. One guy even put on his respirator to avoid the smell." Sam wheezed with laughter.

Clem smiled, she couldn't help it. This was the magic of Sam.

A few minutes later she reluctantly ended their call after a couple banged into the restroom and started having some pretty explicitly narrated sex in the stall next to her. Sam, of course, had lobbied to keep the call going, but there were only so many times Clem could hear someone say, "smack my ass, daddy," before spending time next to Rachel seemed like the better alternative.

THE BAR SEEMED EVEN BUSIER when Clem pushed her way back through the graffitied bathroom door.

Rachel flicked her glance at Clem as she circled the counter.

"Are you done crying in a stall? Lou was just looking for you."

Panic surged through Clem. How long had she been gone? Five minutes, more? "Sorry, should I go find her?" She glanced at the pyramid of limes in the bin next to her cutting board. They were stacked with a precision that was not her doing. There were enough wedges to cure all the scurvy of the twenty-first century. "I thought we had enough limes for a bit."

"I wouldn't go looking for trouble if I were you. And if you haven't noticed, we're a little busy, so now's not the best time for you to go kiss up to the boss. How about you take that guy's order? He looks like a good time," Rachel said with an eye roll before turning back to the very dapper androgynous person in front of her.

The man Rachel had nodded toward did *not* look like a good time, but he did look ready to absolve Clem of some sins and at this point, she'd take what she could get. He was in black pants and a black shirt, but something about the collar was giving her visions of Sunday service. But that couldn't be right. It was probably just a city-look she wasn't familiar with.

"Hi Sir, can I help you?"

Next to her, Rachel let out a demonstrative cough. Right, respect was verboten.

"Is Lou here?"

Clem shrugged. "She's around here somewhere."

"Then I'll just wait if that's okay."

"Sorry, buddy, nobody gets a free ride." Clem tried to sound gruff, but she knew she was missing the mark. "If you're here, you gotta order a drink."

"Alright," the man said as he slid onto a newly vacated stool and put a five-dollar bill on the counter. "Just water then."

Clem nodded and reached for a glass and the soda gun.

Rachel leaned in. "What are you doing?" she hissed.

"He's looking for Lou. I'm getting him some water."

"No water, you know the rules."

"Look, Rachel, he already seems uncomfortable. And what if he knows Lou, and she's okay with it?"

"I've known her a lot longer than you. Serve him water if you want to get fired tonight. It's fine with me to see you go. But because your sad clothes say you need the money, you know what you have to do." Rachel reached under the counter and pulled out what looked to be a police issue megaphone, handing it to Clementine.

Her fingers trembled slightly as she gripped the handle. Alyssa had told her all about the *no water rule*, so she had a sense of what had to be done. And Rachel was right. She needed this job because she needed food and because no matter what, she couldn't return home to her father's house in defeat.

The megaphone screeched when Clem raised it to her mouth. She pulled it away a bit and tried again. "Hey everyone. This guy just ordered water."

The bar fell silent and Clem could feel the eyes of everyone on her, unspoken anticipation crackling in the air. She avoided looking at the man in question. Next to her, Rachel hoisted the clear blue plastic barrel of ice onto the counter.

"Do we serve water at this bar?" Clem called out, her confidence raising a tick at the rapt attention.

The crowd started to chant, "water, water everywhere," as Clementine set down the megaphone and raised the barrel over her shoulder, just like she'd seen Rachel do on her first night.

As she poised herself to dump the bucket on the man like a Gatorade celebration, the crowd's chant shifted to, "and not a drop to drink."

And with that, Clem dumped the ice on him. He shot up from his stool, looking horrified.

"I came with an offering, but I won't stay where I'm not welcomed. Please tell Louise that Father Joe was here to see her." The guy beelined for the exit as the crowd continued their chant.

Clementine felt sick. He *was* a priest and it seemed he knew Lou well, too.

"Oh shit," Rachel said next to her. "He knows Lou's full name, you really fucked up."

Chapter Six
Lou

L ou's office phone trilled, startling her into *remembering* she had an office phone. She'd been deep in spreadsheet-land trying to figure out what cuts she could make that might actually have an impact, but every item was the equivalent of not ordering guac when you were trying to save for a house, a single drop in a bucket full of holes.

"Hello?" Lou nestled the phone between her head and shoulder as she continued her aimless scrolling, clicking into a cell every few seconds for good measure. She should be out on the floor making sure nothing was on fire except the alcohol Rachel liked to spit out of her mouth.

"Hi, honey."

Usually, a call from her grandma set her at ease, a balm for her worries because it was the voice of someone who loved her no matter what. Nothing would change that, not coming out and not even being a failure who had to close her bar and maybe share the spare room with Canoodle. Lou knew to treat that love like it was precious and rare, because, well, it was. But right now, her grandma's call was not a comfort. Lou glanced at the clock on the wall, her alarm amplifying. Her grandma was not one to call after seven p.m. and it was pushing ten-thirty.

"What's wrong, Gram? Are you okay?" She tried to keep her voice steady.

"I'm fine. And Joe said not to worry about the whole ice thing. He was more surprised than anything."

Lou furrowed her brows while she grabbed her keys from the corner of her desk in case she had to rush out. "Ice thing? Are you sure you're feeling okay? Are you confused?"

"Yes, Louise, I'm perfectly fine. I'm sharp as a knitting needle, thank you very much."

"Those really aren't very sharp. I think you can take them on airplanes. Can you tell me what's going on?" Lou's heart was still racing even though her grandma sounded fine. But people could have a concussion or a brain tumor and still *sound* okay.

"I'm trying to." In the background, the dog yipped, and soon the line was filled with a shushing noise that made Lou snap her mouth shut on instinct. "Not now, Canoodle. I'll heat up your shepherd's pie in a minute," her grandma murmured.

"You really shouldn't feed the dog shepherd's pie."

"You know I make him a special one that's fine for dogs to eat, just like every other meal." Eleanor sounded mildly exasperated, like Lou was the one not being rational. "Louise, Father Joe came by the bar earlier to offer a donation to help you buy the building. I told you I might mention your situation to him. To hear him tell it, he was showered in ice when he asked to see you. I said that didn't sound like something you'd do, but he wasn't upset. You know how forgiving he is, it's part of his job description! He also said it's the closest he's ever felt to winning the Super Bowl, so between us, he might have liked it. There are still quite a few layers I need to peel back there."

Wait, what? Lou shook her head trying to make sense of her grandma's words. Then it slowly dawned on her. Of course a priest walked into a bar and ordered water.

Oh, fuck. Lou's stomach sank. She did her best to ignore the fact that her grandma must be working with some powerful voodoo to get her Catholic priest 'friend' to come into a sapphic establishment on a Friday night. On some level, Lou knew it should feel nice that her grandma was trying to solve her problem with Howl. And it did feel nice. It made Lou feel loved but also like she was walking into a trap. Like it was better to run now and never look back than to be beholden to someone's charity. Even if losing any opportunity for money right now could be fatal to the bar.

"Father Joe was here? *Your* Father Joe?"

"Yes."

"Shit."

"*Language,* dear."

"Shoot."

"Much better," her grandma said with a laugh.

"Why would the church donate money to a sapphic bar?"

"Why not? It's a good community place. There are all different kinds of communities, Louise. I just don't understand why you didn't ask me for help sooner." Her grandma sounded hurt, which made her feel bad for *not* taking her money to support a bar that partly drew people in with risqué dancing and bad attitudes.

"Because you need your money. And I was trying not to exhaust every option. I guess I was holding out hope that if I didn't ask everyone, then it wasn't hopeless."

"Mmm. I did that once—I avoided getting an answer I wouldn't like. I thought my boyfriend wanted to break up with me, so I didn't answer the phone for a week."

That was... not really the same thing. "What happened?"

"I married him."

"Okay, I'm not sure that story's really applicable in this situation."

"It is, you need to make yourself—in this case your bar—desirable. Not taking chances can hurt just as much as taking them. Howl has a lot going for it like..."

Lou narrowed her eyes as her grandma went silent on the other end of the line.

"Well, beer, right? And the building is old so... maybe the historical society would be interested. Last year, my town restored an old fire station and made a little museum about the Great Boston Fire. It was really uplifting. There was this great display about all the people who just stood around watching the fire burn because they assumed someone else had called for help. A lot of people died because of that, actually. You need to call for help, Lou."

"Okay, that took a turn. Look Gram, I need to go deal with this ice thing. I'll call you tomorrow."

What Lou couldn't bring herself to say to her grandma was that it wasn't some convoluted hope that kept her from asking for help. Her grandma loved her, she knew that. But Lou had learned a long time ago that sometimes love shouldn't be tested, because if you hit it in just the right spot, it could shatter. So really, it was probably for the best that Father Joe had gotten iced. She'd still go out on the floor and pretend to be pissed at Rachel, but maybe she'd been saved. When people do things for you, they expect things in return. Sometimes they want you to return the favor in kind, but other times they want you to contort yourself into the box they've created to contain you.

That's what had happened with her family. The day Lou had dared to step outside her parents' expectations by having a girlfriend, it was like all the years her mother had cared for her just vanished. Like her love was contingent, something only delivered if Lou didn't breach the invisible contract of her expectations. And she'd be damned if she let the same thing happen to Howl. She'd rather see it closed than tamed.

Lou set the phone back on the cradle gently, just in case her rage could be transmitted through the landline before she stormed out of her office like her heels were on fire, ready to raise holy hell. Just when she was finally about to get a break with Howl, even if it was a small one, it was taken away from her before she even knew it existed.

She rounded the corner out of the back hallway and headed for the bar, vaguely noting the way the crowd parted for her. Howl was Lou's domain, it flowed around her like water.

When she locked eyes with Clementine, the woman immediately busied herself with a lime, even though it was clear to Lou from fifteen feet away that no more were needed, likely for the rest of the night.

Rachel was leaning on her elbows on the bar, talking to a blonde woman Lou had seen a few times before.

Lou called out to her. She didn't raise her voice, just pitched it so she knew it would cut through the music and chatter, something she'd perfected over many years behind this very counter.

Rachel stopped her conversation and straightened up. "Look, Lou, I was just—wait, what's wrong?"

"Did you throw ice on a *priest?*"

"There was a priest in the bar? Oh right, that undertaker-looking guy. New girl helped him."

Rachel started to step away, but Lou shook her head once sternly. "Not so fast, she didn't do that in a vacuum. Clem, over here."

Clementine rushed over, her cheeks glowing bright pink,

and Lou got a little thrill at how innocent that blush made her look. She remembered Clem being quite the opposite.

Lou lowered her voice further, making Rachel and Clem lean in. She did not need any of the customers hearing this. "You two threw ice on a *priest*. A priest my grandma sent here, by the way."

"I'm not the one who threw the ice," Rachel said, raising her hands and taking a step backward.

Clem crossed her arms over her chest and her mouth dropped open.

Lou wondered if she was about to have another front-row seat to this fiery redhead putting Rachel in her place. But Rachel held up a hand to silence her indignation. "I didn't dump the ice, *but* the guy did order water. The rule's the rule."

"Fuck," Lou groaned. "When someone is here asking for me, maybe don't follow the rule."

"Okay, but—" Clem started to speak but Rachel cut her off again.

"Why would your grandma send a priest? Is everything okay?" Rachel asked, her voice infused with concern in a way that was disconcerting to Lou.

If Rachel was starting to care, Lou would have no hope of shutting down concerns about the bar as quickly as they'd arisen. She couldn't let anyone else worry until she had a plan. By the time they started to worry, she wanted to have things figured out one way or another.

"No, it's... look, Howl's fine. I'm fine. *Everything* is fine. Let's just get back to work. Rachel, it looks like Anita is about to cause a scene. She's confronting Mindy and her new girl-friend. Take care of that. And Clementine, go get more ice from the back, and this time try not to dump it on anyone."

Chapter Seven
Clementine

C lem squinted against the sun as she and Alyssa walked down Centre Street, the main drag of their Boston neighborhood, matching iced coffees rattling in their hands. Her favorite heart-shaped sunglasses Clementine's cousin Jane had sent her last year were another casualty of the stolen Corolla.

"Look, Clemmy." Alyssa lowered her own glasses to make eye contact. "We need to get you some new clothes before Lou ruins any more of my favorite tops. Well, my favorite tops outside of the bedroom anyway. I had to skate three seasons before I got that shirt. Do you have any idea how many bruises that is?"

"My best friend from home mailed me some stuff. It should be here in a few days. Can't I just wait for that?"

Alyssa put a finger to her chin and tilted her head to the side, eyes flicking to Clem's legs. "Quick q, are those clothes in the mail anything like the ones you showed up in the other day?"

Clem squinted even harder. She was back in the jean shorts she'd worn on her drive to Boston. She wound her index finger through one of the rips. "Um, yes, they're my clothes, so I'd say they're pretty similar."

"Then no. Absolutely, definitely, assuredly not." Alyssa took Clementine by the elbow and led her down a few doors to a shop called Eastern Exchange. Even as she looked into the window, Clem could tell that the vintage store was almost painfully cool with its low lights and dark leather couches.

"Alyssa. I don't have money for bread, even the kind that might be half styrofoam. You treated me to this coffee, and it's not even a latte because I was worried about spending four dollars. Which is kind of a lot for a plain iced coffee, by the way."

"It's organic."

"Still."

"And fair-trade."

Clem nodded slowly. "O-kay."

"And shade-grown in sacred groves, blessed by a virgi—"

"Look, even if it was made of rainbows, I can't justify spending money right now," Clem interjected. "I'm not going to waste $100 on leather pants or whatever you're thinking."

Alyssa let her mouth fall open as she gazed up at the pants in the window, reverent. "Baby, those pants are an investment that *will* appreciate."

"An investment in what, exactly?"

"An investment in your ass. Appreciated by all. Now come on." Alyssa opened the door to the shop and ushered Clem through. "You've gotta spend money to make money."

Inside the store, Prince's Purple Rain played murmur-low over hidden speakers. A fog floated above the distressed wooden floor dream-like as it skated over her shoes.

They stood in the center of the small shop, a circle of shiny black tables dappled with garments surrounded them. For a clothing store, it really didn't have many, well, clothes. The space itself was sparse—its wares so curated, it was like a forest that had been clear cut, with only a few tiny saplings rising from the wood chips. It was nothing like the thrift stores near Hart's Hollow that Sam loved, packed to the brim with old Nintendo games and nearly every shirt her dad had ever owned.

"Let's start with tights!"

Clem shook her head. "I'm not wearing second-hand tights."

"Don't you mean second *foot* tights?"

"I won't be wearing those either."

"Well, I had no idea someone who's shopping in my hamper would be so picky. Should I be flattered?" Alyssa laughed.

Though her wardrobe might suggest otherwise, Clementine wasn't big on clothes that didn't belong to her. As the track switched over to Thriller, she felt like she was in a dream, except instead of being naked in front of the class she was wearing everyone else's dirty clothes. So, a nightmare. Even adjusting to borrowing a few things from Alyssa had made her squirmy.

Alyssa approached a table that contained five t-shirts, exactly one per stack, and gingerly lifted one up. She squinted at the white lettering that seemed to glow in the milky purple light —Back in Black, how appropriate. It's not that she didn't want an Amy Winehouse shirt, it was that it seemed criminal to pay for one with several rips in it when she might not even need to look hot for much longer.

"This could work," Alyssa said with a grin. "Of course the sleeves would have to go, and we'd need to take about six inches off the bottom. But there's something about old concert tees that rakes in the tips. Plus, Amy's a legend."

Clem pinched the handwritten tag between her fingers, turning it one way and then the other, trying to make it make sense. "Sixty dollars for a t-shirt?" Her whisper echoed in the quiet space of the store.

"It's a classic! These things appreciate over time."

"Are you taking a business class or something? An item that someone has sweat in should definitely depreciate. It has a hole under the arm."

"I told you we're removing the sleeves anyway. And I'm hooked on a show about Wall Street bros, thank you very much."

"Of course." That actually made more sense. Alyssa was a lot smarter than she liked to let on, but the thought of her sitting in a classroom didn't seem right, like she might die of boredom and dry erase marker fumes. "Those sleeves are worth ten dollars each, I'm not removing them."

"Trust me on this one. After this, we should talk about tattoos." Alyssa clutched the shirt to her chest and turned from Clem. "Excuse me, can my friend also see the leather pants in the window? She'd like to try them on."

Beneath her bright blue bangs, the shopkeeper's eyes made a slow appraisal of Clem like one of them was a refrigerator she wasn't sure would fit in her car. Clem didn't like the judgy implication in her gaze. "Good luck," the woman said, a grimace evident in her voice as she retrieved the pants, then slowly walked them over, draping them across Alyssa's waiting arms.

They made their way to the dressing room in the back corner of the store. A black velvet curtain served as her only privacy as Clem removed her top and put on the Winehouse shirt. Though something about the darkness, knowing Alyssa couldn't see her face, pushed Clem to talk about the worry churning through her mind.

"Is this really necessary? I'm not sure if I even still have a job after giving Lou's priest an ice bath."

"Don't be silly, Lou just had a bee in her bloomers."

Clem laughed despite herself. "I don't think that's the expression. It's 'bonnet', isn't it? And also, ouch." She pulled the curtain open and stepped out.

"Well, that's *my* expression. Can you picture Lou in a bonnet? Didn't think so." Alyssa shivered. "The thing you need to know about Lou is, I know she seems scary, but she actually *is* scary."

Clementine's stomach plummeted, followed by a flicker of anger at herself. She needed the money, sure, but there was no reason she had to care about this job. Or about Lou. "Alyssa, was that supposed to make me feel better?"

Alyssa tilted her head to one side and blinked her wide, blue eyes. "No, why would that make you feel better? Do you need to feel better?"

"Apparently not, because everything in my life is great."

"You're damn right it is. Anyway, I've seen how Lou looks at you, you'll be fine. Now get on those pants so *I* can look at you. Respectfully."

"Wait, how does she—"

A firm hand to Clem's lower back propelled her into the changing room again as she swallowed her question. She wanted a few moments in this tiny, clothes-filled closet to bask in the fact that Lou *looked* at her.

A few minutes and many swears later, Clem slid open the curtain with more force than necessary. She was learning to lean into the drama of daily life at Alyssa's urging. It would have been perfect if the leather pants weren't currently halted somewhere around mid-thigh.

Alyssa stifled a laugh. "I see we have a group project going on. Come here."

Clem narrowed her eyes at Alyssa and hopped forward, her

movements hampered by the leather binding her legs like a goth mermaid.

Alyssa closed her eyes for a beat, clearly biting back a smile. When she opened them again, her face was placid. "Pretty good, right? I've been practicing mindfulness after Jazzercise with my friend Esther."

"I'm impressed. Now back to what you were saying about Lou. How does she look at me?"

Clem gripped one side of the pants and Alyssa took hold of the other as they alternated pulling them up in a seesaw motion.

"Well, Rachel called it 'reverent', and you know she's being honest because Rachel hates you." Alyssa bit her lip as the pants' progress stalled just below Clem's hip bones.

"I knew it."

"I mean, you're not special in that way. Rachel hates everyone. Including herself, probably." Alyssa shrugged. "Okay, I need you to hop on three. One, two, go!"

Clem hopped as Alyssa grabbed both sides of the pants to yank them up. Her breathing grew heavy as she continued tugging. "Come on, just a little more Clem, I'm almost there."

"Is everything okay in there?" The shopkeeper's voice called from the other side of the store. "Legally we have to discourage public sex."

Clem's face lit on fire, but Alyssa winked. "Look at these pants, already starting rumors."

When the last button was hooked, Clementine was ready for a lemonade and a nap, but even she could admit that her new roommate and budding life coach had a point. The pants made her body look like a work of art, sleek and sexy, as long as she didn't need to breathe too much. Or use the bathroom ever again. Clem was all about body positivity. She liked how she looked because she felt good and that had nothing to do with her dress size, but this was something different. She'd never looked like something to be devoured.

Clementine spun toward Alyssa with a grin, popping her hips to one side. "What do you think? Do you like them?"

But what she really wondered was if Lou would like them, if this was the thing that would make her eyes linger on Clem just a second longer than necessary, reverent.

FOR THE REST of the afternoon, Clem tried to untangle why she would possibly want to please Lou. It's wasn't though Lou was actually interested in dating her. And it certainly wasn't related to Lou owning the bar, because when it came down to it, this job was a happy accident, temporary. Clementine was only going to stay at Howl long enough to get back on her feet, and then she'd move on with her life just like she'd intended the day she drove out of Hart's Hollow without a glance in her rearview mirror. Nothing against Lou or her chaotic bar, but Clem didn't want to work for someone else long term. That's what had driven Clem from Hart's Hollow in the first place, wasn't it? She didn't like the parallel that was starting to form in her mind.

After her mom died, Clem had done everything she could think of to get her father to turn the diner over to her, but he treated it like a shrine. The years ticked by and nothing changed. Bit by bit Clem lost hope that things would ever be different. And soon enough, everything in Clem's life felt like it was a fork coated in syrup, glued to the tile floor. She'd needed something drastic to pry herself loose.

Frustration with her father welled inside her again, like it did every time she thought about why she'd left. The diner couldn't survive much longer the way it was. Hart's Hollow was changing. Younger families were moving in. Places need to be as alive as people—they have to adapt and grow, but no amount of reason could make her father see that.

Clementine needed a distraction. She couldn't go to work this frustrated. Not when tonight had the potential to be even more of a disaster than last night. After she pulled on her work outfit, she propped her phone up on the bathroom sink so she could do her makeup. Alyssa had gifted her an alarming amount of shimmer products.

When Sam accepted Clem's video call, she felt a wave of gratitude so strong it made her lightheaded.

"Holy hot pants," Sam said, her eyes going comically wide. "Back up a little please, so I can see the rest of them."

Clem rolled her eyes, but then took a step back and twirled. Sam was the most annoyingly lovable person she'd ever known. She knew just the thing to make Clem feel better even when she didn't know herself. Just for a second, another wave of longing for her friend surged through her so strongly that she grabbed the edge of the sink to steady herself.

Sam let out a wolf whistle as Clem swallowed the lump in her throat.

"Sam, I'm not calling about the pants."

"You should be calling everyone you know about those pants. Since when do you wear leather?"

"This is one hundred percent Alyssa's enthusiastic peer pressure."

"I think I'm in love with her," Sam said, fluttering her eyelashes.

Sam being in love with Alyssa was the absolute last thing Clem needed to think about right now. The two of them together would be a glittering parade of sass and zeal. Time to redirect this conversation to the topic she'd been avoiding. "So, have you been by Maine Course lately?"

Sam sighed. "If you're calling to ask if you should call your dad, the answer is yes."

"How could you possibly know that's what I was calling to ask? I was just curious how business was." Clem feigned innocence.

"No, you weren't. I practically raised you, babe, I know you better than you know yourself. You already know business is steady enough with the cottage cheese crowd."

Clem rolled her eyes. "You're only six months older than me, Sam."

"My point exactly. I walked every path before you and served as your personal guide. My wisdom is vast and wide. And I may have stopped in for a muffin this morning and your dad said he hadn't heard from you. Which is very bad, Clementine Darby. Now, I'm going to hang up, and if you don't call your dad, I will drive down there and ruin your life by making out with your roommate."

"The thought of another person in my life falling completely in love with you is distressing."

"That's what I thought. Call. Now."

Clem watched her phone screen fade to black after Sam ended the call. She went back to doing her makeup, thinking she would call the diner on her way to work.

She only made it a few blocks before guilt won out over Red, Taylor's Version. Clem pulled her phone from her pocket and clicked the only number on her *favorites* list: Home.

"Thanks for calling Maine Course, this is Brenda, how can I help you?"

Why was Brenda answering the phone? "Hi Brenda, it's Clementine. Is my dad there?"

"Hiya, kiddo! He's outside taking a delivery, but he should be back in a few minutes if you want to hang on the line. You know how he loves to gossip."

Clem felt a smile creep across her face. She'd been so busy being frustrated with her dad that she couldn't remember the last time she'd thought about the things she loved about him. Denny Darby *was* a world-class gossip. It was one of the things that made him so popular. He was friendly, sure, but he was also looking for the good dirt.

"Sure, I can wait, though I might be holding for hours. Are you working at the diner now?"

"I sure am! Your dad asked me to help out when you left town, and you know I never could say no to that man."

A rush of shame heated Clem's cheeks, even though there had been no reproach in Brenda's voice. Brenda and her dad had been friends for sixty years. Of course he'd asked her to help. "I'm glad he can count on you. How's he doing? Is he eating?"

"He's eating, but not as well as he should. If I had my say, he certainly wouldn't have had chili cheese fries for lunch."

"He did not. I've hardly been gone for a week and already the entire system has fallen apart?"

"Oh honey, my guess is that he was sneaking these fries long before you left. Oh, we better stop our gossip, here he is now."

Clem heard Brenda murmuring against the backdrop of diner noise. She must have pulled the phone away from her ear.

"Oh my darlin' is that you?" Her dad's voice was full of cheer and it made Clem's heart ache. For a year after her mom died, it felt like neither of them had so much as smiled. And then slowly, her dad had become himself again. Goofy and mildly incompetent—frustrating and endearing in equal measure as he burned the elaborate cake he'd made for her birthday, setting off the fire alarms and costing them three weeks of business to clean up the mess left by the sprinklers.

Her dad's voice came on the line, sounding close and painfully far away all at once. "Clementine, are you there?"

"Hi, daddio. I'm here. What's this I hear about chili cheese fries? With your cholesterol levels, that's as dangerous as bicycling without a helmet. Which you'd better not be doing."

"And I suppose you're being a saint there in Boston? No milkshakes or candy?" Denny teased.

"I'm not the one with a heart problem, Dad."

"Okay, fine. It won't happen again. Especially not after I tell Brenda about our diner's non-disclosure policy." He laughed.

"I'd like to see that in action. You'd burst if you couldn't spill secrets you gathered at the counter."

"Well, you've got me there. Not that I'm not glad to hear from you, but why are you calling kiddo? We're about to head into the dinner rush. Everything okay?"

Clem glanced at the time on her phone. 4:25, the early early bird special. "Yeah, everything's fine." Even as Clem said it, tears pricked behind her eyes. "Just calling to give you a hard time."

"Well, mission accomplished. I wish I could chat more, but Mabel and her whole crew from the senior home just walked in. I'll call you tomorrow morning, okay?"

"Oh right, but not before 11, okay? I work kind of late at the bar."

"Eleven is practically lunchtime. I'll call you while I'm eating my super healthy salad," Denny said, a wink in his tone.

"Sounds like a plan. And it's not healthy if it has bacon and eggs and cheese on it," she admonished.

"Goodbye darlin', love you."

The line went silent before Clem could say it back. It had been good to hear her dad's voice, but it had also stung in a way she hadn't prepared for. The way he sounded so completely fine without her there, left her feeling devastated. For years she'd washed this man's socks, and now he was functioning by himself. It should be a crime for life in Hart's Hollow to continue in Clementine's absence. The entire town should have crumbled without her there to hold it together.

But feeling devastated that her dad was doing well made her feel like the worst daughter in the world. She should be happy he was thriving. Leaving was *her* choice, but still, he could pretend to be sad without her. It was just common courtesy.

By the time she rounded the corner onto Howl's block, Clem was only half-dreading going into work. This night had a few things going for it. First of all, she looked hot, as attested to by Sam's wolf whistle. The downside was that also meant the night didn't hold any clothes ripping or mind-melting touches from Lou. That *was* a good thing though, right? Even thinking about Lou's fingers on the inside of her thighs sent a rush of heat through Clem. She definitely couldn't work if she kept thinking about that, because if she hadn't burnt a bridge with Lou over the ice incident, she might actually be trusted with more than just limes tonight.

For the next eight hours, Clem planned to be beyond reproach. She had a sudden need to prove herself essential. She wanted to be needed. Especially after that call with her dad. As much as she would like to be the kind of person who could shrug things off. Rachel's mean trick with the ice had hurt her feelings. No one at Maine Course had ever set her up to fail. Clementine had wanted a change, and it seemed she was getting it.

Lou didn't scowl at her when she walked into the bar, and Clem was taking that as a win. But she did head back to her office, which felt like a loss.

"Hey, new girl." A woman with chestnut brown curls and a bright smile was watching her from the other end of the bar. Her crop top had a ragged, uneven edge that was working with her high-waisted black jeans. Clem wondered if her look was another Lou special.

"Hi, other girl," Clem smiled and breathed out a sigh of relief when the woman smiled back. She would not have survived a Rachel 2.0.

"'Older' is probably more accurate. I'm Megan." The woman held out her right hand. Two of her fingers were bandaged and taped together. When she caught Clementine looking, she raised her hand higher. "The ice machine and I had another dispute, and as always, that bitch won."

"Oh, right! I think that was the first night I worked here. I guess I should thank you for the job."

"My pain and suffering at your service," Megan said with a low bow. "So who trained you?"

"Is there training in addition to the hazing?" Clem narrowed her eyes in a way she hoped was playful and not pitiful.

"So, you've been working with Rachel then? She'll set you up for sure, but she's kind of earned it. She's been at Howl longer than anyone. Well, except for Lou. I'm pretty sure *she* was born here."

Clem nodded. She had been wondering about Lou. It was clear she was devoted to the bar, but there also seemed to be a sadness sitting on her. Maybe it had something to do with the other night. Anyone getting a visit from a priest was probably in some kind of trouble. Whatever it was, Lou struck Clementine as the stoic type who would never let others know what was going on.

"Anyway, let me teach you the register. We keep asking for a POS system, but I think Lou would burst into flames if she had to carry a tablet around the bar. And she'd need to learn how to operate one in the first place."

Clem followed Megan to the end of the counter. The register wasn't that different from the one at the diner that she'd been operating since she was seven.

"The first thing you want to do is enter the code. We all use Lou's."

"Okay." Clem nodded, stepping up to the register, her fingers hovering above the keys. "What is it?"

"80085."

Clem typed in the numbers and nothing happened. "Did I get it wrong?"

"Oh honey," Megan said, shaking her head. "Have you never been bored with a calculator? This thing is like 100 years old, you don't need a code."

Clem laughed. "That's a very dumb joke, but I kind of love it."

"Yeah, I've only been here a year, so I just do baby pranks. Anyway, the drink codes are on this pad right here. Just key those in instead of looking for the item manually." Megan reached under the bar and pulled out a legal notepad that looked like it had been run over by a bus.

"Good system," Clem said, wondering how she could flip through the pages without actually having to touch them.

CLEMENTINE WAS in a groove *and* grooving. She focused on her task, in her lane, thriving. She was also strongly considering testing herself by tossing up a lime and slicing it mid-air. Okay, so she might be a bit fucking tired of garnish duty. Instead of complaining, she nodded along to Tegan and Sara and tried not to worry about the fact that Alyssa had the night off. Her room-mate had stopped by Howl briefly to pick up a sequined jump-suit she'd been keeping at the bar for some reason, but she'd only chatted for a minute before she sent Clem back to work with an *'atta girl* pat on the ass that honestly meant business.

Next to her, Rachel called out drinks, the names What Peaches and What Penumbras and Neon Fruit Supermarket flowing together into a beautiful if confusing poem. Clem could feel Rachel's eyes boring into her, but when she gathered her courage to turn to look, she still wasn't prepared for the rage she saw there.

"Do you think you might be done with those sometime this century so you can, you know, actually help serve drinks? I think we're good on the citrus front." Rachel's voice was less of a grumble and more of a growl. Her words hinted at bared teeth and midnight mischief.

Was she *allowed* to serve drinks now? Clementine wanted to cheer but suppressed the urge. Rachel was going to trust her, Clementine Darby, with the awesome power of a swizzle stick? Her gut told her not to believe it, but then again Lou hadn't fired her after the priest-on-ice incident. Maybe she was the kind of person who could appreciate Clem taking initiative after all. She wiped her hands, cuts stinging, and tossed the towel down.

"Sure. Where do you want me?"

Rachel cocked an eyebrow like a loaded gun and barked out a laugh. Clementine could feel her flush creeping up to her ears so much so that she could nearly hear her own embarrassment. Rachel was definitely going to screw her over tonight.

"I mean, um, who needs help?"

Rachel nodded toward two women at the end of the bar. They were practically leaning over the counter, like kids scrambling for the cookie jar. It looked like the smaller one was about to get a boost. Gotta love teamwork.

"Go get 'em, tiger," Rachel said with a leer.

As Clem made her way over to the pair, the air conditioning from the vent above the bar blew against her bare stomach. She wasn't used to this work 'dress code' yet. Usually dressing for work involved putting on more clothes than she wore at home, rather than taking crucial inches off.

"What can I get you?" Clem said with her best smile before turning it down a bit. Everything at Howl was on a dimmer switch. Brooding was also part of the dress code. Well, unless you were Alyssa.

"How about a shot of whiskey? And one for you, too." The woman's short, black hair was glistening in the light, iced over with enough gel to meet helmet law requirements.

"Oh, thanks, but I'm not a big drinker and I'm working."

Rachel's fingers squeezed into the soft part of Clem's arm. Since when was Rachel even standing beside her? "Never refuse a drink from a customer. House rules."

Was she kidding? Clem searched Rachel's face, but she looked serious. "I can't work if I drink."

"The rest of us managed to figure it out. Unless you want me to go get Lou and see if she'll make an exception for you. Again."

A jolt of excitement passed through her. She wouldn't mind seeing Lou saunter out from the back. Clem's mind flashed to an image of Lou. Dark jeans, a white t-shirt, and boots, a minimal style that somehow surpassed all other attempts at cool. There was something about Lou besides the fact that she looked like every 90s heartthrob poster Clementine's cousin had had up in her bedroom when they were both too young to know boys were a poor imitation of their real desire.

Regardless, Lou McCallister did not seem like the kind of person who liked to make exceptions. Clem's swallow echoed in her ears. "No, it's fine. It's not as though many people will try to buy me a drink anyway."

"Famous last words." Rachel smirked and walked away.

Clem made quick work of pouring the drinks. And after listening to a minute-long weird toast about new friends, she downed hers and got back to work.

She understood why Rachel had been annoyed with her.

The bar was packed, sometimes three deep around the counter, waving hands and money to get their attention. Alyssa had mentioned that it was always busier around Pride.

As it turned out, a lot of people wanted to buy her shots, like a softball team's worth. Whether or not they were an actual softball team was yet to be determined. Clem was feeling it. Her hands were floating and her steps faltered if she wasn't looking at her feet. When Rachel crashed into her with a Stale Beer Afternoon, it almost seemed inevitable. She dabbed at her white shirt with a bar towel, but it felt hard to care.

At some point, Lou had wandered out from the back, and how had Clem missed that? God, she looked good as she stood there examining the bottles and making a list. Lists were sexy. Clem made her way over to Lou, feeling emboldened. Like all of her bad decisions were bubble-wrapped from the hard edges of reality.

She stopped in front of Lou and reached out, finally tucking that rogue strand of hair behind her ear. "I like lists, too."

Lou blinked at her before narrowing her eyes. "Are you okay?"

"Yeah, totally, um, fine. You know, just work shots."

"Work shots?" Lou was squinting at her.

"Lots of people buying the new girl shots. I know Rachel said we have to accept them, but I don't know how you do it. I've lost count of how many I've had." Clem blinked trying to focus on the cute look Lou was giving her. It was like she cared. "Do you think it's okay if I say no the rest of the night?"

"Fuck." Lou's eyes darted to Rachel. "Good luck down here, Rach. I'm going to find our darlin' Clementine a place to lie down."

Rachel started to protest, but then Lou's hand was on the small of Clem's back, leading her to the stairs. Lou's touch could have drowned out air raid sirens, Clementine's world narrowed to the warm press of Lou's palm on her bare skin and the beat of her own heart.

Lou leaned in close, her breath a caress ghosting Clem's neck. "You've realized Rachel is kind of mean, right?"

Clem nodded enthusiastically. *How nice that she and Lou agreed on this*. What else could they see eye to eye on? She tried to turn, but Lou encouraged her to keep moving before she spoke again.

"You might want to question some of the stuff she tells you. But I should have been behind the bar with you two making sure everything was going okay instead of holed up in my office trying to fix unfixable problems."

"What problems?" Clem wanted to pout. *Why wouldn't Lou let her stop and rest and maybe kiss her? And since when were they on stairs? Could she engineer a stumble so Lou's strong arms would catch her?*

"That's not important. The thing with the shots—always accept, but there's no way you can take them. Just pretend to chase it with a beer and spit the shot back into the bottle. Otherwise, you'll be hammered."

Clem leaned back into Lou as they continued up the stairs. "I don't really drink," she attempted to whisper. Not very successfully, if Lou's wince was any indication. "But I think I might be drunk. Is this hammered?"

"You, my dear, are beyond. Here, lean against this wall for a second."

"Where are we?"

"My apartment."

Clem wanted to shout. Lou had brought Clem back to *her apartment*. There was only one reason for that. Clem thanked the universe that her new, revealing work uniform was working its magic. A blessing and a curse. "You live in the bar?"

"No, I live above it. Look, I'll get you settled and then I'll finish out your shift. You just rest here and I'll help you get home after closing, okay?"

Damn. Apparently, there were two reasons. "S'kay."

Lou unclipped her keys from her belt loop and unlocked the door. Keys on a belt loop should not be sexy, but on Lou, they telegraphed her being in charge in a way that made Clem's knees go weak. Or maybe that was the tequila catching up with her. And the rum. And the whiskey. God, she was going to be in for a world of pain tomorrow.

Lou helped Clem inside, and it felt nice not to think about where to step next, to just let herself be guided like a sleepwalker.

Clem settled onto the couch at Lou's gentle prodding. She still felt disappointed, even though she knew she was too drunk to make any decisions and likely too drunk to even read Lou's signals.

"Okay, um. Water! And Tylenol. You stay there." Lou spun from her and rushed away.

Was the unflappable Lou flustered by her? Clem swallowed a giggle that promptly morphed into a hiccup.

Lou came back a minute later with everything she'd mentioned, plus a bowl and a sweatshirt.

She handed Clem the hoodie. "That's in case you get cold. Since your shirt is a little wet."

Clem glanced down, and yup, her bra was clearly visible through the wet fabric.

Lou bent down and set the mixing bowl on the floor. The Tupperware, much like Clem, had seen better days.

"What's this for? In case I need to make emergency popcorn."

"Sure, that. Or," Lou said slowly, "in case you feel sick. The bathroom is that door there but you know you—whoa."

Lou reached out her free hand to steady Clem. She hadn't realized she was tipping over like a tree about to fall until her shoulder thudded against the arm of the couch.

"Shit, are you going to be okay up here alone?" Panic garnished Lou's voice.

"I'll be fine. So fine you won't even believe it. I won't even puke in your bowl." Clem pulled the sweatshirt into a hug and rubbed her cheek against it. Soft. And it smelled slightly of pine, like it had been washed in a forest spring. It reminded her of the woods in Hart's Hollow. It felt like home.

Lou smiled and Clem felt proud of her joke. Wait, had she made a joke? Her eyes started to slide shut as she clutched the hoodie more firmly to her chest.

"Okay, but if you feel sick, don't fight it. I think it wouldn't hurt for you to get some of the alcohol out of your system. Actually, I'll get some food delivered and you just drink that water. I'll be back up as soon as I can."

Before Lou even reached the door, Clem's eyes were closing like automatic doors. She nestled back onto the couch and let herself fall into the comforting woodsy scent of Lou's space.

Chapter Eight
Lou

Lou paused on the stairs, wondering if the metal was too unforgiving to sleep on. With the way her eyes burned from her long day, she might be able to do it, but only if she didn't care about being able to move in the morning. She reminded herself that, a few weeks ago, she'd hurt her back reaching for a glass. She'd then spent the next few days serving drinks in silent pain while Rachel and Megan had a suspicious amount of overlap with their time off requests. Lately, her efforts to save the bar were seriously cutting into her sleep schedule. It turned out bankers' hours were a real thing that meant they were almost never available, except at the crack of 10 a.m.

Had it been a mistake to bring a drunk Clementine to her apartment? Rationally Lou knew she'd done a good thing. There was nothing weird about Lou feeling an obligation to keep her employee safe. It was the same reason she had fire extinguishers around the bar. But Clem sparked something confusing in her, something that felt dangerously like interest.

Lou wished she was the kind of person who could have put her in a car and sent her on her merry, drunken way. And maybe in her twenties, she would have done just that. But the years and the horror stories on the news had made her even less sure of the goodness of others. Besides, considering how drunk Clem was and how new to the city, she probably wouldn't even have been able to give the driver her address.

At least Lou had done the responsible thing and texted Alyssa to let her know. She'd been half-hoping that Clem's roommate would swing by and collect her and save Lou from her own confusion. But when Alyssa had offered to bail on her date after her cabaret show, Lou—like the absolute masochist she was when it came to Clementine—had told her not to.

She climbed the final few steps, the need to crawl into her bed and exhaustion winning out over her trepidation about what she might find in her apartment. No one had ever been waiting for Lou at the end of a long day. And if she was being honest, the thought of Clementine being there to greet her didn't seem like the absolute worst thing in the world. Even if Clem wasn't in the best shape, it wasn't like Lou was a stranger to puke. She practically lived in her bar for god's sake, but it was a lot different when she had to clean it up off her living room floor.

Lou knew she needed to tread carefully. Giving to people who didn't care about her was asking for trouble. It had gotten her heart broken over and over by her family for years, until she'd finally realized if you belong, you can still be cast out. And relying on them was a surefire way to be let down.

Lou opened the door to her apartment and scanned the small living room. When she didn't immediately see Clementine, her heart rate kicked up. Had she wandered outside alone?

As much as Lou told herself she didn't want her guest to stay, now that she was faced with the possibility Clem might have left, it was becoming clear that Lou did, in fact, have a preference. She just needed to *ask* Clem if she wanted to stay over and make it absolutely crystal clear Lou just meant sleep. That was, as soon as she could find her.

Knowing that her fridge was empty, she'd called in an order of hangover-cure food while the restaurant a few blocks over was still open. The absolute best sloppy burger combo money could buy, though the orange soda hadn't survived until closing. Was there anything more delicious than something effervescent and sweet when you were dying of thirst?

Lou set the cardboard box containing the burger and fries onto the coffee table and a movement caught her attention. She turned to see Clem's foot hanging off the couch. A foot that was attached to a long leg that... god, Clem's leg was bare. Her leather pants were in a pile next to the sofa, which meant she was fast asleep in just her underwear and Lou's hoodie. Lou wasn't sure she'd ever get over how sexy those pants looked on her apartment floor.

Clementine had one arm thrown over her head, like she was auditioning for the victim on SVU. The sweatshirt Lou had lent her had ridden up, revealing a sliver of milky white midriff, dotted with just a few freckles the same copper red as Clementine's hair. Those freckles were doing something to Lou, and that was the opposite of chivalrous. She averted her eyes and pulled the blanket off the back of the couch, draping it over Clem.

In her sleep, Clementine shifted, her hand reaching for Lou's. Lou caught her wrist and rested Clementine's hand on top of the blanket. She felt a little like a mortician. Then she flipped open the takeout container and grabbed a fry. Someone might as well enjoy the food before it became inedible. Plus she was ravenous, and unlike her grandmother, she had never been able to let good food go to waste.

When Lou finished eating, she gave Clem's foot a tentative nudge with her knee and... nothing. She leaned a bit closer to be sure Clem was still breathing. Lou released her own held breath when the blanket fell with Clem's exhale. Having a dead employee seemed a lot worse than having one sleeping in her living room. Though neither was great, especially with the way her eyes kept finding their way back to Clem.

It was still dark outside when Lou shot awake, reaching for the baseball bat she kept beneath her bed. It was a small novelty one she'd gotten at a Red Sox game, but the shadows in her apartment made it loom large.

Clementine's scream sounded from the living room, and Lou realized that must have been what had woken her up. Maybe her guest had seen a mouse or a spider. No problem, Lou could take care of that quickly and go back to bed. She was absolutely not afraid of mice or spiders, because there was no logical reason to be afraid. Still, as Lou made her way to the living room, she clutched the wooden bat in her hand until her knuckles ached.

The cast-off glow from the streetlights streamed in through the window, illuminating Clementine who was sitting on the couch clutching her chest. She looked pale, but that could just be the light playing ghostly tricks. Or the fact that Clementine *was* kind of pale. Weren't people in Maine supposed to be obsessed with being outside hiking and, like, taming bears? Maybe she came by it naturally with that whole red hair, blue eyes thing. Not that Lou had a healthy glow with her nocturnal schedule. All the prime sunbathing hours were spent securely in the dark cave of her room, sleeping off the night before.

Lou inched closer, her steps tentative. "Clementine, it's Lou. What's wrong?"

Clementine blinked a few times like she was dazed, but after a moment it looked as though she finally came back to herself. It was like watching a computer reboot.

"Sorry." She let out a low laugh that sounded almost embarrassed. "Did I wake you?"

Lou looked herself up and down, her loose sleep shirt barely covering her. "I'm gonna go with yes. You screamed really loud. Like call-911-someone-is-dying loud."

"Ugh, I'm so sorry." Clem fell back on the couch and pulled one of the throw pillows over her face.

"What scared you?" Lou eased toward the sofa. Clem still had a vacant, haunted look about her that made Lou hesitant to make any sudden movements.

"Nothing."

"Well, obviously something. Unless screaming is just a thing you like to do?"

"You'll think I'm silly."

"What if I promise not to judge or laugh?"

Clementine lowered the pillow and narrowed her eyes at Lou. "Everyone promises that."

Lou smiled then. There was something refreshing about Clem calling bullshit while half awake and underdressed. "Okay, but give me a chance to mean it."

Clem blew out a breath, pressing the flat of her palm to her chest just over her heart. It looked like she was about to rattle off the pledge of allegiance, but what she said was even more confusing.

She rolled her eyes skyward. "I had a bad dream, okay? And the dolphins were being really mean. Like total assholes. And I didn't know how to swim. They ruined my entire birthday." Clementine paused, studying Lou's face.

Lou pretended to be a statue. Calling dolphins assholes was almost unbearably funny, but she wouldn't crack because

Clementine didn't seem to be joking. She seemed upset. "I'm sorry, it sounds like that really scared you."

"I think I forgot to mention that alcohol gives me nightmares? Anyway, that's why I don't drink much because..."

"Because then the dolphins are assholes."

Clem nodded before covering her face with her hands. "God, you must think I'm a ridiculous pest. Here you are being nice to me and I pay you back by screaming bloody murder. I'm sorry I woke you up. I can just head home, in case I, you know, have another nightmare."

Lou tried to stifle a yawn, and the action brought tears to her eyes. "What time is it?"

Clem pulled her phone from between the cushions. "4:22 a.m."

"There's no way I'm sending you out into the world this early. Then I'd just need you to call me when you got home and that would wake me up anyway. So, really, you might as well stay. As a favor to my sleep schedule if nothing else." Lou made her way over to the couch and nodded at Clementine's legs. "May I?"

Clem tucked her legs under her and Lou settled down onto the cushion next to her.

"I didn't expect you to be so..."

"So what?" Lou quirked an eyebrow, leaning close enough that their shoulders brushed. The electricity of the contact rushed through her body.

"So... nice," Clem said and then snapped her mouth closed.

Lou barked out a laugh. "Yeah, well, if you tell anyone, I'll have to kill you. I'm serious, the dolphins don't have anything on me. How's that?"

"Much better. Now can you do that clicking sound they make, like you mean business?" Clem laughed and snuggled back further into the couch.

"Good. Now, tell me more about these dolphins. Are we talking aquarium or the open ocean?"

"That's the thing." Clem clutched Lou's arm, her eyes wide. "It was all in a backyard swimming pool."

Lou nodded, urging her on, thinking all the time that she could listen to Clementine Darby talk until the sun came up. And with the way this story was going, she just might.

Chapter Nine
Clementine

W hat was it with Clem waking up in other people's clothes lately? Especially without an encore of her and Lou's time in the storeroom. It was becoming a trend she wasn't sure she loved. She understood why Lou hadn't made a move on her, but she was still disappointed.

Clem had awoken with a stiffness in her neck that made her worry her spine might shatter if she moved her head. A breath blew warmly against her hair, causing her to jerk to the side, and yup, moving was a definite mistake. She shifted herself just enough to squint at the body next to hers. Lou's head was nestled on Clem's shoulder, the soft ocean rhythm of her breathing the only sound in the room. Well, besides the rumble of trucks outside, people yelling, and other various white noise of the city.

The night came back to her in pieces, like a film reel spliced together. Customers buying her shots at the bar, followed by drinks, then more shots, until finally, Lou had led her upstairs to rest, where Clem had been cool, calm, and collected. A total catch. Yeah, right. She groaned. The moral of the story was that Clem needed to stop believing a single thing Rachel told her.

Her run-through of the night didn't explain what had led to Lou sleeping on the couch, the two of them snuggled together. And then, like a flash of lightning in a horror film, Clem's mind helpfully supplied an explanation that she wanted not to be true with her entire being. A nightmare. Lou had felt obligated to take care of her after she'd gotten drunk on the clock, and then Clem had thanked Lou by having an alcohol-fueled bad dream.

You are winning at life, Clementine Darby.

She considered her nightmares private, mostly because they were humiliating. The first time it had happened she was at Sam's sweet sixteen slumber party, soused on peach schnapps, and the other girls had woken her up by dumping her in the pond outside. Only Sam had been kind about it after as she'd washed the pond scum out of Clementine's hair and stayed awake with her until dawn. Ever since that night, all her drunken dreams had to do with water, though she tried to avoid them by keeping herself from getting past tipsy.

Clem suppressed a cringe as she pulled further away from Lou to scan the room. It was neat but sparse in a way that seemed less like a minimalist choice and more like someone who spent very little time in their apartment. Or who wanted to be able to leave at a moment's notice. A half-eaten container of food on the coffee table was the only real clutter.

Nausea roiled in Clementine's stomach and she lurched off the couch, noticing belatedly that Lou's arm had been around her waist. Damn, she should have enjoyed that while it lasted, since Lou had made it pretty clear their storeroom tryst was a one-time thing.

She froze. The last thing she needed was for Lou to wake up and hear her puke. Lou readjusted without waking, and Clem released the breath she'd been holding, before rushing to the bathroom.

A few minutes later, she splashed water on her face and

studied the red blotches on her cheeks. Sexy. At least her hair looked nice—penny bright where it fell against the black hoodie Lou had lent her. The mirror was ancient and spider-webbed at one corner, little black flecks marred the surface where the silver had oxidized. The porcelain of the pedestal sink was cold against her hip as she leaned closer to her reflection. Looking at herself made her feel like a tintype photo, like her hangover was the plague.

She had to get it together. She was in her boss's apartment, for god's sake. Her boss who'd taken pity on her. What would Sam say? Her friend would tell Clem to run while she still had a shred of her dignity.

Clem needed to leave before she overstayed her welcome and became even more of a burden. She'd clearly made Lou feel obligated to care for her when it seemed like that was the last thing Lou wanted to do when it came to Clem. Flirt with her? Sure. Have a real conversation about what had happened the night they met? Absolutely not on Lou's watch. Actually care about her? Definitely not.

So that settled it. Clem would leave... right after she drank a full glass of water and maybe found some pain meds for the aspiring beatboxer behind her left eye.

There was about as much food to be found in the kitchen as there was on the coffee table. Clementine had been hoping for a pitcher of water in the fridge, but there was only a very sad lemon and a jar of olives. Not even enough for a single hors d'oeuvre. She imagined Top Chef contestants breaking down at a Lou's Fridge Quickfire Challenge.

She opened nearly every cabinet before finding the one full of coffee mugs and glasses. Her mind was torn about whether coffee would be heavenly or the world's worst idea. She filled a glass from the sink and gulped it down before filling it again and wandering back over to the fridge. The contents of her stomach sloshed, reminding her of the Water Baby dolls she was obsessed with as a kid. Companies really sold elaborate water balloons that children were tricked into taking care of.

Unlike the rest of the apartment, the fridge door was dotted with pops of color. Several items were cards that said *granddaughter* on the front. Unexpected but sweet. Every time she learned something new about Lou, Clem was reminded that she hardly knew anything at all. She resisted the urge to peek inside one of the cards and instead her eyes fell on a crumpled piece of paper that had been haphazardly affixed to the door with a piece of duct tape.

The urge to be nosy rose up in Clementine again. Surely there was no harm in glancing at the first page? As long as she didn't flip the paper, it wasn't technically snooping. Clementine realized she should be holding herself to a bit of a higher standard than that. Her eyes snagged only the address of the bar and the word 'vacate the premises by' before she forced herself to turn away.

She started when she caught Lou's eye. Lou, who had woken up and silently snuck into the kitchen like a ghost.

"What are you doing?" Her voice was thick with sleep, her usual gravel almost a growl.

The combination of Lou's low tone and the way her blonde hair was mussed from sleep did something decidedly unprofessional to Clem's insides. Jesus. Ten minutes ago she'd been ill, and now she knew she was looking at Lou like she wanted to have her for breakfast.

"I was just, um, getting some water. I wasn't snooping."

Lou nodded slowly, narrowing her eyes. "Spoken like someone who was definitely snooping."

"Fine, but I would like the record to show that I tried very hard not to snoop." Clem leaned against the counter and crossed her arms.

Lou laughed. "There is no record. So, did you find anything that piqued your interest?" Lou's eyes flicked down. She looked almost nervous, vulnerable.

"Yeah, but I'm not sure how to ask about—"

"Clem, you're standing in my kitchen in your underwear and a hoodie that you definitely appear to be naked underneath. Just... ask."

Clem looked down and indeed, she had shed her clothes at some point.

"Are you getting evicted?"

Lou's face fell as she stared at the floor before walking to the sink and getting her own glass of water. "That's, um, that's nothing to worry about. I'm figuring it out."

"I guess I assumed you owned the building."

"No, when I took over the bar from Jude Eakins who ran it for years, her daughter got the building, but then she sold it to my current landlord. I always planned to buy her out, but I could never quite save up the money I needed. Other things always came up—the bar needing new appliances, caring for my grandma. And then by the time I almost had enough, it was too late. Property values had started to skyrocket." Lou scoffed. "This time next year, this place will probably be a microbrewery or cupcake shop."

Clem liked cupcakes but she sensed that wasn't the point.

"Right." Clem nodded. Her eyes tracked the way Lou bit her lower lip. "So now she's just going to sell the building out from under you?"

"I mean, not exactly. The notice you were snooping on informs me of her plans and gives me right of first refusal. Basically, six months from the letter date to decide if I want to buy the building on the same terms she wants to sell it."

"Well, that's good, right?" Clem asked.

Lou laughed, but there was no joy in it. "Did you not get to the offer price?"

Clementine made her way back over to the fridge. It was more zeros than she had ever seen strung together consecutively, interrupted only by little comma teardrops. "I wasn't aware the building was worth a railroad baron's fortune."

"It's less the building and more the neighborhood. Every new restaurant or condo that opens its doors raises the value of everything. Only a miracle would get me enough money to buy at market value."

"But you have six months, right? That's so much time to figure things out." Clem squinted at the paper. Maybe Lou could get a loan for that amount.

Lou looked down at her feet. "*Had* six months about, um, five months ago. I've been striking out on finding financing ever since."

"Why didn't Alyssa mention this to me? I thought she'd told me everything about the bar."

"She doesn't know." Lou fiddled with her glass. "No one does. Well, except my grandma. And her priest. I apparently couldn't bear six months of people seeing me as a failure because I couldn't fix this on my own."

How could that be? Clementine couldn't imagine how Lou had coped all these months on her own with the threat of losing the bar hovering over her. It seemed lonely, but also needlessly stubborn. It could be that Lou was waiting for someone to offer and if that was the case, Clem was her girl.

"Why would you have to do this all on your own? There has to be something that we can do. Howl's a cultural institution, I've seen the writing on the wall. Literally, that graffiti is amazing. So that's why the priest came by the other night??"

"Don't worry about Father Joe. It was probably just a good-will gesture of like fifty dollars because he's in illicit love with my gram. Plus, I have tried. I've gotten more rejections from men than I ever thought possible. Of course they all work at banks and are denying me loans, but still, the nerve. I'll keep trying until September first when I have to throw in the towel and accept my fate, but it doesn't look good. All this is just between us. I don't want anyone else to worry."

Clementine nodded her agreement as her brain revved with ideas, but she paused when she caught the quiver in Lou's chin before she steeled her expression. Jumping to solutions might not be appreciated. It had been a hard lesson for Clem that solutions weren't everyone's love language—that sometimes hearing her ideas didn't make people feel helped or hopeful, it only made them feel worse. Her father's resistance to changing the diner flashed through her mind. Clementine couldn't understand why he believed change would erase her mother instead of honor her by helping her favorite place thrive, but eventually, she'd had to accept it.

Clem had craved change, had driven hundreds of miles to find it, which had led her where she needed to be. Well, not exactly where. She never expected to be in Lou's kitchen, but still, a new life with new problems made her feel a little heady. She wanted this challenge. And if it just so happened to save Lou and this amazing bar, that wouldn't be so bad either.

"Sorry, Lou. I didn't mean to imply you weren't trying. But I'd love to help if you'd want that. Especially since I lost you that investment."

"You've worked at Howl for like two minutes, how could you possibly help?"

Lou wasn't wrong, but Clem still flinched as the words hurtled toward her. "Right." Once again her help wasn't wanted. When would Clem learn that people didn't trust her to know what to do?

"Hey, I didn't mean—" Lou blew out an audible puff of air

and raked a hand through her hair, making the messy blonde strands look tousled and perfect. "Look, I'm not saying no to your help, I'm saying let's table it and go get breakfast. You need something that's terrible for you and I know just the place."

FOR BREAKFAST, Lou had taken her for pancakes, because she thought Clementine probably missed diner food from home. All the waitresses greeting Lou by name warmed Clem's heart. It did feel just a little like home, and Lou had thought to take her there. Afterward, she caught the Orange Line back to her apartment. The whole way home, she was grateful for Lou's hoodie, and not just because it was a soft reminder of Lou caring for her when she really didn't have to. It also turned out that the clothes that got her tips and compliments at Howl got her some very unwanted attention on public transit. She wished the whole world could be a sapphic bar where people dried each other's tears in the bathroom.

It was nearly one p.m. by the time she fit her key into the front door lock, only to find it already open.

"Hey Lyssa," she called out. "Did you know the apartment was unlocked?"

When she got no response, she made her way down the hall. Alyssa's door was ajar, and Clem gave it a push with her index finger so she could peer in. Being a roommate wasn't unlike being a cop in that if something was open, she figured she didn't need a warrant, but still, she felt uneasy even if she was just checking on her. She'd been watching far too many proce-durals. Clem really needed to examine how often she was excusing her own detective-like behavior. This was twice in one day, and her first investigation hadn't ended with a cold case.

Alyssa was sprawled on her bed, sound asleep. One arm was thrown over her eyes to protect them from the sun streaming through the window.

Ever since her car had disappeared, Clementine had been fastidious almost to the point of obsession about checking locks. Not that anyone was likely to steal her three dirty t-shirts and scraps of denim that passed as shorts, but still.

She considered nudging Alyssa awake, but this was a conversation they could have later. Alyssa must have the day off from her second job as a receptionist, and her third job as an exercise instructor. For someone who put a lot of effort into seeming like a ditz, she was one of the most together and hardworking people Clem had ever met. One wall of her room had a burn-down chart where she tracked progress against her student loan balances. Clem glanced at the whiteboard, noticing the teeniest progress on the line since last week, before she pulled the door shut.

It was probably for the best. She wanted to tell Alyssa about Howl's peril, but she also didn't want to betray Lou. She just needed to find a way to convince Lou to go to the mattresses for Howl.

Clem grabbed her towel from her room and made her way to the shower. As the water heated up, her thoughts drifted back to Lou. The woman was an enigma. From second to second Clem wasn't sure if Lou wanted to kill her or kiss her. Though if Lou wanted to kiss her, Clem hadn't given her any reason to hesitate after the night they met.

She pulled back the curtain and stepped into the clawfoot tub. Before she could overthink it, her hand drifted between her legs. It remained a great injustice that she hadn't gotten to touch Lou that night or any night since. She'd never hear her own name gasped from Lou's lips as she made her come. The heat of Clem on her own fingers was a stark contrast to the cool porcelain pressing into her back as she came with Lou's name on her lips.

)O(

SINCE HER SNOOPING INCIDENT, things at work had been stilted. Lou asked Clementine to drop the issue, and she had, even if doing so felt physically painful. It was hard for her to understand why Lou wasn't doing everything she could to fight for the place she loved, and that included letting other people help. It was the same thing that had driven Clem away from Hart's Hollow, and she felt that old desire to leave kicking up again.

Plus, Alyssa had been relentless in trying to figure out what was going on. She knew that Clementine had spent the night at Lou's and seemed absolutely gleeful about it. Clem had been forced to offer her newly arrived clothes from home for alterations as a sacrifice to distract her roommate. Everything she wore now had about fifty percent less fabric than before, and with each passing day, she felt a little more confident showing her ass to the world.

When she'd opened up the box Sam had sent her, right there on top was what she first thought was a ring pop but was actually a jeweled plug for a... much different area. Clem counted the fact that she'd obscured that horrifyingly inappropriate addition from Alyssa's prying eyes a win. She was already planning a way to get back at Sam for that little prank.

Clem's head was buzzing, a low vibration pulling her from sleep like a child being dragged from a toy store. She wanted to kick and scream and cling to the automatic doors. Instead, she reached beneath her pillow for her phone—the ruiner of dreams. An image of her best friend filled the screen and Clem slid the answer button across Sam's smiling mouth.

The video call connected and Sam, Blair Witch shaky, came into view. Clementine squeezed her eyes shut so Sam's gait wouldn't make her seasick.

"Sam, what's wrong? Are you okay?"

"Why wouldn't I be okay?" Sam huffed.

Clem cracked open one eye in time to watch her friend take a sip of her coffee, which was... not the most flattering from this angle. She snapped a quick screengrab. You never knew when you'd need the worst picture in existence of someone you love. What if Sam got married and Clem needed to make a slideshow for instance?

"You're calling so early, I was still asleep." Clem pulled up her white duvet, snuggling beneath it to make a point. She tried not to think about how rough she probably looked.

Her room was still mostly bare. Even if Clem had money to replace what she'd lost and set up her space into something that didn't resemble a jail cell, she'd hardly had the time or energy these past few weeks.

"Clem, it's 11 a.m. This is a normal-person time to call. See, there's the sun." Sam angled her phone up at the sky.

Clem squinted on instinct, even though that same sun was currently streaming in through her window that she'd not yet put curtains on. At least there was a tree outside—nature's privacy screen. "Well, not for me. Not anymore. I didn't even get home until 3:30. Every part of my body hurts. My wrists, my feet, my legs, my—"

"Clementine, please do not list every part of your body, unless you're about to launch into a rousing rendition of My Neck, My Back." Sam paused and quirked an eyebrow. "No?

Okay. The whole world is tired, darlin'. I was calling to see how you're doing since—no shade—it feels a little bit like we never talk anymore. Now that we're done with your yearly physical, why don't you tell me about your life?"

"My life?" Clem fought the urge to close her eyes against the overly cheerful sunlight, which seemed amplified by Sam's enthusiasm. "I'm pretty much either home or at Howl, just trying to save money and get back on my feet."

"Right," Sam said slowly.

At the scrutiny in her friend's voice, Clem gave in to the urge to close her eyes. "I'm not avoiding you, Sam, if that's what you're thinking."

"That's not what I'm thinking."

Clem let out a slow breath of relief, allowing her body to relax just a fraction into her pillows. "Okay, good. Because you know I would never—"

"I think you're fucking Lou."

Clem's eyes shot wide and she glanced over to make sure her door was shut, only to see it wide open. "Sam," she whispered. "I am *not* and if you could keep your voice down, that would be great."

The sound of footsteps echoed in the hall, and a moment later Alyssa's head popped into view. "Hey, is everything okay? Who are we fighting with?"

Clem glared at Sam before forcing a smile. "I'm just talking to my friend Sam. No fighting."

"Damn," Alyssa said. "I'm feeling all fired up after my morning tai chi in the park."

Clem frowned. Fired up was not something she'd ever associated with gentle calisthenics, but knowing Alyssa, the movements were probably synced to Like a Virgin. Sam cleared her throat with an exaggerated "ahem" and Clementine reluctantly turned her phone around so her friends could see each other.

Alyssa bent down to get to eye level with the phone. Her tank top gaped open and Clem could imagine Sam gaping in kind on the other side of the screen. Clem would have said something if she wasn't absolutely certain Alyssa was doing it on purpose.

Alyssa liked attention, and she used flirting as another way to disarm people. It had taken Clem a few days to realize her roommate wasn't coming on to her. Alyssa was just the kind of friend who saw no issue with wandering into Clem's room in her underwear and asking her to snuggle. She was actually a lot like Sam in that way. There was something comforting about it, now that Clem was so far from her best friend. Not that Alyssa could replace Sam, no one could.

Sam had always been a tactile person. In high school, everyone thought the two of them were dating, because Sam had an affinity for holding hands and calling her *darlin'*. Some things never changed. But Clem had always seen it for what it was: affection not hemmed in by societal expectations of what might be appropriate. "Why shouldn't we adore our friends?" Sam had asked her once.

"Hiya, Sam," Alyssa said, turning the phone back toward the pile of blankets that was Clem. "I was hoping you were a sexy intruder."

"Well, maybe next time. I'm due for a visit," Sam said sweetly.

Clem suppressed an eye roll by closing them until the impulse passed. When she opened them again, Alyssa was looking between Clementine and her phone.

"So, Sam," Alyssa said, "Has Clemmy told you about being in love with Lou?"

Sam's eyes lit up like the sparklers they'd loved as kids, all excitement and danger in the name of good fun. "Wait, is this the Lou you fu—"

Clementine had never hung up a phone so fast in her life. She would have thrown it through the window if she had the money to replace it. She'd gotten the impression that under no circumstances did Lou want anyone to know they'd slept together. Of course, Clem had told Sam she'd slept with someone but not who, partly to prove she'd taken her friend's advice, and partly because she wanted it to be more real than it was. Clementine had been hoping the night in the store-room was the start of something, even though that was the opposite of the goal she'd walked in there with. You probably had to be casual to have casual sex, and Clem was anything but.

Alyssa tilted her head to see the phone screen. "Weird, did you lose the signal? Sometimes the service is spotty in here."

Clem got the feeling she was being given a graceful out. "I think my hand slipped a little. She'll call back once she stops talking and realizes the call disconnected."

"Okay," Alyssa said, returning her attention to Clem. "I'm headed to my Sweatin' to the 80s class I teach at the Y."

"You're going to another exercise class? I'm not even out of bed yet."

"Do you want to come? It might help you seize what's left of the day."

The only thing Clem wanted to seize right now was her duvet so she could pull it over her head and shut out the world. "No, I don't think I—"

"If you're worried about not being able to keep up, the class is for seniors and Mrs. Blaine or one of the others could help you."

Oh great, now Alyssa was showing concern that Clem couldn't keep up with the clique from the senior citizen community. The fact that she probably couldn't was *so* not the point. What happened to having faith in people? She shook her head, hoping to convey disappointment she definitely didn't feel. "Maybe next time."

Clementine's phone screen lit up and she accepted Sam's call. "Hi, Sam, one sec. Alyssa's on her way out."

"Okay! Bye Clemmy! Bye Sam!" Alyssa said with a wink and a wave before whirling from the room.

"God, she's so hot. Did you see her neon pink sports bra? I love that color."

"Right, the color." Clem quickly turned her phone back around, nearly dropping it on her face. "Can you keep your voice down? And I didn't look at my roommate's bra."

"Why? She said she wants me to be her sexy intruder. I *have* been meaning to come visit, you know."

"Sam. Absolutely not. She's my roommate."

"Fine." Sam sniffed and took another thoughtful sip of her coffee. "New topic."

"Thank you."

Sam's brown eyes sparkled, and damn if Clem shouldn't have known better. A new topic with Sam was just another minefield.

"What are you and Lou up to, because it's either crimes or sex with how much time you're spending together?"

"Wait, who have you been talking to? Are you and Alyssa texting? Do you even have her contact info?"

"Hmm, I don't think so. But to set your mind at ease, why don't you tell me her number so I can make sure that I don't have it written down somewhere?" A grin split across Sam's face, and Clem's heart warmed despite her annoyance.

"Very smooth, Sam. I'm hanging up now."

"I'm hoping it's sex, by the way."

Clem choked. "What?"

"You and Lou. I hope you're up to sex. Wait, no, crime."

"Sam!"

"Sexy crime! Final answer."

"Goodbye, Sam."

"Love you! Call you tomorrow!"

She let the phone fall to her chest as she stared at the ceiling, trying to make sense of what her friend had said. Had everyone caught on to her hopeless lust for Lou? Was she so obvious that even her friend in another state could pick up on it? Because if that was the case, she was in trouble. But that was a problem for seven p.m. Clem, when her shift started. Right now she had an entire day stretching before her and she planned to seize the mid-afternoon right after she got a few more hours of sleep.

Chapter Ten
Lou

S he could see it now, the way Howl carried its age—its laugh lines showing. The chipped paint revealed hints of horsehair plaster and brick beneath it, makeup that was no longer covering the wrinkles. It made Lou think of the first time she'd looked in the mirror and saw a glimpse of her mother's face. That unsettling moment of recognition. There was something in the tiredness in her eyes that made her look less and more like herself.

Lou let her fingers trail along the wall, tracing the graffiti and love confessions scratched deep into it. *G + L = 4Ever. Sarah + Jude* inside a heart. *I luv boobs.* That last one was practically universal, on par with Peace on Earth and Joy to the World. This was history. This was the place she'd fallen in love with. She kept walking, trailing her finger over the old paint until she found what she was looking for—a small house like a child would draw, and inside it was her own name. She remembered the night she'd scratched it there as surreptitiously as possible with the tip of the key to her terrible apartment.

After her parents disowned her, Lou had yearned for home, ached for it but also couldn't imagine it. Home seemed as elusive as happiness, something she knew was possible but couldn't quite remember. And then one rainy night she'd taken a flier on the train from a woman with a shaved head and no bra, a getup Lou recognized instinctively as welcoming. The paper advertised a drag king show in an area of the city she'd been to a hundred times, but she couldn't picture a bar there. Just the Heating and Cooling shop her dad used to work at and some warehouses scattered among the cobblestones and broken beer bottles.

"So," the woman had said, a metal ball glinting on her tongue, "any chance I'll see you later at Howl?"

Lou had squinted at the information written in magic marker. In the bottom corner of the sheet was a wolf sporting a pompadour. "Howl?"

"Yeah." She tapped the paper to emphasize her point. "Home of the Wayward Lovers. Though most of us just think of it as Home."

By the time Lou had finished her first beer, she was starting to think of it as home, too. A place where she could take off the expectations of her family and society and her Catholic upbringing and just *be*. And it didn't hurt that she could openly stare at the women, many of whom had looked back at her.

This was also the story of Lou's first one-night stand, a new ritual for her.

She let her hand drop from the wall and got back to examining the bar, taking in every dingy thing about it while memories floated through the air like smoke.

Howl was there the first Christmas Eve she'd been devastated not to hear from her mom. Sure, Lou had lined up a date to hedge against being lonely, but when the call didn't come from her family, and the attraction with her date didn't materialize either, she'd wandered into Howl with snow glittering on her red scarf like she was on a fucking Hallmark card desperate to stave off her sadness with a scotch or two. Only she'd found Jude and Sarah behind the bar, and they lit up when she sat down. She'd expected the place to be deserted due to the holiday, but it was packed.

"I don't like that look on your face, but I'm happy you're here, my dear." Jude had grinned at her and rummaged beneath the bar, triumphantly pulling out a red stocking with white, faux fur trim. "This is for you."

"Oh." Lou had taken the stocking like it was a baby, cradling it to her chest because she could tell without looking inside that it was precious. "This is so kind, but I'm sorry I didn't get you two anything."

"Hmm, well, there's a favor we've been meaning to ask you. It's in there. If you want to do it, that's a gift to us and if not, you owe me some socks and a new wallet."

"I just had a flashback to every holiday with my dad," Lou said through laughter. "I'll be sure to get you the trifold with the picture insert, pre-filled with my class photos."

"You sure do make me proud, Lou. Now open it before people riot over lack of service."

"*God bless us, everyone,*" Lou said with an eye roll, but she got to work excavating the stocking. She pulled out a few standards: gold chocolate coins and an orange, a pair of rainbow tube socks, and finally a simple key chain sporting a brass key. Lou studied it, trying to remember if keys had some special Christmas meaning, but all her years of Catholic school had her coming up blank.

"Do you like it?" Jude asked.

"Yeah, it's..." Lou hefted the cold metal in her palm, searching for a word that might obscure her confusion until she could work out what was going on. "...sturdy. The key chain is nice too."

"Well, sure, but it's more about what it represents."

"Right." Lou nodded. "Symbolism."

Jude squinted at her in that way that showed both affection and annoyance, like Lou was the densest person she'd ever met, but also the most cherished. "It's a key to the bar. I could use more help around here and I know you love this place like I do."

Lou did. Plus she really, really needed the money. She was already three weeks late with her rent since she got fired from her waitressing job. An inconvenient lump of emotion rose in her throat. "Oh Jude, that's, it's just—"

"What?"

"Everything I've ever wanted."

"Well then, welcome home, you are now an official wayward lover. Any chance you could start tonight? I still need to wrap Sarah's gift," Jude said with a wink.

Lou swallowed hard, her chest so full she thought it might burst. "I thought you'd never ask." And with that, Lou had slipped behind the bar, and in the thirteen years since she'd barely been on the other side of it.

Lou paced the interior of Howl, taking in every dingy thing about it. The small stuff she overlooked, like peeling paint and rundown barstools with faux leather seat covers, split open, little kernels of stuffing bursting their way out.

Clem's words from breakfast the other day kept running through her head even though Lou had done her best to shoot down her every idea. People didn't come to Howl for fancy. They came for stiff drinks and to feel a little less alone. They came to run with their pack.

Lou was in the middle of scratching a marker rendering of a suggestive peach off the bar when the door flung open, a stream of sunlight filtering through, along with a buoyant Alyssa. That woman always seemed a half step away from skipping, just hopscotching her way through life.

"Hiya grumpy, what are you doing there?"

Lou pulled her hand back from the counter and shoved it into her pocket. "Nothing, just taking stock of the bar."

"Oh, exciting! Are you thinking about renovating? Because I have *a lot* of ideas, like at least seven."

Seven ideas was... pretty specific. Alyssa's question pinged in Lou's chest. How much had Clementine told her? And had Lou specifically asked her not to? Or had she just assumed they both understood what 'private' meant?

"No, not exactly. Why do you ask that?"

"Well, the stack of paint swatches there, for one."

Lou's eyes followed Alyssa's. Shit, she'd meant to throw those away. Even if she wanted to spend money on paint, closing the bar for several days and losing that money simply wasn't feasible.

"What did Clementine tell you?"

"What did Clementine tell me about...?" Alyssa trailed off.

Was Lou being bated? A flash of annoyance flared in her chest. "Don't play dumb, Alyssa."

Alyssa tilted her head to one side, blinking coquettishly. "Have you considered that maybe I *am* dumb?"

"No, because I know you're not. You have two master's degrees. Everything you do is based on strategy, regardless of what you want other people to think."

Alyssa brought a hand to her chest, covering her heart. "Thank you, Lou. I always knew you really saw me. But truly, Clementine didn't tell me anything about bar renovations. She's been in her own world, holed up in her room the past day or so. She said something about a business plan. Maybe you'll have some more competition soon."

Lou laughed, but there was no humor in it, just a mean

edge, sharp enough to flay. "Well, good luck with that. She's in for a world of heartbreak."

"Lou, what is going on?"

"What's going on with what?" Clementine's voice rang out bright as sunshine.

"Nothing," Lou muttered at the same time Alyssa said, "something's wrong with Lou."

"I thought you said something was always wrong with Lou." Clem's brow furrowed and then she slapped a hand over her mouth as her words seemed to catch up to her. "I didn't, I mean, I..."

Lou considered letting her squirm, but she found she didn't want to. Something about Clementine was pulling her toward comfort. "It's fine, I know I'm the wicked bitch of the northeast."

Clementine started to object, but Alyssa's laughter cut through it. "At least you come by it honestly."

Lou raked the paint chips toward her like she'd just won a poker hand, hoping to conceal them before—

"What are those?" Clem asked.

"Oh, nothing, I was just thinking." Lou shoved the cards into the back pocket of her jeans.

"She wants to renovate, which I think is a brilliant idea," Alyssa offered.

Clem's face lit up and Lou attempted her best Jedi mind trick to keep her from opening her mouth, but she failed miserably.

"That's great! So you're going to try to save the bar?"

Alyssa tilted her head, a sweet, innocent, glitter-covered puppy. "Save the bar from what?"

Lou glared at Clementine and felt a small hit of satisfaction when she flushed—only her frustration quickly turned to something else, her stomach swirling as Clem's blush deepened. Lou was taken back to their night in the storeroom, Clementine coming undone beneath her fingers, the way her face had had their afterglow written all over it.

"Save the bar from an intervention," Clem said, looking only at Alyssa. "I threatened to wallpaper everything if we couldn't at least wash the walls."

"I saw the cutest wallpaper in the nursing home the other day," Alyssa said. "Like flowers in a blender."

"Why don't you tell me more about it while we get set up?" Clem took a few steps forward, mouthing a *sorry* and widening her eyes at Lou as she passed.

And Lou found she wasn't mad at all, even if she didn't quite know how to be honest about what was happening with Howl with anyone besides Clementine yet.

Chapter Eleven
Clementine

I'm not sure what you did to piss off Lou and the universe to be in charge of the Terrible Tues." That's what Alyssa had said to Clem as she'd walked out the door two hours ago for her shift at Howl. What Clementine realized now was that "terrible" referred to a lack of anything at all happening. It was a special blend of bad, with undertones of bone-deep boredom paired alongside the full-bodied prospect of non-existent tips. Plus she was working the night with Lou, who had barely acknowledged her since she'd slipped up and mentioned saving the bar in front of Alyssa the other day. It felt a little like being in silent detention, except instead of reading, she had to just think up random things to clean.

Clementine was a few hours into her shift, and business was still the kind of slow that made her wish for a crisis just to pass the time. Nothing major, just a little something to keep it interesting, a broken glass or a group of confused, mildly inebriated tourists. But that was before Lou started talking to her. When Lou spoke, Clem clawed back those wishes for distraction. She wanted to focus entirely on her in this little bubble they had.

"So what would it look like?" Lou didn't look up, just kept

her eyes focused on the bar top, which she was polishing with methodical precision.

It was probably as shiny as it would ever be, but Clem was already on thin ice. With those few words, Lou's voice had pierced the quiet stretched between them, deflating some of the tension. Other than one customer nursing a beer at the other end of the bar, they were the only two at Howl.

"What's that?" Clementine asked, looking up from the glass she was drying. Even though it was already very dry.

"If I tried to save the bar, *not* on my own. What would that look like?"

Clem set down the glass, her heart picking up its pace. Was this what she thought it was? Was Lou McCallister going to accept her help? Dreams really did come true.

Clem cleared her throat and forced her voice into a casual register. "I think it could look a lot of different ways, as long as you were comfortable with it. My first thought was that we could hold a community meeting and explain the situation."

"I don't want to ask people to donate money. They already pay for drinks, they're not responsible for this problem." Lou slung her bar towel over her shoulder and crossed her arms. She looked like a boxer about to step into the ring.

"I get that. And I wasn't thinking we'd pass around Rachel's cowboy hat like a collection plate or anything like that. This would be less of a fundraiser and more of a brainstorming session. It could be as simple as one of the regulars knowing a loan officer. Or maybe people with grassroots organizing experience can help petition the city to get the building on the historic register? That might lower the rent. It might even change the landlord's mind about selling."

Lou started shaking her head before Clementine finished talking. "I don't think anything will change her mind about selling, not when the market is this hot and she has her sights set on one of those retirement communities in Florida where everyone drives golf carts around to their sex parties."

"O-kay," Clem drew out the word while she tried to decide if she actually wanted to know more about these communities. She did not. "Well, if her plans are set in stone, maybe there are grants we could apply for to preserve pieces of LGBTQIA history. Plus with this happening so close to Pride Month, I think harnessing public support will be easier."

When Clem looked up, Lou was leaning back, her elbows resting on the bar and one hundred and ten percent of her attention on Clem. It felt glorious. Like Clementine wasn't just one of the only people in the bar, but the only person in the world.

"That actually sounds... reasonable. I've been focused on getting approved for a mortgage that would cover the sale price, but you're right. This isn't just any building being sold in a developing neighborhood. One thing I love most about Howl is its history. It's literally written on the walls, past love and heart-breaks, people celebrating who they are in the safest space available. The legacy of acceptance. I know it saved me." Lou cleared her throat, her eyebrows drawing together as she shook her head. "I just mean that I can see your point."

Clementine wasn't sure what had shifted, but Lou seemed to withdraw into herself the second she started hoping too loud. "I think you're right. This place means so much to so many people. You should be proud of that."

"I don't want to jinx it, that's all. If I get my hopes up now, I only risk being let down later."

Clem frowned and tried to think of something to say that didn't dismiss Lou's statement, a way to counter it kindly, but before she came up with anything her phone rang. It was her dad's ringtone, the only one that came through.

"Do you need to get that?" Lou asked.

Clem fished the device out of her pocket and rejected the call, then dashed off a quick text that she was at work. No sooner had she slid her phone back into her pocket than it started ringing again.

She grimaced at Lou and retrieved it. "Is it okay if I take this quickly? It's my dad and I'm worried something might be wrong because he never calls like this."

As soon as the words left her mouth, Clementine felt a shiver run through her. *Was something wrong?*

Lou nodded and then busied herself with straightening some cocktail napkins.

"Hi, Dad, is everything okay? Did you see my text about work?"

"Hi honey, it's Brenda."

"Oh." Clem's heart leaped to her throat. Why did Brenda have her dad's phone? He could have just forgotten it somewhere random. She used to get calls all the time to pick it up, except she didn't live in Hart's Hollow anymore and Brenda definitely knew that. Clementine forced out the question she wasn't sure she wanted the answer to. "What's going on?"

"I just brought your dad to the hospital. They're triaging him now, but he was having chest pains."

Clem's own heart clenched in response. "Chest pains? Like a heart attack?"

Lou stopped what she was doing and Clem looked away so she didn't have to meet her gaze. Just moments ago, she'd wanted all of Lou's attention and now she wanted to run. The last thing she needed was for cool, calm, collected Lou McCallister to see her have a breakdown. The little voice in her mind rang out like a siren screaming that this never would have happened to her dad if she hadn't left home.

"It's too early to tell, hon. I just wanted to let you know

what was happening. I can update you later, once they figure out what's going on."

"No, that's okay. I mean yes, let me know what's happening, but I'm on my way." Clem patted her pockets, searching for her car keys before she remembered she no longer carried them since their usefulness had disappeared right along with her car. "I'll be there as soon as I can, just text me the address," she said, ending the call.

Did Ubers cross state lines? Probably not for less than the price of a kidney. Clem turned, and Lou was still watching her intently. She was no longer even pretending to be busy.

"I'm so sorry but I have to go. I'm not usually this flaky but my dad—I have to figure out a way to get home."

"Of course." Lou's hand came to rest on Clem's back. "Is he okay?"

"I'm not sure. Brenda just got him to the hospital. Brenda is his...hell, I don't even know. I just... I have to figure out a way to get there and my brain is spinning in too many directions at once to make a linear plan."

"Okay," Lou drew in a deep breath, motioning for Clementine to do the same. And goddamn it, it worked the slightest bit. "There. Now, let me drive you."

"What? You can't. Someone has to stay and—"

"Hey, Sue," Lou called out.

The woman at the end of the bar looked up from her beer. "Yeah?"

"We gotta close for a family emergency. Next time you're here your tab's on me, but right now I have to kick you out."

"You got it, Lou." Sue raised her glass and finished her drink in one impressive gulp.

Clem grabbed Lou's wrist. Was she out of her mind? "You can't just drive me to Maine."

"You're right. Usually I couldn't, but I just so happen to

have my grandma's car. It's a funny story really." Lou's hand found a place on Clem's lower back and stayed there as she ushered her toward the door behind Sue.

Clem's feet moved on autopilot. She tried to make a list of everything she should do, starting with locating her dad's healthcare proxy paperwork and insurance card, but her thoughts swirled like dust. She could text Sam once they were on the road to get the card and papers and meet her at the hospital.

Behind her, Lou was still chattering as she locked the door. *Chattering* was not a word Clem would have previously associated with Lou, but there was no other term for the words rushing from her mouth.

"Well, my grandma called me yesterday and said—I kid you not—that she'd just gotten carjacked by a big, strong guy, and after I calmed down enough to realize she meant that she got a flat and a man stopped to help her, I offered to get the tire replaced. I meant to take it back to her earlier, but ran out of time before work. So anyway, that's why I have a car. I'll just give her a call and let her know I'm going to keep it a bit longer."

Not far in front of them, a car chirped unlocked and flashed its lights in greetings. Clem barked out a laugh.

"A fucking Toyota?" Clem was sure the universe was absolutely bullying her tonight. Not only was she headed back to Maine to be there for her dad, but she was doing it in a simulacrum of the car she'd left in.

Lou frowned, pausing with her hand on the driver's door. "What do you have against Toyotas?"

"Not a thing." Clem's continued laughter sounded nearly hysterical to her own ears, but she couldn't stop it. If she didn't laugh, she'd cry, and the unfortunate thing was that Clem was an ugly crier. Blotchy and hiccupping—the whole bit. "This is almost identical to my car that got stolen. Which, incidentally, was once my grandma's."

"I'm not really seeing why that's funny, but let's build on this and get on the road. Can you pull up directions on your phone while I call my gram?"

Clem was clicking on the hospital address Brenda had sent over as she slid into the passenger seat. A rosary hung from the rearview mirror along with a plastic sunflower photo frame on a green string. At the center of the flower was the face of a young girl, her smile full of gaps beneath the brim of her batting helmet. Even with most of the teeth missing, the smile was unmistakably Lou's—slightly higher on one side, like she knew something no one else did. It felt like a little peek at who Lou had been before the world got to her and taught her trust was a vulnerability.

She was surprised when the phone started ringing through the car speaker. The thought of having to talk to Lou's grandma sent a shot of panic down her spine. If she had to be polite right now, Clementine might implode all over the inside of this nice Corolla.

"Hello, my dear." A kind voice filled the car.

"Hi, Gram. Sorry to call so late, but I need to borrow the car. I'm going to drive Clementine up to Maine for—"

"I'm so glad you're going on a little getaway, Louise. I told you you need to focus more on romance." Lou hit the button to take the phone off speaker like she was buzzing in on a game show, then fumbled the phone to her ear.

In the dusk, Clementine could just barely make out the color rising on her cheeks. In her wildest dreams, she wouldn't have imagined Lou McCallister blushing. This emotional roller-coaster of a night was turning her world upside down in more ways than one.

As soon as Lou ended the call, a blast of music filled the car.

Lou reached for the volume knob, but Clem touched her hand to stop her. This was just too good to let pass.

"I didn't peg you for a Britney Spears fan."

"Like I said, it's my grandma's car." Lou turned down the volume slightly as she pulled away from the curb.

"But you drove it last, right?" Clem could be tenacious when she wanted an answer, and she was prepared to go full detective on Lou's love of Britney.

"Okay fine, you got me." Lou turned to Clem and winked before belting out the lyrics to Work, Bitch loud and off-key and Clem couldn't help herself, she was laughing, and this time the only motivation was joy.

Lou continued her performance until they reached the entry ramp to the expressway, and Clementine laughed until her chest ached and something just behind her heart loosened a bit. She could recognize the gift Lou was giving her, and she didn't take it lightly. Lou did not seem like the kind of person who went out of her way to care for others. Not that she was mean. Just that she was contained, an island unto herself, but apparently her grandma's Toyota was the bridge to reach her.

THE THREE-HOUR TRIP passed like three years and three minutes all at once. Both of their phones kept losing service on the drive, so she hadn't had any updates from Brenda. Clem had twisted her fingers so much that she half expected them to hold their contorted shape like pipe cleaners. She'd shared some of her guilt about the distance that had formed between her and her dad, how the miles had separated them like their love had to hitchhike its way across state lines. Lou talked a bit about being estranged from her parents, but any time Clem asked a follow-up question, Lou steered the conversation back to the bar or why Clem had left Maine.

It was only when they were pulling up to the hospital that Clementine realized she never texted Sam. She'd been so wrapped up in talking to Lou that she hadn't even thought to organize what she needed here.

"Why don't you run in while I park the car?"

"Oh," Clem paused. She wasn't sure why she'd assumed Lou was simply dropping her off. Now that it was clear Lou was going to stay with her, a little weight lifted off her shoulders. She nodded and lingered by the automatic doors until the tail lights of the car disappeared around a turn. Then she rushed inside. She had to put out her arms to keep herself from crashing into the nurses' station.

"Hi, I'm looking for my father. He came in about three hours ago with chest pains."

"Name?" the woman asked without looking up.

"Clementine Darby."

"No, hon, what's your father's name?"

Clem swallowed hard, wishing Lou was still with her. She wasn't sure she could face this alone. "Denny Darby. Dennis."

The nurse's fingers flew over the keyboard in front of her. Her typing speed must be astronomical. Clem crossed her arms to keep her fingers from tapping on the counter as the nurse adjusted her glasses and squinted at the computer screen. "Dennis Darby, okay, he was transferred to cardiology. Go to the nurse's station on the third floor and they can help you. Elevators and stairs are just down this hall." The nurse pointed to her left.

"Okay, thank you." Clem's heart was racing. Cardiology. That didn't sound good. She'd been gone for a month and her father's heart had given out? She turned toward the hallway but hesitated. She didn't want to leave Lou, but she needn't have worried, because a second later a rush of blonde hair sped through the door.

Without thinking, Clem reached back and grabbed Lou's hand, pulling her down the hallway. She pressed the elevator button three times and watched the number six light up on the panel and stick there. Clem thought she might explode if she had to wait for five floors of people getting off and on. She pulled Lou toward the stairs and took them two at a time, nearly gasping by the time she pushed open the metal door marked "three."

Brenda was pacing in the hallway in front of some uncomfortable-looking chairs.

"Oh, Clementine. You didn't need to come all this way."

Clem started to stutter a protest, but Lou's voice cut in strong and clear. "Of course she did, her father's sick."

Lou's fingers squeezed hers.

Brenda nodded. "You're right. They think he's going to be fine. The doctor was just finishing up some tests, but he might even be able to go home tonight."

"Oh, that's incredible." Clem breathed out.

Lou disentangled their fingers and wrapped her arm around Clem's shoulder. Clementine let herself relax into the warmth of Lou's body.

A young man about Clem's age in aqua scrubs walked into the hall. "Are you here for Dennis Darby?"

"Yes," Clem and Brenda said in unison. She was glad Brenda was there and had gotten her dad to the hospital, but it just occurred to Clem to wonder *why* she was there. It was nearly midnight now, which meant Brenda and her dad were together at nine p.m. But they were old friends. He could have called her when he started feeling off.

The three of them followed the doctor into the hospital room where her dad sat propped up in the bed smiling, absolutely housing a tapioca pudding cup.

"H2 blockers and some calcium carbonate really work wonders in cases like this." The doctor grinned.

Were they in the twilight zone? Why weren't her dad and the doctor taking this more seriously? Clem gritted her teeth. "Calcium carbonate for a heart attack?"

"Oh no," the doctor said with a chuckle. "For heartburn. My recommendation is no more spicy foods and taking antacids as a preventative before big meals or anything acidic, especially tomatoes. Are there any questions I can answer?"

Clem shook her head. Heartburn. The emergency had been *heartburn*. She couldn't believe it. She felt a pang of guilt for dragging Lou all the way here.

"Is there anything we need to do once we get him home?" Brenda asked.

The doctor shrugged. "Sure, try keeping him there."

Clem dragged her eyes away from Lou to study Brenda. She didn't love the way the word *home* had slipped out of Brenda's mouth. Which was absurd. She liked Brenda and was grateful for her, but something felt off.

"Okay then." The doctor flipped through a few pages of the chart before closing it. "A nurse will be by shortly to go over the discharge instructions, and then we'll get you on your way."

Once the doctor left, Clementine turned toward her dad. "Spicy foods?"

"I was eating a home-cooked meal, thank you very much. You were the one who told me not to eat all my meals at the diner."

"Oh no, you are not pinning this on me after we left work and drove three hours in the night to make sure you were okay." Clem took a step toward her dad. It was as much her own guilt at the new distance between them as anything.

Relief and frustration were warring inside her, but in the end, his sheepish smile disarmed her. It wasn't his fault she'd dropped everything and rushed here. And dragged Lou along with her—Clem really owed her a huge favor when they got back to Boston. "But I suppose you're right. I did say that. So what was the home-cooked meal?"

"Chili cheese fries." Her father sat up a bit taller. "I was using that air fryer you got me for Christmas."

"That was four Christmases ago."

He shrugged. "I got the holiday right.

"And you followed the letter of my ask, but not the spirit of it. I wasn't saying to make diner menu items at home." Clem folded her arms across her chest.

"What else is there?"

"Salad? Fruit?"

"I'm not a rabbit, honey. And the fries were delicious. I hardly used any bacon fat at all."

Chapter Twelve

Lou

The only soundtrack on the drive from the hospital to the house was Clementine's stream of babbling apologies. She placed her hand on top of Clem's to keep it from flailing in another mea culpa for dragging them up to Maine for some heartburn. It was oddly adorable, even though Lou was running out of ways to tell Clem she had nothing to apologize for because it was always better to be safe than sorry. Even after Clem settled a bit, Lou kept their palms pressed together, almost in prayer. She didn't feel ready to examine why her hand kept finding Clementine's tonight and why her commitment-phobic self wanted to cling to her like a lifeline as though she was the one in crisis.

The pitch-black Maine night surrounded the car like deep water, unsettling for all the unknown, but also full of possibility, new discoveries. Lou couldn't remember the last time she'd seen true darkness. There was always more than enough of a glow from the streetlights in the city to make out the shapes in her apartment, if not their details. But here, next to Clementine, she couldn't see a thing beyond the headlights. She was going on faith that Clem would lead them where they needed to go safely.

Denny and Brenda had stayed at the hospital to finish up the discharge paperwork while the two *girls,* as Lou and Clem were repeatedly being called, went on ahead to get settled in for the night. The drive had tired Lou out a bit, but she was used to late nights that stretched into the early hours, even though she rarely saw the sunrise from the bar.

Gravel churned under the car's tires as they turned into the driveway. The house was glowing, lit up like a lantern in the darkness.

"Always with the damn lights," Clem muttered as she led them inside. "Sorry I didn't think to book a hotel to stay at."

Lou paused, frowning. "Don't you want to be here anyway?"

"I do. But it's not exactly spacious or fancy." Clem bit her lip. "That doctor gave me big wrong-a-lot-but-too-confident-to-notice vibes though. I'll probably just sit up on the couch tonight to make sure my dad's okay. You can take my bed."

Lou followed Clementine into the living room, where they both stopped to gape at the mess. It looked like something had been spilled on the couch and someone then attempted to cleanse it with fire. The charred foam showed through a crater in the cushion.

Lou shot out an arm to protect Clementine from stepping any closer to the mess. *What in the hell?* "That couch looks like a portal to hell. I'm not sure you should be near that unless you want to follow Dante's journey."

"What the fuck is going on?" Clem brought a shaking hand to her brow and shook her head. "I'm too exhausted to deal with this right now." Clementine took a tentative step forward and poked the cushion with her foot. It didn't budge. "He always did hate this couch, I just never thought he'd resort to arson. I can just... take his recliner."

Lou glanced at the chair in the opposite corner, which could most generously be described as well-loved. Another descriptor might be *thrift store reject*. "It's an inventive use of duct tape, I'll give him that."

Clem sighed. "He's not very into new things. I think that's where I get it from. When my mom got sick, money was tight. We had insurance, but her treatments cost so much, and the diner was never going to make us anything more than comfortable. We all got used to making do. Those leather pants I bought to wear to Howl are the first new thing I've purchased for myself in longer than I can remember, and even those are vintage. A very chic word for 'used'."

Lou had noticed that about Clementine's clothes—everything seemed worn in, soft and well-loved. That made it easy to spot the nights Alyssa had dressed her. She never looked bad. Clementine was beautiful—she could probably wear a paper bag and look sexy—but there was generally a broken-in factor to her outfits. Even if she had recently taken scissors to all of them.

Okay, she definitely didn't need to think about Clem in cutoffs and midriff-baring tops. Their hookup that first night had been depressingly fully clothed, and this wasn't the first time Lou had wished she'd had a chance to take in all of Clem. But that was over now. Their time had come and gone. A neat little memory, just the way Lou had always liked it. Clean and simple, with absolutely no danger of leading to the complications of feelings.

Lou was fine with things in her life just the way they were. And she and Clementine were both adults. They'd agreed on the terms and would stick to them. Still, Lou's heart pounded as she said, "Let's just share your room. I'm worried if you sit in that chair, the tape will adhere and we'll need a pry bar to get you out. We need to be on the road by mid-afternoon tomorrow."

"Are you sure?"

Lou laughed, trying to play it off like this was no big deal when everything in her mind was screaming *danger*. She didn't share a bed and she didn't do sleepovers. Lou McCallister liked to be clear, and there was nothing more clear than a quickie in a semi-public place. No one misread that for a relationship. Lou certainly wasn't misreading that either. Clem had been quick to walk out without a backward glance when Alyssa had interrupted them.

The door to the house clattered open, bringing Lou back to the moment. "No chance you have bunk beds, right?"

"Sadly, no. I begged for years, but bunk beds are a hard sell for an only child. I do have a full though." Clem delivered the statement with a wink.

"Luxurious." A full bed would definitely be big enough for her not to touch Clem at all as long as she didn't move or breathe. But the bunk beds would have been an easier sell, especially if Denny was going to react anything like her own father had. Would he actually be okay to find out Lou was sharing a bed with his daughter? Past experiences of her own dictated that parents could react badly to a discovery like that.

"Hey girls, thanks for coming all this way. Sorry to ruin your night," Denny said as he leaned against the doorway into the living room.

Lou gulped and stood stock-still. The thought of sharing a bed with Clem under her dad's roof had her thinking she should start looking up hotels now before they got kicked out.

Clem's red hair flashed as she spun toward her dad. "What happened to the couch?"

Behind him, Brenda's eyes went wide, and she excused herself to grab something from the other room before heading down the hall to what Lou assumed were the bedrooms.

"What, can't I treat myself to a solo date night gone awry?"

Clem narrowed her eyes. "Start talking."

"I cooked myself a nice dinner the other night like you've been suggesting, thank you very much, and I thought it would be a good idea to light a little candle for ambiance. But you know how it is after a long day on my feet. I was exhausted and dozed off. At some point, the candle tipped over, because I woke up to a lot more ambiance than expected. An ambiance emergency. But it was nothing some cold water couldn't handle."

Clem's eyes looked wild, almost like she wasn't there at all. "That's it. You cannot be trusted with food. First a fire and now tonight, with the hospital visit. All meals at the diner until I can arrange proper supervision."

Lou shuffled her feet, waiting for the moment Clementine would push too hard and they'd get kicked out. She couldn't bear the thought of driving back to Boston tonight. But Denny didn't seem angry.

Clem's dad blushed as he looked down at his boots. "Darlin', it was fine."

"Why haven't you gotten rid of the couch?" Lou asked, hoping to diffuse the situation.

"It's salvageable."

Lou glanced at the charred mess but kept her mouth shut.

Clem shook her head. "I assure you it is not. I'll drag it outside before we leave tomorrow. And don't even think about bringing it back in. I'm going to send Sam by to make sure you don't."

"Oh good, it will be nice to see Sam." Denny smiled dreamily. "I miss her. She hasn't been coming into the diner much since you left, which I've been trying not to take personally."

Clem's face dropped as she seemed to consider what her father had said. There was something about it she didn't like, that much was clear. But what?

"Okay, well, I better get going." Brenda's voice sliced through the tension. "It was good to see you, hon," she said as she pulled Clementine into a hug.

Clem's eyes were trained on the novel and the electric toothbrush clutched in Brenda's hand, her mouth stretched into a tight line. "Good to see you, too," she mumbled.

"You girls come see us at the diner tomorrow before you leave."

"*Us?*" Clem mouthed, seemingly to no one. She certainly wasn't looking at Lou.

Once Brenda had gone, Lou made a show of yawning, hoping to move the night along. Plus, watching Clem and her dad work out their issues was making Lou squirm. How badly she'd wished for this with her own parents. For years, she wanted closure or just the faintest glimmer that she still mattered to them, but that's not how life worked. If you disappointed someone, they could cut you loose at any time and that hurt a hell of a lot worse than never caring in the first place. Lou had built her adult life around that philosophy, and with the exception of her grandma, it was a rule she never broke. Casual friendships, casual sex, a heart as safe as a fortress.

"You know, I'm pretty beat too, after all that excitement," Denny said. "I'm going to hit the hay. Do you girls need anything?"

Clem glared at her dad, opening her mouth like she wanted to demand a duel, and Lou felt a little flutter of panic at the prospect of pistols at dawn.

"We're okay. Thank you, though. Sleep well," Lou added hastily.

Once he had disappeared down the hall, Lou linked her arm through Clem's pulling her close. "Shall we?"

)o(

IT TURNED out a full bed was... even narrower than Lou had thought. Even if she held her breath all night, there was no way to avoid their bodies touching. She longed for bunk beds or even the crispy couch as she settled next to Clem, their arms brushing together and igniting little fireworks in Lou's stomach. But these reactions were only a problem if she acted on them and she never would.

Clem's voice cut through the silence. "Do you think my dad is dating Brenda?" Her voice was quiet, like she was afraid to speak this into being.

Lou turned toward her. Clem's eyes were the gray-blue of the Atlantic in June. "I think that's a distinct possibility."

"The toothbrush?" Clem's eyes were damp, and she blinked quickly, clearing her wave of emotion.

"Yeah, the toothbrush." Lou nodded. "Are you okay?"

She drew out a breath, dragging a hand through her messy red waves. "After my mom passed away, he never dated. I never even saw him flirt with another woman while I was here. Was he waiting for me to leave to start living again? Sometimes I wonder if I held us both back by staying to help. And then other times I feel certain I messed up everything by leaving."

Lou wanted to ask more about Clem's mom. She was transfixed by these little glimmers of the past Clementine was revealing. And Lou wished she could reassure her so badly that everything was okay, but some things had to be felt. And this

137

seemed like something that deserved time and space to breathe. "Change is hard. And I'm here if you want to talk about it."

"That's okay." Clem shook her head and rubbed at her eyes, leaving little red marks at their edges. "But thanks. It's been a long day, and we need our rest—we have a couch to haul in the morning."

"*We*? I distinctly remember that conversation and I made no such commitment." Lou widened her eyes in mock accusation.

"If I get hurt, who will serve drinks to the beautiful wayward lovers?"

"Okay, okay... fair point. I'll help you, but first, sleep." It was far too easy to give in to Clementine.

Lou rolled to face the wall, needing every centimeter of space she could get to breathe through the intimacy of the last few minutes. What she wanted was to pull Clem against her and fall asleep in the safety of this bubble. Instead, she said, "Don't have any dolphin dreams, okay?"

Clem groaned, and the sound was delicious. "I'm not drunk enough for those jerks to haunt me."

Lou laughed. Clem's tone had all the fierceness of a toddler raising their fists. "Not even punch drunk?"

"If I were you, I'd hope not." Clem sighed out a yawn. Adorable. When did all of her noises become so appealing to Lou? "Goodnight, Lou." And then, after a long pause, "I'm glad you were here."

Clementine moved beside her, and then the bedside lamp switched off.

Lou whispered, "me too," into the darkness.

HOWL

)O(

FULFILLING EVERY POSSIBLE CLICHE, Lou awoke with her arm wrapped snugly around Clementine's waist. Clem was facing her, and her hand was fisted in Lou's shirt right over her heart. It felt like some grand metaphor for the way Lou had gotten herself tangled up with Clementine even as she'd tried not to.

But Lou didn't see the point in metaphors any more than she saw the point in love. Both were pretty ways to convince you of something you didn't need to believe. She'd leave the flowery language along with the first date bouquets, thank you very much. She lifted her arm from Clem's waist and attempted to roll away, but her shirt pulled, still clutched tightly in Clem's grip until the collar cut into her neck, making Lou feel like she couldn't breathe. This escape would need to be delicate. Could she contort herself out of her shirt? It couldn't be too much harder than taking off a bra without removing her top—a few awkward elbow motions, and voila. And if you were lucky, no noses were bloodied in the making of that miracle.

Lou pulled her legs out from under the covers one at a time and bent her knees, bracing her feet against the mattress. Then she scooted as close to Clem as possible to get a little slack in the fabric before pulling the collar up over her head. With her arms raised, she inched her body down the bed, working her way to freedom. When at last she felt the cool rush of morning air on her chest, Lou hurried off the bed triumphant and fucking topless. Shit. Why didn't she calculate that removing her shirt would keep her trapped in Clementine's bedroom half-naked

139

until she woke up, at which point she would presumably find Lou exposed and likely shivering?

She made her way to the dresser and tried to shimmy open its ancient drawers, but the creaks were too loud. She went to the closet and nearly collapsed in relief when she saw a flowery silk robe hanging inside. She wrapped herself in it and made her way out the door.

First, coffee. Caffeine was always the first, and sometimes only, good thing that happened to Lou each day. Certainly, nothing good ever happened to Lou *before* caffeine. She padded quietly down the hall on bare feet until she reached the icy tile of the kitchen, where she froze. Grinning over his paper was Denny. She hoped this wasn't going to be trouble now that he had Lou alone. He raised his mug that said *World's Best Grandpa* in a mock salute.

Lou squinted at the cup.

He shrugged. "It's aspirational. There's more coffee if you want it, kiddo. I'm not sure I caught your name last night."

"Lou." She felt her shoulders dropping. "It's nice to officially meet you, Mr. Darby."

"Likewise. Thanks for bringing Clementine all this way, even though I really am sorry about the false alarm. But the true travesty is that I'll never eat chili cheese fries again with these women in my life watching me like hawks."

Lou studied him. "Not to be another woman telling you what to do, but you might want to consider reframing that before Clem gets up. She was really worried about you and I know she's relieved."

Denny looked down at his coffee. "She seemed kind of angry last night."

"I think she was coming down from the stress and adrenaline. Look at it this way, it's better you're okay, and she's a little mad than the alternative."

"Very true." Denny swirled the coffee in his mug before downing it. "Well, I need to go open the diner. Be sure to stop by before you leave town, okay?"

"Of course. I wouldn't miss out on the famous Maine Course."

"And I wouldn't want you to. Nice robe, by the way." He winked at her on his way out the back door.

Lou stood at the counter, a mug of the worst tasting coffee she'd ever experienced steaming before her, wondering what she'd done to deserve it.

)O(

EVEN LOU HAD to admit that Hart's Hollow was charming. They'd gotten ready quickly after wrestling the couch outside. Clem had a few stops she wanted to make before they hit the road this afternoon.

Clem squinted against the sun, studying Lou. "You're walking like a zombie. Are you sure you're okay? The bed was uncomfortable, wasn't it? Did I snore? Dolphins?"

"No snoring and no dolphins. It was actually eerily quiet without the noise of traffic and people yelling 'screw you' on the street. Hard to relax, you know?" *Also, I spent all night wanting you*, Lou thought, but what she said was, "I just need coffee."

"Of course. I saw you barely drank your mug at home. I wish I had warned you. My dad is a snob about coffee, but his taste is terrible, like the hipsters who cling to lukewarm cans of PBR. It's the grocery store, tin can stuff or death for that guy." Clem shuddered.

"That explains a lot, actually. The powdered, non-dairy creamer was an almost palatable touch." Lou grimaced.

"I have been saved by that chalk substitute many times. Here, I know the best spot for coffee in town."

"Is it the diner?" Lou asked incredulously.

"Nope, the coffee there is terrible. My dad does the ordering." Clem shuddered. "Now, follow me."

"Where else would I go?"

"Fair point." Clem's smile rivaled the rays peeking over the low buildings of the main street, which was, of course, called Maine Street.

Lou followed her tour guide down half a block, with Clem pointing out a new little landmark every few feet: her and Sam's names scratched into the sidewalk; the crack in the pavement that caught her roller skate and caused the little scar on her chin that Lou hadn't noticed before. A very kissable crescent moon-shaped scar that—

"Here we are!"

Lou nearly crashed into her as she stopped abruptly in front of a dusty-looking store with a hand-painted red and white sign that read Shop: Hammer Time.

"You're going to love this place," Clem said enthusiastically.

"This looks like a hardware store."

"It is. The best one in town." Clem smiled. "Like everything, it's also the only one in town."

"What's up with the name?"

"Tommy let his daughter rename it for her eighth birthday. Pretty sure he regrets it daily. Want to guess what it was before?"

"Tommy's Tools?" Lou asked, more a statement than a question. People sure did love alliteration.

"Hey, you're good at this. If you ever want a future in naming small-town stores, Hart's Hollow might be the place for you."

Lou rolled her eyes playfully. "I'm still confused about why you promised me coffee and then led me to a hardware store."

"Just trust me, okay?" Clem extended her hand and Lou took it as she followed her through the door and to the back of the shop.

Sitting on a scarred piece of wood atop two sawhorses was the most beautiful espresso machine Lou had ever seen. All glinting chrome and serious-looking levers. "This is like an oasis in the desert."

"Lou McCallister, have I pleased you?" Clementine's smile jolted Lou's heart with the force of a triple shot.

A smile curved Lou's lips despite her trying to suppress it. She had a grouchy image to maintain, but it was harder and harder to do that around Clem. "Ask me again after proper caffeine."

Clem got to work grinding beans and tamping the grounds before firing up the heavenly machine.

"Who's there?" A gruff voice called from the back.

"Just me, Tommy," Clementine replied.

A bearded lumberjack of a man, Buffalo plaid shirt and all, emerged from the back. "Clementine! I didn't know you were in town."

"Just here taking care of something for my dad. We're leaving in a few hours. This is Lou."

"Hi, Lou. This one's always sneaking in and stealing my coffee." He jerked a thumb toward Clem.

"Excuse you! Stealing? I buy you a coffee subscription every year for your birthday."

"A birthday present should be for the person you're gifting it to. Not for you to secretly steal."

Lou laughed, accepting her espresso from Clem. "I think he's got a point."

"I can't believe you'd betray me like that after I provided you with coffee." Clem lifted a hand to her heart.

"Fine" Tommy sighed. "You can buy me a coffee subscription any time as long as you come over to make it."

"Deal." Clementine grinned.

"Well, kids, I better get up to the register. Tell your old man *hi* for me and that I'll be by Sunday for the cookout."

What was it with everyone calling them *kids* here? That, mixed with the almost parental affection, was doing a number on Lou's psyche. She wanted to cocoon in it and push it away all at once.

Clem tilted her head. "The cookout?"

"Just a little thing he and Brenda are throwing. See you later."

The smile fell from Clementine's face.

"Does it bother you?" Lou whispered.

Clem blinked. "Sorry, does what bother me?"

"Your dad, dating."

"I know it shouldn't," Clem said, biting her lip. "It hurts more that he didn't tell me."

"Yeah, I get that. If you can, you should ask him about it."

Clem nodded and checked the time on her phone. Lou took the hint that she was done talking about it for now.

"WE SHOULD GET GOING TOO." Lou drained her mug.

"You're right. You still have almost an entire block to see."

On the corner of Maine Street, next to the hardware store, was a beat-up little building, as worn in as a pair of Clem's jeans, called Dirty's. "Is this what I think it is?"

"If you think it's the best dive bar for a hundred miles, then yes, it is."

"Ugh, I wish it was open. I love a small-town dive bar.

They're so homey. You know, I could definitely afford a place for Howl here." Lou stepped to the window, spotting an old jukebox in the corner.

She caught the reflection of Clementine's frown in the glass. "Sure, but why would you want to?"

"Why *wouldn't* I want to? The town's charming and the people are nice and there's a hardware store with an espresso machine. It's like a tiny little heaven."

"Huh. I guess I haven't seen it like that in a long time."

"Well," Lou said, turning to face Clem. "Maybe I should take over as tour guide."

"The student has become the master."

"Breakfast time?" Lou tilted her head toward the sign for the Maine Course just across the street.

"You've gotta get the pancakes."

They were halfway across the street when a voice rang out that stopped Clementine, and by proxy, Lou, in their tracks.

"Clementine Darby, if you leave this town without spending time with me, I will shoot out your tires before you even hit the highway."

The voice was loud and very close and coming from the mouth of a woman who looked like a 60s pin-up model. And Lou meant that as the highest compliment, because who wouldn't?

"Sam," Clem said, eyes widening. "I was just about to call you."

"You always were a terrible liar. That's one of the things I love about you." The woman grinned, her eyes flashing. "And you must be Lou. I've heard *so* much about you."

Lou gulped. Sam looked far too happy at the prospect of grilling her, and it probably wasn't a wise idea for her to hold Clementine's hand to get through it.

Chapter Thirteen
Clementine

For the second time in a month, Clementine woke up the entire house with her screaming. She had come to before sunrise to a pair of beady eyes staring directly at her from the tree outside her bedroom window. Her first thought was murder, and her second thought was also murder, but it was a turkey—so, basically the same thing. Just a giant, fucking bird right there, three stories from the ground, staring her down. Turkeys flying seemed wrong somehow. Usually, it was confusing when birds *couldn't* fly, but these fowl seemed decidedly land-bound.

Clementine was still exhausted from the emergency trip to Hart's Hollow a few days ago. There was so much she had yet to unpack, like how she'd woken up in the middle of the night wrapped in Lou's arms. And how, when she woke again, she was clutching Lou's t-shirt to her chest like she'd dreamed her up. She had nearly choked when she'd found Lou in the kitchen wearing her robe, knowing she was topless underneath. Clem could imagine the feel of the smooth silk caressing her skin. She'd wanted to bring the robe back to Boston because she hadn't meant to leave it, but she didn't want to risk seeming creepy.

The turkeys of Boston, it seemed, had no such qualms. But she was okay with thinking about these feathered beasts, because anything was better than obsessing about how Lou had seemed in Hart's Hollow: open and soft and hopeful. It was as though the town revealed a Lou without all her armor. It had almost been appealing enough to make Clementine want to stay there.

Well, except for the part where Sam had entertained the entire diner with the story about the time Clem couldn't find her gym shorts in second grade. She'd been wearing a nice dress, and the best solution her developing brain could conjure at the time was wrapping herself in paper towels like a mummy. Which is how she'd wandered out onto the kickball field, only to be immediately beaned by a large, red rubber ball. And Lou —this woman she'd been trying to impress for weeks—laughed so hard, she'd nearly choked on her pancakes.

To be fair to Sam, she'd also snuck in some not-so-subtle statements about what happens to people who hurt Clementine.

She'd been so excited to see Lou opening herself up to new ideas for a split second, like maybe Lou cared about the things Clem had said... cared about *Clem*. She needn't have gotten excited though. Since then, Lou hadn't given any more indications that she wanted Clem's help to save Howl.

Lou was being so stubborn after their talk on the way back, that she was willing to let things die rather than compromise, and Clementine just couldn't understand it. Maybe Clem's enthusiasm about saving the bar had been too much. Her dad had done the same thing with Maine Course. He resisted even the smallest changes, like one day her mom might come back to life and be hurt if the salt shaker wasn't precisely where she'd left it. Clementine could have saved that place, made it her own. Or maybe she couldn't have. For all she knew, she'd only put everything on hold, delayed the inevitable. What if, as long as she was there, her dad was never going to move on? Seeing him with Brenda had upset her, but the more she thought about it, it was nice to see him happy. A positive change.

As the days between her and her life in Hart's Hollow stretched into weeks, she had more and more trouble seeing herself happy there. Sure, visiting with Lou had thrown some of her resolve about never going back into question. But even if she could have brought the diner into this century, all of her other problems wouldn't have been magically solved. She'd never taken the time to figure out what *she* wanted. When her mother died, Clem had simply stepped into *her* dream of running the diner. She loved where she'd grown up, but there were times that the small town felt more like the pressure of a boot on her neck than the comfort of a warm hug.

Nerves wracked through Clem as she walked into Howl for her shift, wondering how she'd move past the tension with Lou. But she shouldn't have been worried. Lou was still pretending things were normal and Howl wasn't in dire straits. Which meant *Clementine* had to pretend like nothing was wrong, even though basically *everything* was wrong, because all of this was about to go away if a whole bunch of people didn't pull together to do something drastic. And who better to save the world than a rag-tag group of queer people? It's the only thing that ever had.

An uneventful hour into her shift, the music was skull-shattering, and the crowd at the bar was already rowdy when the siren went off. The noise reminded Clementine of the tornado warnings she'd heard the summer she'd spent in Michigan—

those first Saturday of the month tests as regular as clockwork. Were tornados a thing in Boston and she just didn't know about it?

She froze, gripping the silver shaker full of tequila and sour mix near her shoulder as she tried to remember the protocol. Stop, drop and roll didn't seem right, but probably couldn't hurt. Frantically, she looked around at the other bartenders who had kept on mixing drinks like the world wasn't ending.

The siren wailed again, low and mournful, and this time everyone stopped. Behind Clem, a voice boomed out over a megaphone. "You all know what that sound means!"

Cheers rose up from the crowd in the bar, which seemed incongruous with the prospect of an impending disaster. So it would seem that Clementine was the only one who did not know what that sound meant. She turned toward Alyssa and widened her eyes in the universal sign of *what the hell is going on?*

Alyssa winked. Not super informative.

The lights went out and the crowd cheered again. This time when Lou yelled into the megaphone, Clem felt every syllable rattle in her chest like Lou's words had replaced her pulse. "Rumor has it we have a birthday this fine evening. Lovers, it's time to do your thing."

Was Clem a Lover and more importantly, what *was* their thing? She sent out a silent prayer that it wasn't *howling*. Or stalking prey at a city park.

"Christi, happy twenty-first!" Megan yelled. She didn't work with Megan much, but Clem always had fun when she did.

"I'm twenty-nine," someone—presumably Christi—called back.

"Well, then happy anniversary of your twenty-first. This one's for you! Ready, Lovers?"

As the lights came back up to their dim glow, the opening notes of Peaches' Fuck the Pain Away resonated through the bar, taking root in Clem's chest, making her feel young and wild and ready to make bad decisions.

She stepped aside just in time to avoid the heel of Lou's boot as she hopped onto the bar.

Clem caught Alyssa's wrist. "I still don't know what's happening."

"Oh, I keep forgetting you're new to all this. Birthdays mean a bar dance, babe. How's your rhythm?" Alyssa's grin had something wild beneath it, nearly feral.

"Kind of like when one tire goes flat but you keep driving anyway? Don't places usually do that clapping thing for birthdays?" Clem's face heated, she was sure it was glowing like a birthday candle. "Or couldn't we just stick a candle in a shot of vodka?"

Alyssa tilted her head. "Don't be silly, that would be a Molotov cocktail."

"Those are... festive. Put that in the suggestion box." Lou took hold of Clem's free wrist. "Think of this as team building, then." Lou crouched down, leaning close to whisper in Clem's ear. "Besides, I'm not sure arson is covered by insurance, but I appreciate that you're still trying to sneakily make money for the bar."

As Clem let her roommate and Lou lever her up onto the counter, her boots—okay, Alyssa's boots—threatened to hydroplane on whatever spilled drinks and glass condensation they'd failed to wipe up. Almost immediately, Alyssa, Rachel, Megan, and Dana launched into a complicated and very suggestive version of a line dance. Lou stood off to the side, arms crossed over her chest.

Clem stood shakily, her boot barely avoiding a glass of What Peaches and What Penumbras as anxiety flowed through her limbs like a low electric current. She wasn't sure if she was nervous about dancing in front of a crowd or dancing in front of Lou, who was still looking at her. Clem did a quick check of her clothes and yup, they were still bordering on obscene, but all the important parts were covered.

Clem tried to match their movements, but kept sneaking glances at Lou instead of looking out at the crowd. She knew they weren't leering, but she felt self-conscious, on display. So instead, she took in the way Lou's hand rested gently on her own arm, fingers loosely wrapped around her bicep. Clementine had an almost visceral sensation of the way it had felt to hold Lou's hand in Hart's Hollow, a comforting anchor keeping her from drifting into despair.

Lou looked strong. Strong enough to hoist a case of tequila —or Clem—over her shoulder. The thought sent a current of pleasure through her and her feet faltered, missing the beat. The thought of Lou's lips on a bottle, Lou's lips on her... Tequila, the patron saint of bad decisions.

Before long, the other bartenders split into pairs and Clem was left off to the side, like a wallflower not being asked to dance. Middle school Spring Fling now on a bar top. She debated getting down, but worried that might draw more attention to herself. Clem both knew herself well enough and was realistic about her abilities, and years of self-knowledge dictated she would almost certainly take a tumble if she tried to hop off the counter with leather boot soles that were slick. She tried swaying a bit, but that felt worse somehow, more mortifying to acknowledge her solitary, unwanted state of being. Her body heated, and she knew it had nothing to do with the way Rachel and Alyssa were dancing obscenely close.

Clem knew at that moment that she *had* to jump, pull the ejection lever, and parachute to safety before she spontaneously combusted. The bar should obscure most of her fall, anyway.

And the rubber mat would ensure she wouldn't get too banged up.

She had just about worked up the courage to jump down when she felt a sure touch on her lower back pulling her back from the edge. Strong fingers curved against the dip of her spine. Clementine turned slowly to see Lou. Lou, who didn't smile at her but nodded once decisively and took a half-step back as her hips began moving to the music. And my god, those hips had to be illegal in at least eleven states. Though not Mass-achusetts, probably. Always a true leader when it came to bodily autonomy. Truly, this New England state was blessed. First gay marriage and now this—Lou's hips moving to Fuck the Pain Away in a manner that made Clem think maybe Peaches was onto something.

Even though she and Lou had already had sex, maybe once more really would get it out of their systems. Even as the thought strobed across Clementine's mind, she knew she wanted more than that. She wanted the Lou she'd seen in Hart's Hollow who held her hand when she was scared and teased her over coffee. Clem wanted time to get to know everything about her, to understand and disarm all of Lou's defenses. A lifetime of road trips still wouldn't be enough.

Clementine tried to shove her fists into her pockets, but they were fucking tiny because women's pants colluded with the handbag industry and couldn't even fit a quarter. Finally, she laced her fingers together behind her back because really, what *was* she supposed to do with her hands in a situation like this?

Lou reached for her, running her fingers down Clemen-tine's arms, starting at her shoulders until Clem's grip broke free and she gave in, reaching back. And then, Lou was in her space. Lou's sure hands gripped her hips, index fingers resting on Clementine's bare skin just above the waistband of her shorts. Lou looped a finger through her belt loop and gave a tug, causing Clementine to stumble into her. Good god, had belt loops always been an erogenous zone?

That thought was a tripwire.

As the music continued to vibrate the bottles, Lou's arm snaked around Clem's neck, drawing her in. Now that they were so close, she could feel rather than see Lou's hips moving to the beat and that brush of Lou against her was more potent than any birthday shot. Suddenly, Clem had a very clear idea of what birthdays meant at Howl and she didn't mind one bit.

Lou's eyes and hands were all over her as Clem let go of her anxiety and started to move. She reminded her body that this was for show. Just another way to get tips, like her short shorts. Only the ache she felt in her clit as Lou slid a leg between her thighs told Clem that if this was a show, she was fooled by it.

Lou's hips pressed into Clem and the rest of the world flew away. The cheers of the crowd faded until it was just her and Lou and Peaches, their bodies moving together in a way Clem desperately wished was horizontal and not on this bar. Or maybe on this bar, but without all the other people.

And then even Peaches faded away, the song a self-fulfilling prophecy as the bass of the music dwarfed in comparison to the cacophony in her chest. Her heart was beating against her ribs like it was vying for freedom, as a vision of Lou seated on the countertop, legs slung over the shoulders of a kneeling Clem, gripped her imagination. Followed by an answering rush of heat between her legs that she would be surprised if Lou couldn't feel it.

Clem drew in a shuddering breath, mentally pinching herself to remember this was just pretend. Lou had made it clear that what happened between them in the storeroom was a one-time thing. Exactly once and no more. But this didn't feel like *no more*. Lou's movements had intentions.

Commotion caught her eye as Alyssa and Rachel pulled a person onto the bar who Clem assumed was *the* Christi of birthday fame.

The beats of the song wound down and suddenly Clementine was alone as Lou slipped from her arms.

Alyssa caught her hand and squeezed. "You must be some kind of magic, girl. How did you get Lou to actually dance?"

Nothing was making sense. *She* hadn't done anything. "What do you mean?"

"I don't think I've ever seen Lou partake before. It looked like you two were pretty cozy."

Clem's throat went dry. If even Alyssa could see what was going on with her and Lou, then maybe Clementine didn't need to pretend it wasn't happening. Had Lou changed her mind about not wanting anything more? Clem had to find out. "I, uh, have to go to the bathroom."

Clem hopped down on unsteady legs. A quick glance around confirmed that Lou was nowhere to be found. Hopefully, she'd just retreated to her office and not fled the premises. Clementine nearly ran toward the back hall.

"You know the bathroom is in the other direction..." Alyssa's voice faded behind her, absorbed by the noise of the bar.

As Clem made her way toward Lou's office, the bass of the music buzzed up through her feet, settling in her chest like her heart was set to vibrate. She felt excited and turned on and something else beneath that. Hopeful? Maybe. Delusional? Perhaps. Nerves shouted into the wind of her desire, their wise words lost to the roar of her need to see Lou right now. To understand what that dance meant. Even if it meant nothing. Even if it meant Clem was reading into things that weren't there. It would be better to know that, too.

She drew closer to the office and a fresh feeling of want

coursed through her. Maybe it wouldn't be better to know that last part. She'd already tried to be a new version of herself that first night she'd met Lou, and if the ensuing weeks of her pining over the surly blonde were any indication, she was still the same-old Clementine.

But would the old Clementine push Lou's office door open and lean against the door frame in what she hoped was an appealing pose and not a slump? She would not. Maybe who she was now, was a hybrid of old and new. An evolution.

The door opened beneath her light touch. Lou sat perched on the edge of her make-shift desk, head in her hands. She looked up when Clem entered. Clementine's heartbeat was loud in her ears. Even disheveled, Lou was beautiful. Not some kind of perfect beauty, but like something made better for the tiny knicks life had left on her, something to be cherished and cared for. Those were certainly not one-night stand thoughts.

She cleared her throat, and Lou looked up to meet her gaze.

"What was that out there?" Clem asked, her voice raspy.

"Nothing." Lou leaned back a bit, folding her arms over her chest, muscles taut. Every movement seemed to showcase a new breathtaking detail. Clem had never thought she was a shoulder woman, but the sleeves of Lou's white t-shirt were doing God's work.

Clem narrowed her eyes but didn't say anything.

Lou shrugged, and those damn shoulders again... "It was just a dance."

"That," Clem said slowly, turning to shut the door and lean against it. "Was not just a dance."

"What was it then?" Lou raised an eyebrow. A master at not giving anything away. Clem was the opposite, sure that every-thing—her confusion and desire—were plain on her face.

She pushed off the door before she knew what she was doing. Lou's knees parted slightly, and Clem stepped into this newly offered space. She held Lou's gaze before dipping her head to meet her kiss.

Everything stopped. Every warning in her head telling Clem this was a bad idea was silenced like a bedside alarm when Lou's hands came to her hips, tracing the same pattern on her bare skin as they had during the bar dance.

Clem moaned and Lou took the opportunity to deepen their kiss. With a swift tug on her belt loops—a move she would now forever associate with Lou—Clementine stumbled forward. Lou urged her up until Clem was straddling her hips. Clem had never wanted anything as badly as she wanted Lou right now. The touch of her fingertips beneath Clementine's shirt felt electric. She grabbed one of Lou's hands and pressed it to her chest.

A thunderous crash in the hallway startled them. The loud swearing that followed was way too close. Clem pulled back quickly, her body tense with fear and want. She pressed her forehead to Lou's as they both gasped for air.

"It's okay," Lou whispered. "Probably just a drunk customer looking for the bathroom. They'll be gone in a minute."

Lou's fingertips traced the cups of Clem's bra, nearly over-riding reason. But slowly Clementine came back to the reality of their situation. Another illicit hook-up where they could be interrupted was not what she wanted. She didn't want to lie to people. She didn't want to sneak around and be somebody's secret. A life of being queer in a small town had been more than enough of that. Whatever the opposite of casual was, she wanted *that* with Lou. And if Lou couldn't give her that open-ness, then Clementine needed to walk away.

She drew in a hitching breath. "I want you, Lou. But not like this. I want to take my time. I want to enjoy every moment knowing that there are more nights to come. Think about it, I'm not going anywhere."

Clementine kissed Lou softly before easing herself off of Lou's lap. As she smoothed her clothes, her thumb snagged on the open button of her shorts. How had she missed Lou's fingers doing *that?*

On shaking legs, she headed back to the bar to finish her shift.

Chapter Fourteen
Lou

I am once again asking, can priests go on dates?" Lou stood in the small entryway of her grandma's house, trying not to stumble into the walls as Canoodle swarmed her feet. Just as she had been rolling out of bed at the crack of one p.m. on this fine Saturday, Lou had received an urgent text from this woman who had been busy batting her eyelashes in the hallway mirror since Lou had arrived breathless five minutes before.

She loved her grandma, but they seriously needed to discuss what counted as urgent at eighty-five. Health issues, home invasions? Yes. Dates? Decidedly less so. With false alarms, her gram was as bad as her college roommate texting her during an exam to ask Lou, a certified lesbian, if she had any spare condoms for emergencies. "What kind of emergency, an identity crisis?" Lou had typed back before getting caught with her phone and kicked out for cheating.

"Louise, my dear, dinner at Chippy's is not a date. Maybe if you're in junior high and think anywhere with utensils that aren't plastic is nice," her grandma said as she applied lipstick in the hallway mirror, "but when you're my age, you want a little nicer than that."

The emergency, it turned out, was dog-sitting. Lou had already planned to bring her grandma's car back today, so it wasn't entirely inconvenient, except for the part where she had a life and also couldn't even keep a plant alive, let alone her grandma's featherweight pride and joy. Lou had had the old Toyota washed after driving it back from Maine. She'd even vacuumed up all the crumbs from their snacks and blotted out the little stain where Clementine had spilled her coffee.

But erasing all signs of their trip had done nothing to dissipate Lou's memories of how great she'd felt to be there beside Clem, calm and safe, the weight of the world lifting for a few hours. Until Clem had brought them crashing back to reality by focusing on Howl's woes during the drive back to Boston. She wished she could forget every perfect thing between them since the night they'd met. Not wanting to feel good might seem counterintuitive, but feeling that way with Clem now was obliterating her memory of their simple hookup. And then last night, when Clem had come to her office, Lou's already shaky resolve had faltered. Clem's mouth on hers, blurring every line between her head and her heart.

As a rule, Lou limited her involvement with women to the early moments: flirting and laughter and sex. And that had always been fine. In her experience, there was nothing enjoyable about opening yourself up to someone, about letting them decide at any moment they no longer liked what they saw. Lou had been confident in her approach: all the fun and none of the heartache. But her carefully constructed safety measures had shattered when she'd held Clementine's hand in the hospital and felt like, for the first time in years, she wanted to be there for the hard stuff, too.

"Did I lose you, dear?"

"No, I was just thinking about... taxes." Lou hoped her grandma wouldn't ask why anyone would ever be thinking about taxes when they didn't need to. She stilled, waiting for a follow-up, but none came. Her grandma was busy fluffing her hair. "I guess you're right about Chippy's, that place seeps into your clothes. Still, are you sure about this? Won't it make things awkward at church?"

Canoodle jumped on her hind legs. The dog's full extension came up to Lou's knee and she crouched to ruffle her ears.

"Not at all. Besides, it's more of a working meeting. I plan to talk to Joe about the upcoming food drive. Did you know that last time, they didn't collect menstrual products? Macaroni and cheese does diddly when you're bleeding through."

"Okay Gram, wow. I mean, I agree with you, obviously, but still. And if it's not a date, why do you need me to keep Canoodle *overnight*?"

"I thought it might be nice for my two favorite gals to have a little sleepover."

Canoodle scrunched her eyes and yawned before jumping into Lou's knee again. "I think when one of the sleepoverees is a dog, it's just called pet sitting."

"Nonsense. Invite your girlfriend to watch a movie and order pizza then, it will be fun. Besides, you know how long all those planning logistics can take."

"Logistics, huh?" Lou raised an eyebrow. "Is that what you kids are calling it these days? And Clementine is not my girlfriend."

"Is that *not* what you kids are calling it these days?" Gram smiled sweetly and opened up the hall closet. "Here's her leash. And here's her emotional support stuffed elephant. And don't forget she needs a second dinner before bed. I made her goulash, there's enough for you, too. You could also give her a special version of whatever you're having."

It exasperated Lou, but she did admire her grandma's dedication to treating Canoodle as a regular member of the family, albeit one with some pretty serious dietary restrictions.

"So we're just done talking about your date then?"

"Make sure it's something nutritious, otherwise she gets night pukes."

Lou grimaced. "Okay then. I'll save my pizza crusts for her."

Gram sighed before scooping up the six wriggling pounds of fur and thrusting the dog into Lou's arms. "If you get her a pizza, make sure it's dog friendly, but it's probably better to make it at home to avoid cross-contamination."

"I'm not sure what a dog-friendly pizza is."

"Then look it up on googly, my love. Now, I have to finish setting my curls."

"It's not googly, it's—" Before she could finish her thought, Lou found herself standing on her grandmother's stoop with the screen door clanging behind her in the light summer breeze. She tucked the dog under her arm like a football and she started her walk to the subway station, praying to the gods above that it wasn't a Red Sox game day. Otherwise, she'd be fending off drunk dudes who thought invading the space of someone with a dog somehow got a pass for being creepy.

WALKING her grandma's toy poodle always felt to Lou like she was a little kid pulling one of those toy dogs on wheels behind her. Only Canoodle's latest thing wasn't just tipping over if she hit a bump, but instead going after every other dog they passed, teeth bared like she meant business. She came mere inches from making contact with a Great Dane's Achilles tendon before the oaf of a dog skittered away, nosing her owner's elbow. A cartoon elephant fleeing from a mouse.

Lou rounded the corner to Howl, dreading the call she'd have to make to Rachel about needing her to cover tonight. But if the pint-sized terror could wreak that kind of havoc on the city's streets, Lou shuddered to think what the dog might do to her apartment unsupervised. She felt a small wave of disappointment as she realized that meant she wouldn't work with Clementine tonight. They were meeting Sunday to go over some ideas to raise the capital to save the bar, but Lou didn't want it to be all business.

She sighed and pulled out her phone to get the task over with, scrolling to find Rachel's contact: Rachel two skull emoji (for emergencies only under threat of bodily harm). Lou should really shorten her name now that she was confident Rachel would only hurt someone if she stood to win money for doing so. Boxing had become like a lightning rod for her rage. She hadn't threatened a customer in months.

Somewhere in front of her a woman yelped, causing Lou to glance up from her phone. She was glad she did because Canoodle was currently scaling Clementine's leg, her little paws gaining purchase in the rips of Clem's jeans. And my, were those some rips. Entire sections of Clem's thighs were on display. For a full minute, Lou's brain just stopped working. Usually, after she slept with someone, she stopped wanting them altogether. With Clementine, the exact opposite had been happening. This woman was upending the law governing Lou McCallister's world.

"And who is this little one?" Clem asked as she slipped her hands around Canoodle and lifted her into the sky. The light from the sun caught in the dog's golden fur as Clem held her aloft like Simba on the rock.

"That's Canoodle."

"Canoodle the toy poodle? I didn't peg you as an Instagram pet name person."

"A what?"

"Like when people give their pets catchy names and social

media accounts. I once saw an account for a Weiner dog named Foot Long in Tucson."

Lou cackled, her laugh was rich and deep in a way that she wasn't used to hearing. It felt... good. And the way Clem was staring at her with a twinkle in her eye? That felt good, too. "Well, that's just savvy marketing. But this is my grandma's dog, and she's definitely not 'on the computer'."

"Is your grandma here, too?" Clem's gaze traveled over Lou's shoulder as she scanned the street behind her. "I'd love to thank her for letting you drive me to Maine in her car."

"No, I'm hanging with Canoodle tonight while my gram has a... meeting."

"Oh fun, a slumber party! Will you be hanging out at the bar?" Clementine turned to Canoodle, directing her question to the dog.

Lou hesitated. Did she expect Canoodle to answer? "I, um, was going to ask Rachel to cover for me since I have the dog. Canoodle is tiny but she's fierce. I don't trust her in my place alone, but it hadn't occurred to me to bring her to work. I'm not sure I could watch her *and* serve drinks though."

"Why not? You're the boss. Besides, look at this face." Clem clutched the dog to her chest and ruffled Canoodle's ears. "I can help watch her. Especially if I'm on garnish duty again."

"Well, I'll see what I can do about that." Lou felt a slow smile dawning across her face and she could do absolutely nothing to stop it, with Clem looking at her like that, like they were a team. That whatever the problem was, Clementine might appear beside her and offer to help.

"Alright, well, I should go. The owner's pretty strict about being on time." Clem nodded to the door.

"Someone should tell her to relax." Lou winked. She didn't even care that she was fully flirting with Clementine. She'd been thinking about what Clem had said last night in her office.

Clem wanted her, even knowing that the bar was in trouble and Lou wasn't perfect. It was doing something very weird to the inside of her chest, her heart aching like a waking limb.

Clem set Canoodle back down. "See you in there?"

The dog immediately tried to throw herself back into Clem's arms. *Same, Canoodle. Same.*

Lou reeled the pup in on her retractable leash like a wily trout.

"Yeah, we'll be right down after I get changed."

Clem's eyes slowly perused Lou, like soft fingertips tracing over her body. Lou tried not to squirm as she let herself be examined like she was something worth looking at in her tight old jeans and a beat-up black t-shirt. Clem's eyes dragged up to meet Lou's gaze, and she bit her lip. Lou held back a groan.

Clem gave a little wave and turned toward the door, calling over her shoulder, "you won't change too much, I hope."

SETTING Canoodle loose at Howl had been a mistake, but a fun one. It had Lou thinking a dangerous thought, that maybe sometimes it was okay to lose a little control. Tonight was possibly worth the price of admission just to listen to Clementine laugh as she chased that tiny, bouncy ball of fur around. Lou would not have been able to make this work without Clem. That seemed to be a common theme in her life right now. The few ideas Clem had thrown out for saving the bar didn't even seem like Hail Marys. They seemed within reach. And sure, Lou hated the thought of asking for help, opening herself up for rejection, but maybe, very very rarely it was worth it. It all seemed a little less scary when she thought of asking for help with Clementine there by her side.

"This is so much fun!" Clem said.

Lou glanced down to see that she'd found a way to tuck the dog into the front of her apron. It was almost unbearably cute.

"I didn't even realize we had aprons."

Clem shrugged. "I found it under the bar. Canoodle was sleeping on it. Hey, does the bar have an Instagram? Or other social media?"

"I think you know the answer to that. If Canoodle doesn't have one, then the bar definitely doesn't."

"Here," Clem said, sliding her phone from her pocket and holding it out to Lou. "Take a picture of me and the noodle."

Lou took her time getting Clementine in the frame. The lighted bar shelves glowed behind her. She looked almost ethereal. Once Lou was happy with the shot, she crouched down and took a few more from different perspectives.

"You'd be a perfect Instagram girlfriend, you know that?"

Lou felt the color drain from her face. "I'm not sure what that means," she said, handing the phone back.

"Don't panic. It means you worked hard to get my angles," Clem said with a head tilt that showcased that little crescent of a scar on her chin. The one Lou had first noticed in Maine. She scrolled through the photos, looking pleased. "These are good. Maybe you could just follow me around from now on?"

"Hmm." Lou made a noise she hoped was noncommittal, because right now that proposal didn't sound half bad. "So what are those photos for anyway?"

"We're going to make Howl's first post. It's only right that it features two fan favorites." Clem pointed between herself and the dog.

The idea of one more thing on her list made Lou's breath catch. "Clem, I can't maintain social media for the bar. I don't even know the first thing about it."

"Lou." Clem shot her a pointed look that did something

165

swoopy to Lou's stomach. "You manage a business. How do you not know about delegating?"

"Rude. I *delegate*." Lou crossed her arms over her chest. Surely she handed things off to others. It wasn't like she served every drink herself, although sometimes she wished she could.

"Last night, you took over slicing limes for me because I was doing it wrong."

Lou thought back to the night before. The way Clem was holding the knife had been a safety hazard. She was legally obligated to intervene. Plus, maybe she wouldn't have been able to bear watching Clementine get hurt. Seeing her panic at the hospital was enough fear when it came to Clem to last a lifetime. "You *were* doing it wrong."

"There's a difference between not the exact way you would do something and that thing being wrong. You didn't even cut the limes differently—you know what? That's not the point. Delegation! That's the point." Clem's speech was undercut a bit when Canoodle squirmed free of the apron and snuck a kiss with lightning speed.

Lou tossed her a napkin, sending gratitude to Canoodle for putting an end to this pointless discussion. Only the second Clementine wiped her face and threw the napkin out, she picked up right where she'd left off.

"When I helped my dad with the diner, nothing would have gotten done if I had tried to do it all myself. So I outsourced things. I bought the muffins from a local bakery. You've got to stop trying to make the muffins yourself."

"Why are you talking about muffins? I'm a savory breakfast person. Except for Maine Course's pancakes."

"Yes, I know." Clem met Lou's gaze then quickly glanced down, a flush spreading across her cheekbones, highlighting the smattering of freckles there.

Lou felt the same heat bloom in her chest, like the first sip of whiskey on a cold night. Pure comfort with a promise of more to come. When Clementine looked up again, a fire burned in her eyes. "Let me and Canoodle make the damn muffins."

Lou cleared her throat, glad to shift away from thinking about being with Clem in Maine and already missing it at the same time. She had felt safe there with Clementine, and she'd learned long ago not to trust feelings like that. "Fine," she relented. "As long as no muffins are actually made in this process. I won't agree to changing the menu."

"Not a single egg shall be broken. Trust me, I can handle this. What do you think about a series for Pride Month where we highlight the history of the bar and the patron's personal stories?"

"You came up with that just now? While we were arguing?"

Clem frowned. "It was more of a lively discussion, but yes."

Lou wasn't sure she ever could have come up with an idea like that to promote Howl, and Clementine had conjured it from nowhere while engaged in a *discussion*. How many other great ideas had Lou missed out on because they weren't hers? While she loved the grungy vibe of Howl, she was starting to see the appeal of making it a little more, well... appealing.

A FEW HOURS LATER, the bar had emptied out. Clementine had offered to watch the dog for a bit while Lou finished up a few things. She'd spent a lot more time than she'd planned earlier, chatting with Clementine. But once she started, she found she didn't want to pull herself away. Spreadsheets were far less appealing when the company was good. Talking to Clem about the bar *was* technically work anyway.

That, along with the tornado of distraction that was Canoodle, meant that Lou was behind schedule on pretty much everything today. She'd been putting off emailing her landlord to make her interest in buying the place more clear because doing so felt a little bit like tempting fate. And also a little like she might break her own heart and let everyone down, including her landlord, if she failed to find the money. But still, after her talk with Clementine, knowing she was still around made the message a bit easier to send.

Clem had also encouraged her to ask for an appraisal of the building to see if the price her landlord cited was possibly over market value. Lou doubted it was, with the way real estate prices had been booming in Boston, but it couldn't hurt. Also, it would force her to commit publicly just a little to saving the bar. She slowly released the breath she was holding as she pressed send. As soon as the confirmation chimed, Lou closed her laptop and stood. She had more things she'd intended to accomplish, but right now all she wanted to do was tell Clementine that she was in.

Chapter Fifteen
Clementine

C lementine wasn't sure how long she'd been asleep on the harsh metal stairs leading up to Lou's apartment, but if the pain in her back was any indication, it was not an insignificant amount of time. The furry creature in her arms was wiggling to get free. She cracked open one eye in time to see strong hands swoop in and lift Canoodle.

"Okay, who's ready for goulash?" Lou asked.

Or maybe it was some dream version of Lou who wasn't making any sense. This sure beat the dolphins.

"Goulash at two a.m.?" Clem shifted so she was sitting up, her body unfolding as gracefully as a broken umbrella.

"It's three, actually. But I was talking to the dog."

"I'm not sure how that makes more sense."

"I bet I can find some food for you, too. Come on, it's the least I can do to thank you for your help tonight."

Clem followed Lou up the stairs. As she was pushing the door closed, she saw her opportunity to get Lou on board with her nascent vision for Howl's social media. "I'm not saying 'no' to food because I'm not a fool, but if you really want to thank me, you could be the first interview for the series on Howl that tells stories about its past, present, and future. I was thinking of calling it 'Finding Our Way Home.'"

"Let's make a deal. You can interview me first, but just for practice. This part of me is just for you." Lou immediately busied herself setting the wriggling pup down.

That last statement sent a shiver of excitement through Clem. Lou didn't mean it in a sexual way, which made it more intimate somehow. A tiny flicker of trust that Clementine wanted to guard against the winds of Lou's doubt.

"I can accept those terms," Clementine said with a nod. "I'm ready when you are."

"What, now?"

"Go get the dog her old Hungarian lady dinner, then we can sit in the living room for the questions."

Canoodle yipped, clearly in agreement with Clem's stellar plan. It *would be* good practice, and if it just so happened to bring her and Lou a bit closer, that was an outcome she supposed she could live with.

Lou returned with three bowls of red soup filled with noodles and tomatoes.

"I thought this was for the dog?"

"It is. My grandma makes a special version of every meal she eats for Canoodle. This will be pretty bland, but I could always order a pizza if you're hungry. I've actually never seen her encounter a meal she can't adapt in some way. The dog gets her own tiny table at Thanksgiving."

"I have a lot of questions."

"Off the record?" Lou raised a perfect eyebrow.

All Clem could do was smile and nod, the questions leaving her mind as though someone had just asked her for her favorite book. She could never remember a single title she'd ever read.

"I'll take that as a 'yes'. Between us, I think it's bananas, but

I love my gram, so when I cook for her once a week, I also cook for this wild child."

Canoodle hopped up onto the couch, shoving her small body between them. Clem mourned the opportunity for her thigh to brush Lou's. *Accidentally*, of course. But another small part of her was grateful for this miniature Wall of Jericho to keep her thoughts in check.

"Well, bananas or not, I think that's very sweet of you."

Now it was Lou's chance to look uncomfortable, and Clementine felt a little rush of confidence that she had evened the playing field after Lou's home run of an eyebrow quirk.

"Okay, so." Clem angled her body toward Lou. Her mouth went dry as Lou's intent gaze met her own. Or maybe that was just due to the lack of absolutely any flavor in this mush. "Let's start with where you grew up?"

"That's easy. Here."

"Alright, so you're a Boston native." Clem grabbed her phone from the coffee table where she'd set it when she'd picked up her bowl. She opened her voice memo app. "Any objection to me recording this?"

Lou shook her head. "No, that's fine."

"Is your family still local?"

Lou's face lost a little bit of its color. "Pass."

"No problem, moving right along. How old were you when you realized you were queer?"

"Pass. But I identify as a lesbian."

"Got it." Clem made a note on her phone. "Thanks for telling me. How about you share your coming-out story?"

"Which time?"

"The very first time or to your family?"

"Pass."

"Lou," Clem said, trying to catch her eye. "You can't pass on every essential question."

"It's not a happy story." Lou closed her eyes and opened them slowly. Her irises glittered like she was on the brink of tears. The most un-Lou-like thing Clem could imagine.

"People need to hear those, too. But if you can't talk about it or don't want to share it with me, I understand."

"No, it's okay." Lou sniffed and nodded. "This is just between us, right?"

"Yeah, just us."

Lou cleared her throat. "I was in college, senior year and my parents came to surprise me. I didn't even know they knew where I lived, but I must have given them the address for a birthday card or something. My roommate let them in and, well, I was in bed with the girl I was seeing at the time, celebrating the end of finals. And then she left too."

"Oof. How did they take it?"

Lou sniffed, her lips curling inward before she released them and spoke again. "They didn't take it. They rejected it completely. Mostly my dad, but my mom went along with it. They didn't even let me come back to the house to get the things I'd left there."

"What happened with your girlfriend?" Clem asked.

"Hmm?"

"You said they walked in on you and that she left too?"

"Oh, right. It turned out that she was already planning on breaking up with me that night, and the events of the afternoon did nothing to dissuade her from that decision," Lou said with a sad smile.

"Lou, that's horrible. I'm so sorry. Did your parents ever come around?" Clem couldn't imagine not having her dad's support. She'd told her parents early, partly because keeping secrets in a small town was impossible, and partly because Sam had come out the year before and held her hand throughout it, but had also paved the way for Clem. If she hadn't had that encouragement, her life might look a lot different.

"No, after a little while I stopped trying. I get the sense that sometimes my gram still tries to reason with them, but a friend from high school said she asked after me once, and my parents claimed they didn't have any kids. It's, um, yeah. I try not to let it get to me."

Lou shifted on the couch, pulling her knees up to her chest, and Clementine's fingers itched to reach out and touch her, offering any comfort she could. But Lou's posture didn't telegraph someone who was seeking comfort from others. It conveyed someone who had spent a long time learning to comfort herself, and Clem's chest burned with the truth of her realization.

"Things improved a lot when I found Howl. It gave me a sense of home again. I've always been welcome and cherished at my grandma's house, but I never lived there. In a lot of ways, my parents' rejection made me who I am. And I think I'm lucky that I learned early that anyone you let close has the power to push you away and destroy you in the process. So I'm careful about being vulnerable. Asking for help with the bar actually hits every nerve."

"So why did you agree to it?"

"Because I trust you." Lou stood abruptly as soon as the words left her mouth and started gathering dishes. "Let me just get these out of here. I'll be back."

LOU WAS GONE for a long time. Clem wanted to respect her need for space, to respect Lou's needs in general. What had just happened was nothing short of monumental. As Lou spoke, Clem could practically see the war inside of her as she opened up. That kind of vulnerability after years of being trapped

173

inside armor must have felt like prying open a car with the jaws of life. Clem wanted to be the sunshine and fresh air and safety that met Lou on the other side. And right now that meant staying put while Lou processed, or took a shot, or whatever she was doing.

Clementine waited a few more minutes before going back to her phone and tooling around on Instagram. She wanted to look busy when Lou re-entered the room so she wouldn't feel uncomfortable, or like she had to apologize for stepping away. So Clem did what she did best, she started formulating a plan. But also she'd be lying to herself if she didn't acknowledge she was hurt by the way Lou ran from her. She searched out some LGBTQIA history accounts and some Boston historical accounts to gather ideas. But before long, her own ideas started rolling into her like a runaway office, reply-all email thread. She could do a series on the graffiti wall, maybe get interesting frames for a few of the pieces. She had her eye on a simple house that had Lou's name inside where the door should be. Could she convince Lou to get a neon sign, maybe? A purple wolf howling for the wall? Something people would want to take selfies in front of. It would be good, free promotion for the bar. She made a list of these ideas in her notes app to talk through with Lou later.

She was searching for local, sapphic neon artists when Lou came back into the room carrying two glasses of water.

"Sorry, that took so long."

"That's okay, Canoodle's snores are soothing white noise, optimal thinking conditions. Plus, it gave me time to strategize. Are you okay?"

Lou nodded but her brows were furrowed. Clem considered asking more about it, but decided not to push.

"Do you want to talk about something else? Work maybe?" Clem didn't particularly want to work. What she really wanted to do was hold Lou while she felt her feelings, but Clem also lived in reality. She knew Howl was Lou's comfort zone, that work was the place she retreated to when things felt like too much.

"Yes." Lou's face lit up with a relieved smile.

"Okay." Clem opened her notes app and cleared her throat with a silly a-hem. "If we did a series on the graffiti wall, would you provide some context or a few stories?"

"Do I even want to know?"

They talked for another hour, planning ways to celebrate the history of the bar while saving its future. Finally, Clem felt her energy flagging. Lou seemed to be pushing too.

"Did you want to go look through the graffiti now and pick what to showcase?" Lou asked through a yawn.

"Maybe tomorrow? It's getting pretty late. If I stay any longer, I'll catch the sunrise."

Lou's face fell a little, but she recovered a neutral expression quickly. "You're right, I didn't realize. Maybe you'll see a glimpse on the way home. The city pollution really does wonders for the colors."

"Oh, one more thing before I go."

"Yeah?" Lou leaned in a bit and Clem wanted to close the distance between them, but she wouldn't take advantage of Lou's vulnerability, not after she'd been the one encouraging her to open up. Clementine swallowed hard and pulled herself back.

"So for the community meeting, are we really on for that? I don't want to push you."

"You're not. Or maybe you are a little bit, but I think it's in a good direction. Let's do it this week, that way I won't have time to change my mind." Lou nodded.

Clementine couldn't help but smile. She'd been told for so long that she was too pushy about the diner that she'd worried she no longer knew how to be supportive in a way that people wanted. "It's an opportunity to bring people together. The sapphic world is small. Somebody definitely knows someone who dated someone who dated someone else who then dated the first person who can help save Howl. It's time to call in the brain trust. I'm smart, but I'm not that smart, and social media will only get us so far. We need boots on the ground."

"You're right. Howl is home for so many people, not just me."

Lou's words rang in Clem's chest. "I agree. This week it is."

Lou jammed her hands into her pockets, the relaxed posture from a few minutes ago snuffed out. "Do you think we can pull it together in time?"

Clem bit her lower lip and tapped quickly on her phone before turning the screen toward Lou. A graphic announcing the meeting showed on the new social account Clem had created for the bar. "I sure hope so!"

Chapter Sixteen
Lou

E verything was perfect and Lou hated it. It turned out she had very little practice dealing with people supporting her. She hated how the nice things Clementine said made her eyes sting. If Clem kept being so understanding, Lou would be at risk of dehydration.

For years Lou had starved herself for affection after her parents rejected her. She did it so long that the sharp pain of loss faded into a dull and sturdy armor. And Clementine had pierced it, undoing years of hard work with her questions and photos and kindness. She'd pierced it with her social media posts and the way she brought Lou coffee just the way she'd liked it at the hardware store. Clementine wasn't thoughtful in a generic way. She was thoughtful of *Lou*. It made Lou want to stop hiding. She was ready to be seen.

With each passing day, Lou found herself thinking of Clementine more, too. She'd been waking up early and then counting down the hours until Clem would walk in the front door of Howl and they would get to work on strategizing their next plan of attack. It all felt so *good*, and that unnerved her. Lou didn't know who she was without the walls she'd built and at this rate, she was worried her support beam was about to get taken out by Clementine's smile and that sweet little head tilt she did when she was listening intently. Lou had noticed it when she'd told her coming out story on the couch and Clementine had stopped taking notes, her head angling to the side as she paid Lou all of her attention.

But if Lou really was tough, why couldn't she handle letting someone in? She thought about calling her grandma for advice, but that woman was like a dog with a bone when it came to wanting Lou to be happy.

Lou paced back and forth in her apartment. It was another beautiful summer day and Clem had suggested they work in the living room to take advantage of the natural sunlight. One thing her office didn't have was a window, which Lou usually loved. Fewer distractions, no birds chirping outside the glass with their obnoxious joy. Lou caught herself whistling Rockin' Robin and rolled her eyes. Who was the obnoxious one now?

She was sure of one thing: something had changed between her and Clementine since their emergency trip to Maine. Those hours Lou had spent lying awake in bed being tortured by Clementine's proximity had been illuminating, even if it had taken a few days to admit to herself that she hadn't wanted to run away. She wanted to be the kind of person who opened her arms to Clementine.

It had been over a week since their kiss in her office, and Clementine had made her interest in Lou clear, but only if Lou wanted more than a quick hookup. The fact that she did was scaring the hell out of her. Every day this week she'd resolved to ask Clementine out, and by each evening she'd decided that was the thing that would destroy her. Because what happened when this was all over? Whether they saved the bar or failed, Clementine wouldn't work at Howl forever. Hell, she'd only just moved to Boston. She might return to Hart's Hollow. And then Lou would be back where she started, undertaking the painful process of reconstructing her walls.

If she'd survived a big loss once, she could do it again, right? Lou might not recognize the smiling and vulnerable version of herself that greeted her in the mirror every morning now, but she was starting to like her. How long had it been since she'd liked herself? Had she *ever* liked herself? If the joy she was feeling now was any indication, the answer to that second question was a resounding no.

Maybe by saving the bar, she would also find a way to save herself. Ugh, did happiness always come with a side of corny? That part seemed fatal, but the rest of the side effects, she thought she might be able to get used to. Even the whistling.

Lou shook out her hands, bouncing on the balls of her feet like a boxer about to enter the ring. She'd made herself a promise that she would make progress toward telling Clementine how she felt before the community meeting. Those three little words were sticking in her throat like a sideways pill. How did anyone work through the terror of saying them for the first time? Her hands were unsteady whenever she ran them through her mind. The three most terrifying words in the world: *I like you.*

Clementine's knock saved her from totally decompensating. She ran a hand through her hair and ruffled some papers on the coffee table, too. Even if she had spent all morning obsessing over this moment, she didn't need Clem to know that.

Lou opened the door and Clementine was in a fucking sundress. Only it was all black with little lightning strikes all over it. Like if a sunny day and a storm cloud had an adorable, grumpy baby. That comparison was not lost on Lou. Though she absolutely should not be thinking of babies where Clementine was concerned.

Clem took a step closer, but Lou didn't move. It suddenly

felt like now or never. She grabbed the doorframe to keep a hold on something that would anchor her to reality.

"Is it okay if I come in?" Her guest laughed nervously, and Lou knew she was being weird.

"I have something to tell you."

"Oh." Clementine's face fell. "It looks pretty serious, from your expression. Please don't tell me you decided not to save the bar." Clem frowned. "Like, obviously you can do whatever you want, but we've got a really good shot and I want this for you. I want this for all of us."

"I definitely want to save the bar."

"Okay, so what is it then? Are you firing me?"

"No." This was going all wrong. If she didn't say what she needed to soon, Clementine might leave, thinking Lou hated her. "Clementine I—"

"Please just tell me, Lou, I can take it. There are other jobs and I've probably way overstepped—"

"I like you." Lou let out a startled laugh. Saying those words felt euphoric.

Clem tilted her head to the side, a smile crinkling her eyes. "That's a weird way to fire someone."

"I'm not firing you, I'm trying to do this." Lou leaned forward into Clementine's space. She held her gaze and gave Clementine time to pull back. But Clementine leaned forward, tilting her head up slightly.

Lou closed the last bit of distance between them. Clementine's mouth was warm and strawberry sweet against hers. Lou let go of the doorframe and her fingers found Clem's hip. The fabric of the dress was surprisingly soft, like a favorite t-shirt. Which only led her to imagine Clementine in one of her old shirts. Or that sexy robe of hers that Lou had borrowed and secretly wished she'd absconded with.

Lou ran the tip of her tongue along Clem's lower lip,

wanting more instead of less. She wanted mornings in bed and all the bad movie nights that she always told herself she hated. The bar hadn't kept her from having relationships, her fear had done that. And it was time she stopped letting trepidation control her.

Clem broke their kiss a full twelve hours before Lou was ready for it to end, but her hands lingered on Lou's waist like a promise.

"As much as I would love to do this all afternoon, and believe me, I would *really* love to, we have so many things to do before the community meeting tomorrow. I'm worried that if we start, I won't ever want to stop."

"Are you always so practical?"

Clementine shook her head. "Almost never. Right now it feels physically painful. But someone I care about has a dream she needs help with."

"Fine. I suppose we should still try to save Howl." Lou stepped aside so Clem could come in and followed her into the living room.

"Wow," Clem said as she set her bag on the couch. "I see you've been burning the 11:00 a.m. oil. What's this?"

She reached for a letter on top of one of the piles. Lou had wanted to show it to her as a joke, but the way Clem's eyes narrowed as she read it did not look like she was finding humor in it.

"Wait. Founding Charter Bank—isn't that one of the banks that rejected your loan application?"

"One and the same. Can you believe they sent that letter asking to partner with Howl on a Pride event where we'd share our liquor license and we'd 'get exposure' in return?"

"This is great." A smile spread slowly across Clementine's face, causing the edges of her stormy blue eyes to once again crinkle slightly, like a ripple in a calm pond.

Clem's reaction made no sense. Lou took a step closer to read the letter again over her shoulder. What had she missed? She did a quick scan and yup, still very inconsiderate. "Wait, why is it great? Ironic maybe, but I also found it pretty insulting."

"That's the thing. These big corporations are happy to take from the queer community. They make merchandise and want our money, but there's no actual support. Like these banks make such a big deal at Pride with their floats and rubber wristbands that end up killing birds for months to come. But when a sapphic bar, a real part of the community, needs help, they can't be bothered. They want us to invest in them, but they have no interest in investing in *us*." Clem paced back and forth next to the coffee table, the letter fluttering in her hand.

"You're definitely right about that, and I hate it. But I still don't see why that makes this letter a good thing."

"Lou, we can use this. We could take this to the paper, or I could post about it and tag some queer websites. Our follower base on social media has really taken off. With enough outrage, they'd probably reverse their decision. How would it look for a bank that sponsors Pride to deny a loan to the last surviving sapphic bar in Boston? And how long do you think they'd hold out once that fact was widely known? Or before another bank seized the opportunity to come out of all of this looking good just in time for the parade?"

Clem wasn't wrong, but Lou didn't love it, maybe because it felt strangely close to charity. "I can see your point, and I'm sure people would find it all absurd. But I don't want to bad-mouth them, you know?"

Clementine paused and frowned. "It's not bad-mouthing someone to say what they did to you."

"You're right. I just don't want people to feel bad for me or the bar. We don't want pity, we want a party."

"I'm putting that on a t-shirt." Clem pulled out her phone to write a note. "What you're saying makes a lot of sense. But if you don't want to contact the press or let me post about it, we should go to the bank and talk to them. Try to negotiate."

"What would we negotiate? They already said 'no'."

"That was *before* you had leverage." Clem set the letter on the table and took a quick photo of it. "Now you have something they want, and I'm guessing they don't need their decision to *not* help save Howl to come out right before their Pride events. It would seriously complicate their narrative about being an ally."

"Are you sure this isn't blackmail?"

"Not if it's hypothetical. I think this is a job for Rachel. Is it okay if I bring her in on this?"

Lou squinted at Clem. *Rachel as a mediator, really?* "Sure, but I'm still not seeing what good it will do to bring the letter to them. I doubt they're going to suddenly approve me for the loan."

"Maybe not. But hear me out, what about corporate sponsors for the HowlQueen event?"

"Fuck corporations. They are soulless."

Along with the community meeting, they'd been busy planning HowlQueen—the bar's annual big Pride event—part drag show, part auction. It would be their big push to raise enough to buy the building. Usually, the funds they made at the event went to the local shelter for houseless queer youth, but this time, the money would benefit the Save Howl fund. Lou felt bad about diverting it, but rationally she knew it would be better to still be around to donate next year and for many more to come. Though maybe they could get a sponsor for another event in a few months, and still get money to the shelter.

Clem grinned, and at that moment Lou knew she could be

convinced of almost anything that beautiful person came up with.

"Oh fuck corporations for sure," Clem said, "but what about taking their money and not doing what they want with it? For this one month a year, banks are desperate to seem like they care. Instead of helping them serve lukewarm beer on the sidewalk, let's accept their donation and put on the gayest show on earth."

Lou couldn't help it, excitement pinged through her in response to Clem's enthusiasm. She reached out and pulled Clementine close until their lips were just an inch apart. "This is devious. I've never been more attracted to you."

"Babe, I'm just getting started."

Chapter Seventeen
Clementine

The interior of Howl was giving off church basement vibes, but that wasn't necessarily a bad thing. It was a combination of the industrial champagne-brown, metal folding chairs and the paper cups stacked next to the coffee carafe that really pushed it over the edge. Both *had* been borrowed from Lou's grandma's church.

Pulling together the event hadn't been easy, but it went smoother than Clementine could have imagined, thanks to a lot of help from Alyssa, Megan, Dana, and Rachel. Today was the day they would lay it all out on the table, or rather the bartop, and ask for help. The future of Boston's queer past and present was on the line. And she was confident the community would come through to save Howl.

Between managing the online presence and planning events, Clem felt like her whole life was suddenly Howl, as though she and Lou lived in this little bubble together, and she was more committed than ever to saving it.

The bar's Instagram had taken off after Clementine posted a few photos of the graffiti wall, along with people's stories, and had launched it into the stratosphere with sapphic cultural celebrities like Tanner Tavish and Arden Abbott resharing the posts. An hour ago, their new purple neon wolf sign had arrived. She'd watched as Lou affixed it to the wall with a quiet confidence that had done strange things to Clem's chest. Fluttery things. When she'd handed Lou a screwdriver, their fingers had brushed and it was like a string of lights getting plugged in, bursts of sensation tingling throughout her body.

Several people had contacted Clementine wanting to add their own graffiti to the wall, like a sharpie in a sapphic bar was the equivalent of those memorial bricks people bought for walkways. It would be an easy way to raise a little money and get people from all over promoting Howl and its story. Still, even though the benefits were clear, Clem had been surprised when Lou had agreed to sell wall space to people online. She'd opened up to Clementine's creative ideas to save the bar in a way that was encouraging and also, for reasons Clem hadn't had time to examine, a huge turn on.

A half-hour before the meeting was set to start, she found Lou standing next to the coffee, stiff as a statue. "I still can't believe you actually agreed to let people help save the bar."

"I haven't been that bad, have I?" Lou leaned toward her, and Clem reached out to place a steadying hand on her hip for the briefest moment. No one else was here yet, but they'd both decided to keep whatever was happening between them just that, between them. Though not forever, she hoped.

"No, not at all." Clementine served up a devious grin, holding her pause for maximum impact. "You've been worse."

"Hello, girls," a voice called from the darkness of the entryway.

The cutest old lady Clem had ever seen came into view. Her gray hair was in a wavy bob and her bright pink glasses were a stunning contrast to her all-black outfit.

"Gram, what are you doing here? And *what* are you wearing?" Lou asked, taking a few steps forward.

So *this* was Lou's grandmother.

She scoffed, bringing a hand to her chest in a very Lou-like gesture. "Can't a lady dress up for a day on the town?"

"She can. I've just never known you to do that." Lou smirked and ducked a swat from her grandma.

Clementine watched silently as the two women went back and forth. Sarcasm and teasing were love languages she understood well. Clem was best friends with Sam, after all.

"Fine," Lou's grandma relented. "I *might* have a lunch date at a fancy restaurant."

"A date, huh?" Lou raised an eyebrow.

"A friend date, *Louise*. You can stop being weird about it now. Look, I didn't stop by to answer all these questions. Now, introduce me to the pretty lady next to you."

Clem's face heated, but her shyness was countered by a rush of pride. She had gathered that her grandma was the most important person in Lou's life.

"Gram, this is Clementine. She works here and is the driving force behind this meeting. Clem, this is my grandma who is here for some undisclosed reason," Lou said, gesturing between them.

Clem knew they weren't ready to tell anyone about them. And what would they even say? They liked each other and had tentative plans to go on a date later this week? Still, as a descriptor of someone you'd slept with, 'she works here' left something to be desired. But Clem swallowed her pride and offered a warm smile. "It's really nice to meet you. Lou talks about you all the time."

"She'd better." The woman smiled and then narrowed her eyes at Lou. "I have a name, Louise." She turned to Clem with an exasperated-sounding sigh. "I'm Eleanor, dear. And can I just say I love your hair? I always wished mine was red like that."

"Thank you, that's—"

"Aren't you a bit cold in that outfit though?" Eleanor cut in before Clem could finish.

And, well, Clem was a bit cold, actually. "You're not wrong about that, Eleanor."

"Darling," Eleanor said, turning her attention back to Lou, "get this lovely human a space heater or at the very least a sweater."

Lou unzipped the hoodie she was wearing, the same one she'd lent Clem the other night, silently handing it over.

Clem slipped it on and closed her eyes to soak in the warmth of Lou's body heat still clinging to the black fleece. When she opened them again, Eleanor was watching her with a glimmer in her eye. *Sneaky.*

"Not that I'm not glad to see you, Gram, but what brings you in? It's just that people are going to be arriving soon and I don't have much time to spend with you."

"You act as though I came to hang out. You mentioned the event the other day, so I just wanted to drop these off for your guests." Eleanor pulled a glass container out of her bag and patted the lid. "My special brownies."

Clem widened her eyes at Lou.

"*Not* pot brownies," Lou clarified. "'Special' as in her recipe that she *refuses* to share with her favorite granddaughter."

"If you don't have the recipe, how do you know what's in them? I never said the special ingredient was love," Eleanor said with a shrug.

"Sure you didn't. Gram, you didn't have to go through the trouble of baking these."

"I wanted to. I thought it would be nice for you to offer snacks, but looking around, I see you've had a hand with that.

I'm happy you're letting people help," she stage-whispered, "I know it's not easy for you."

Clem wandered behind the bar to give Lou and her grandma some privacy, but it turned out voices really carried in the mostly empty space.

"Well, you should have let me pick them up at least," Lou grumbled. "I can't believe you baked and had to come all the way here."

"It was practically on my way to lunch. Besides, Louise, you come to my house all the time. I like doing things for you, I tell you that all the time. It makes me feel good to care for you even if you never want to let me. I've learned it's best to be sneaky about it."

"Well, thank you. I'm sure people will love them."

"Of course they will. But that's only if you share them. Make sure Clementine has one at least. She seems nice. Nice enough that you might bring her by sometime?"

Lou shook her head and said something Clem couldn't catch. A moment later, Eleanor threw up her hands before hugging Lou.

"Goodbye Clementine," she called over her shoulder as she headed to the door. "Knock 'em dead today."

Lou walked her grandma toward the door, and their heated whispering continued.

For her part, Clementine was trying exceedingly hard to scrub away thirty years of intractable water spots from the bartop. She was not focusing *at all* on how nice it would be to spend time with Lou and her grandma. She also wasn't thinking about that little flicker of hope she'd felt at Lou having her interact with someone she adores.

Nope, she'd extinguished that hope immediately, and dropped a bucket of ice right on it. It was too much to think about now, especially so long as what they had was secret. Lou was independent and so sure of herself most of the time that it was hard to imagine her coupled. Though Clem may have dreamt about it once or twice. Even now, Clementine knew that Lou letting her help was more of an indulgence. But she wanted to prove to Lou that she could move mountains, and maybe today would be the first seismic shift.

"Sorry about that," Lou said as she approached the bar after walking her grandma out.

"Nothing to be sorry for, she's lovely."

"She is. She's all I have, you know." Lou swallowed audibly and Clementine stopped wiping the bartop.

She wanted to ask more, but she could practically see Lou retreating into herself. "Eleanor seems really special," Clem said instead. "And she clearly adores you."

Lou cleared her throat and reached for the container. "She wasn't kidding about these, you know. You should eat one now before they're all gone."

Lou opened the lid and took out a brownie. Clem held out her hand to take it, but Lou leaned forward, raising the treat to Clementine's mouth. *Was this really happening? Dreams coming true on a regular old weekday?* Clem's heart was pounding to the beat of The Wedding March. Her thoughts spiraled into full-on reception fantasy mode with images of Lou in a white dress shirt and loose tie under a leather jacket, smiling at Clem like she hung the moon. What would their colors be? Probably purple like Howl's sign and—her thoughts stuttered as Lou withdrew the brownie from Clem's lips. She had to remind her brain to close her mouth.

Lou seemed unaffected, as though they hadn't just gotten married in Clem's head, while she casually lifted the brownie to her own lips and took a bite. "Amazing, right?"

"Yeah, those are, um, life-changing." Clem swallowed hard. She needed anything to get this back on track before she made a fool of herself. She glanced around, her eyes landing on the stack of informational fliers she'd printed. "Do you feel prepared for today?"

Lou shrugged, chewing thoughtfully. "As ready as I'll ever be to admit I'm a failure in front of a roomful of people I know."

"Hey," Clem said with a frown. She wanted to pull Lou into a hug and stroke her hair, but that would probably have the opposite of her desired effect of comfort. "You're so far from a failure. You've been running this amazing bar that has been a home to so many on your own. And you've kept it going for years despite drastic changes in the neighborhood around you and the market. This is a success story, Lou. All you need to do today is to remind people that Howl is worth fighting for, and not because it's a bar. Well, not just that. But because of what it means for the sapphic community. If Howl had to close, nothing would replace it. It's not like regular bars."

"It's not like regular bars, it's a cool bar." Lou shot her a jaunty wink.

Clem froze. She was in a perfect dream of some kind where suddenly, she could see a future with Lou. One where they cuddled and watched nostalgic things. "Did you just riff on Mean Girls?"

Lou shrugged. "What? I love that movie."

"I never would have pegged you for a fan of early 2000s comedies."

"Why not? There's something so comforting about watching movies from that time in my life. Imagine Me & You, Coyote Ugly, Ten Things I Hate About You."

"I'm going to force you to have a movie night with me before this summer is over."

"Is that a threat?" Lou quirked an eyebrow.

"Nope, it's a promise." And it was.

Chapter Eighteen
Lou

Lou needed to get her shit together immediately. She'd been flirting with Clementine like a lovesick teen as a way to distract herself before the community meeting, only now she was too distracted by the way Clem laughed and seemed to want to make plans with Lou for the future, to remember what the meeting was even for. Plans that included watching movies in a way that didn't seem like a euphemism. Like Clementine wanted to spend time with Lou and not just sleep with her. Sure, she'd told Lou as much last night, but it was hard to trust that someone would want her. And even if Clem wanted her now, what was to stop her from rejecting her later if Lou turned out to be not the person Clem thought she was?

It had been a hard lesson that not meeting people's expectations could make them stop loving you. Not that Clementine loved her. She liked Lou, and that was scary enough.

"Okay," Clementine's voice cut into her brain's doom-scrolling through its worst memories. "I think we're about ready to start."

Lou blinked her surroundings back into focus, surprised to see all the folding chairs occupied. Her stomach lurched. When Clem had suggested holding this meeting with Howl regulars, Lou had expected maybe five people to show up, but there was even a small crowd standing in the back.

She grabbed the stack of fliers and shuffled them. The paper stuck to her damp palms, making her plan to hand them out clumsy and frustrating.

Lou talked to people all the time while working. Hell, sometimes she yelled at them through a megaphone. But now that she had to be serious and ask for help, her throat was dry. Why weren't they serving alcohol instead of coffee and brownies? Right, because it was barely noon and alcohol actually didn't solve anything, it just sanded off the edges of reality for a bit. But we need those edges to make the pieces of our lives fit together.

Once the fliers made their way around, a sea of expectant gazes focused on Lou. And she... couldn't do this. She couldn't ask for help.

A warm touch on her back steadied her and she relaxed into it. Clementine gave Lou a warm smile and reached to take the remaining flier—that was now crumpled—from her, clutching it like a lifeline.

"You can do this," she whispered.

For a second, Lou believed her. And then she looked out over the crowd again. The crowd that would probably stop liking her as soon as she started talking about losing this place they loved.

"Maybe just say a few things about the bar's history and why it matters to start," Clem suggested.

Lou remained silent. In the back of the room, someone cleared their throat.

When Clementine's cheerful voice filled the room, Lou exhaled in a rush. She thought she might collapse in relief.

"Thanks so much for coming, everyone! We're all here because Howl means something to us, right?"

Around the room, a chorus of 'yeahs' and 'hell yeses' resounded.

"It's given so much to so many people. It's not just a place to go drink. Howl is where you celebrate your birthday—"

Clem paused while someone let out a wolf whistle. Rachel emerged from the shadow near the door and made her way up to the front next to Lou and Clementine.

"It's where you come on Thanksgiving for Wild Turkey shots and no political arguments. It's the place you come to on Christmas Eve when you want to be surrounded by love and warmth. Howl is home for so many, including Lou McCallister. For years, Lou has shared her home with this community. I know many of us don't take *home* for granted. And we don't take acceptance for granted. We've had to build those things ourselves and they're worth fighting for." Clem paused and offered Lou a smile. "And now Rachel is going to talk a little bit about the history of the bar."

Rachel leaned into Clem and whispered something Lou didn't hear over the rushing in her ears. Did Clementine really believe all the things she had said? The thought that she did made warmth bloom behind Lou's ribs.

Rachel rehashed the history of the bar and its early mission to serve as a space where people could finally be themselves in a world that wasn't accepting. Afterward, Clementine calmly laid out the facts of the situation and then opened the floor to the community. One by one, people in the crowd stood up to say what Howl meant to them. How it was the first place they'd ever felt fully like themselves. How they fell in love here, and nursed broken hearts, and fell in love again. Sometimes all in the same week.

The room filled with laughter and misty eyes. Or maybe just Lou's eyes were misty. Though she could have sworn she saw Rachel surreptitiously dab hers with a cocktail napkin.

And then the ideas started to flow. Putting local art for sale on the walls. Renting out the bar during the day as a meeting space. Someone had an in with the Boston historical society and thought maybe Howl could be certified as a historical LGBTQIA site. Another person mentioned corporate sponsors for a Pride party, and Lou caught Clem giving her a sly smile. As much as the idea had turned Lou's stomach when Clementine had presented it yesterday, there was also something satisfying about taking money from people who only supported the queer community one month a year, and even then their support ended at rainbow tchotchkes. Plus, Rachel was stopping by the bank later to have what she kept calling a 'cage match discussion'.

Before Lou realized the meeting was over, Clem was collecting people's email addresses on a form, and Rachel was thanking them for coming. She wasn't sure she'd ever heard Rachel say 'thank you' before.

A few people wandered up to Lou to offer support and encouragement, and she stumbled through a few words about how important the bar was to her, but soon enough it was just her, Rachel, and Clem. And then Rachel was picking up her gym bag with a wink, saying there was a sparring date she had to run to.

"I think that went well," Clem said.

Lou let out a long breath. "Really? I was so nervous I barely took in what anyone said." *Except you*, Lou thought. When Clementine spoke, it was the rest of the world that faded away.

"Do you want a quick recap?" Clem's hand found Lou's lower back where it was pressed against the bar.

"Sure." The thought of Clementine telling her what happened didn't scare her nearly as much as experiencing it in real-time.

"Basically everyone loves the bar and they love you. Oh, and we're going to save Howl. We've got about thirty plans and I have everyone's emails so I can start organizing. I think it makes sense for the big push to be a Pride event. A few people mentioned HowlQueen. So that lines up with what we talked about."

Lou nodded. "People really get into it. The hybrid drag show and dance party is what Howl is famous for."

"Huh, I would have thought it would have been the buckets of ice you dump on people. Or the bar dancing. That Peaches song? God damn." Clem quirked an eyebrow.

"Well, those *are* pretty memorable, too."

"So we can build the rest of the ideas around HowlQueen as the main event."

Lou nodded. She was focusing on Clem's words, but fear rushed in to drown out everything. "Be honest with me, do you really think we have a shot at raising enough money to save the bar? It's going to take more than a bake sale."

"Lou, we have a shot. And if we do decide to have a bake sale, I'm going to need you to call your grandma for some more of those brownies."

Lou's heart soared. For the first time in months, she had hope for the future. The future of Howl and her own future. And it was all thanks to Clementine, who didn't owe her anything but was showing up for her all the same. Before Lou could think too much about it she leaned forward and pressed her lips to Clem's. The kiss was sweet, almost chaste, but it felt deeper than any desperate makeout Lou had had before.

When she pulled back, Clem blinked at her. "What was that for?" she asked.

"Because you make me feel like things are possible. And like I'm worth showing up for."

"Well," Clem said, pulling Lou into her arms. "That's because you are."

Chapter Nineteen
Clementine

Y ou are *such* a bad liar. And I imagine that's hard for you to hear because there aren't many things you're bad at." Sam said, tilting her head to the side, her eyes narrowed.

The effect was powerful even through the small screen of Clem's phone.

Her best friend was sitting down for this video call, which had Clementine worried. A Sam not in motion was a dangerous creature, ready to pounce. When the call came as she had just walked into her apartment after another long day with Lou, it wasn't totally unexpected. She hadn't talked to Sam in a week, which was basically treason. But when Clem wasn't at the bar, she was exhausted. And her fledgling 'seeing where things go' with Lou had made leaving Howl at a reasonable time a little harder each night.

"Ugh, like comically bad at lying, right?" A voice from behind Clementine agreed cheerfully. Even her roommate's cadence had a bounce to its step.

Clem turned to see Alyssa leaning in the doorway to the

living room like she'd been hanging out there long enough to get comfortable.

"What is happening here? How can I be lying when all I said was 'hello?'" Clem asked, looking back and forth between the doorway and her phone.

"What's happening is that you're being super evasive lately," Alyssa said as she stepped into the room. She settled so closely next to Clem on the couch that they were sharing a cushion. This was the same amount of personal space Canoodle liked to give her. Seemed extreme, but okay.

On her phone's screen, Sam continued to stare her down. "*And* dodging my calls."

"We're worried about you." Alyssa leaned her head on Clementine's shoulder, a weird move even for her. Clem knew she was doing it to better catch Sam's eye.

Everything about this felt like a trap, and all Clem had wanted to do tonight was to cue up a Top Chef rerun and fall asleep three minutes into the episode.

Clem sat up straight, causing Alyssa's cheek to slip off her shoulder. "Oh my gosh, Sam, if you are FaceTiming into an intervention you planned behind my back, consider our friendship over."

"Calm down, Clemmy. We literally couldn't have planned anything even if we wanted to. It's a small miracle you're not with Lou and actually took my call."

"What's that supposed to mean?" Clementine definitely knew what that meant, but was secretly hoping she was wrong. Maybe her friends thought she had a drug problem, or like, recklessly spent all her money on lattes. Though she did need to review her coffee budget.

"I think what Sam is trying to say is that you and Lou have been spending a lot of time together. Like *a lot*, a lot." Alyssa widened her eyes.

Well, damn, it was hard to deny that. No problem, Clem could be honest without sharing too much. "We're trying to raise money to save Howl. It turns out a project like that takes a lot of time and we don't exactly have much of that to spare."

"I think you're doing a bit more than project planning." Sam winked.

Oh, god. Clementine had thought this was Sam being hurt by her radio silence or being a little jealous, but it was somehow so much worse that she'd sussed out that something was going on between her and Lou from 200 miles away.

"Hey, I get it," Alyssa said. "Lou's a sexy—"

Sam let out the fakest sounding cough Clementine had ever heard.

There was no way around this. Clem sighed. "Okay, I admit it. There's something there, but we've been taking it slow."

Sam leaned closer to the camera, her face enlarging on Clem's phone. "What's the point in taking it slow when you've already hooked up?"

Alyssa gasped and a split second later, her hand slapped Clementine's arm. "I *knew* it. It was that first night, wasn't it? You said you were talking about her hiring you, but no one gets that flushed from an informational interview."

Clementine sighed and buried her face in her hands, letting her phone fall to her lap. She felt Alyssa scoop it up. It was so much harder to feign getting disconnected when one of the people interrogating her was there in person. "Sam, how would you even know that? I mean if it were true, and I'm absolutely not saying it is."

"When I ran into you in town, I could tell by the way she looked at you." Her friend's voice had lost its accusatory glint.

Clementine bit her lip, trying to stifle the question, but her curiosity was too strong. She'd tried to commit everything from that trip to memory, but she had been so busy watching Lou that Clem hadn't noticed Lou looking at *her*. She raised her head from her hands to discover both of her friends watching her with absolute glee.

"How did she look at me?" Clem rasped.

"Like you were a pile of blueberry pancakes she wanted to take her time with. I'm talking syrup *and* whipped cream."

Clem swallowed hard. Is that really how Lou looked at her, even then? Her stomach nearly grumbled with her want for that look.

"Wow, that's descriptive." Alyssa bobbed her head. "Very nice analogy."

"Clem's family diner makes the best blueberry pancakes. I'll have to take you there." Sam smiled at Alyssa.

"Wait, what?" Why did Clem feel like the third wheel at her own intervention?

"I mean if Alyssa ever visits or anything. Look, we can all go! Lou, too." The way Sam's eyes were twinkling would have been demonic on anyone else, but Clem had known her long enough just to be mildly unsettled.

Clementine narrowed her eyes. "Okay, there is clearly something happening here that I'm not aware of."

"I wouldn't say that. Sam sent me a mixtape with her phone number written on it, so we've been chatting a bit." Alyssa shrugged, like what she had just said wasn't the textbook definition of *something happening*.

"A mixtape?" Clem leaned back and let her head rest on the cushion. "Do you even *have* a cassette player, Alyssa?"

"Of course. One of the women in my Sweatin' to the 80s class gave it to me last year for my Olivia Newton-John Halloween costume."

"I'd love to see a picture of that," Sam said.

"Sure, I'll call you later and show you." Now it was Alyssa's turn to wink.

Clem glanced between her best friend and roommate. "I'm sorry, do you two want to be alone?"

"No, Clem, this is about you," Alyssa said without looking away from Sam.

The amount of tension between Alyssa and Clem's phone was so intense, that she might need to get rid of her rainbow ice cream cone case to dispel the memory. Or maybe she'd get a new phone, really start fresh. She couldn't be sure if the spirit of their love wouldn't get trapped in there like a poltergeist.

Or, perhaps a less drastic option would be to redirect the conversation. Maybe it would be nice to talk to her friends about Lou. She let Alyssa and Sam gaze at each other for a few more seconds before clearing her throat. "Lou and I are going on a date tomorrow."

"No, Lou doesn't date." Alyssa shook her head, breaking eye contact with Sam.

Clem shrugged, a feeling of pride swelling inside her. To be someone's exception was a heady thing. She didn't want Lou to change who she was, but Clementine couldn't help being glad she was worth bending the rules for.

"What are you doing for your date?" Sam asked. "And I swear, if it's something work-related, you're grounded."

Clem rolled her eyes. "It's *not* work-related. Lou suggested maybe going to the aquarium and having dinner afterward at Legal Seafood, which I gathered is a particularly grim pairing that's popular here."

Sam shivered. "Thinking about that makes me feel like someone just walked across my grave. That date's got major 'murder you later' vibes. Does the aquarium food court also serve fish?"

"I don't think so," Alyssa said. "I've only been there once, but that would cross a line."

"Right." Clem gave an exaggerated nod. "It's much better to eat at the seafood restaurant directly across the street."

"Okay," Sam said. "So you turned down the 'see fish, eat fish' date."

Clem held up her hand. "Do not make another fish joke or I'm hanging up."

"How? Alyssa's still holding your phone. But fine, because I love you, I will not make a joke about how eating fish is something best done *after* dinner."

Clem glared. "*Anyway.* We're going to walk around downtown because I haven't had a chance to explore, and then she's going to cook me dinner."

"Can Lou cook?" Alyssa asked.

"Of course she can. She makes meals for her grandma all the time. I don't think people give her enough credit. Though I don't think she gives herself much credit either."

"Well, Clemmy," Sam said with a genuine smile, "if anyone excels at helping people see their own goodness, it's you."

Clementine swallowed the lump in her throat. Could she really be the support Lou needed? Or would there always be this push and pull of trying to convince Lou that letting people in didn't only lead to them letting you down? Sometimes it led to them lifting you up instead. She felt the prick of a tear forming in her eye and stood up abruptly. She did not need to be tag-teamed with friendship. Already Alyssa and Sam were a duo that could strip down her defenses. Maybe this uncomfortable vulnerability was how Lou felt, and if Clem didn't stop pushing, she'd want to run, too. Still, Clem needed to leave this room five minutes ago.

"Okay, I'm off to shower." Clementine reached out her hand for her phone.

"Love you," Sam said over the speaker.

Alyssa didn't relinquish her grip on the device. Instead, she blinked innocently up at Clem. "You don't need your phone to shower, do you?"

Chapter Twenty
Lou

L ou hardly recognized herself as she unlocked her apartment door. She had a canvas bag for god's sake, like a regular public radio listener. A tote she'd been talked into by Clementine and a perfectly nice and far too enthusiastic lady who had a pineapple stand at Haymarket. To be fair, that surprisingly prickly fruit was rather awkward and uncomfortable to carry. No matter how long Lou had lived here, it always surprised her what a different world Boston's outdoor food market was compared to the tourist chaos of Faneuil Hall, although they were right beside each other. The narrow street had been filled with produce vendors, card tables piled high with vegetables she'd never even heard of and a few she was pretty sure were legitimately fake.

Most concerning of all was how much Lou had *enjoyed* it. And now she was the proud owner of a tote bag that said Beets Me, a metric ton of broccoli, and everything else she needed to make dinner for Clementine tonight. And, of course, the pineapple Clem had talked her into buying that would make her mouth burn when she inevitably had a piece later.

On a scale of perfect days, this one was up there with the one when Jude had given her a key to Howl. Both had felt like the start of something. Everything about spending time with Clem lately just felt good—it felt right. When she'd left Howl in the early morning hours, the bar had felt not just empty but lonely too, and that wasn't something Lou had experienced before.

Walking through the narrow streets of the North End with Clem earlier, their hands brushing every few steps until Clem's fingers had intertwined with hers, had felt oddly normal. It was what Lou imagined Saturday felt like in other people's lives, free of obligation with plenty of time to wander with her favorite person. That was something that occurred to her on the outing, too, that Clem was her favorite person.

Lou had wanted to do something nice for Clem after everything she'd helped her with. She also wanted time away from saving the bar to see if the crisis was all that had drawn them together, because if it was and she lost Howl, she'd rather avoid having her heart decimated twice in quick succession.

She was perfectly comfortable showing up for others. But these past few weeks, it had been others showing up for her, and that had set Lou back on her heels. It was so vulnerable to admit you needed people. She wanted to balance the scales a bit, and if that also happened to mean more alone time with Clem, well, that was a win-win.

So although Clementine had rejected her aquarium idea, Lou still wanted to show her the city, since knowing Boston meant knowing Lou. Plus, cooking was her default method for showing care, something she knew she could accomplish with a certain level of proficiency because she did it weekly for her grandma.

Only now it was nearing seven and her messages to Clem

had gone unanswered. The vegetables were getting peaky sitting in the June heat on the counter in her apartment. And her confidence was wilting, too.

She considered sending another text, but what would she say? To keep trying made about as much sense as continuing to press the elevator button hoping it would come faster. Lou didn't do *desperate*. And she was starting to think this was why she didn't do relationships either. All the little letdowns.

If someone didn't want her, she didn't gaze back longingly, hoping they'd change their mind. Why Clem didn't think she could handle a direct rejection, Lou didn't know. Maybe she had misread their attraction, but that didn't seem right. Had she done something earlier that put Clementine off, proved herself to be unlovable again? Or had Clem simply changed her mind or gotten a better offer? Lou never thought of herself as some great prize, but these past few weeks with Clem had made her see that she was good, solid. Clementine seemed to feel that way, too. So why wasn't she here?

Lou checked her phone for what felt like the thousandth time but was more likely only the hundredth, and she felt... pathetic. The second she started to care about someone, the world gave her a reason to regret it. She'd been good on her own, and why mess with a good thing?

Outside, lightning cracked across the sky, and like some cosmic force, the idea hit her. Sure, it was the most obvious realization in the world, but it was also a revelation, as the simplest ideas usually are. Lou would make the dinner for herself. It wasn't often that Lou showed herself the care she so readily offered others. Clementine's teasing about Lou's bare fridge before the Haymarket trip was proof enough of that. But why shouldn't she care for herself? As her new plan sank in, she liked it more and more. There was simply no reason to date at all.

Lou pulled out her pristine cutting board, a far cry from the scarred one at her grandma's. Next, she unboxed a copper pan —another concerning sign. Why did she buy nice things and then not use them as though she needed the excuse of caring for someone else to use something new? Soon enough she hit her rhythm, chopping the broccoli and sautéing it along with the chicken. She made the teriyaki sauce from scratch and it felt good. Even though there was no one to share it with, cooking still felt like love to Lou. She was amazed she hadn't made that connection sooner. That doing nice things for herself could feel just as good as doing nice things for others.

The entire time she cooked, the sky darkened and thunder rolled. Occasionally, bright streaks of light lit up the kitchen like flashbulbs.

When the food was ready, Lou took her time arranging it on her plate until it looked like the picture in the recipe. She poured herself wine in the nicest glass she had, one fit for the purpose. She knew she should be embarrassed that she often drank wine or beer out of mason jars—she was a bartender after all—but it never occurred to her to get the best ones down just for her.

She'd taken her phone off silent before she started cooking, thinking it might help her stop torturing herself by checking for a message from Clem. And it had. Mostly. Even though her absence still snagged at the fabric of Lou's thoughts like a loose thread.

The bowl steamed in front of her, and now that the excitement of cooking had waned and her phone remained silent, fear and worry and dread combined in her stomach. She washed the feelings down with another sip of wine.

It hurt that Clem had disappeared tonight, but maybe there was a reason. Even if it wasn't a particularly good one. And maybe there wasn't. Either way, when this rain stopped, Lou was going to climb out onto her fire escape and enjoy the sunset bathing her dirty little part of the city in its Neon Fruit Supermarket glow.

Chapter Twenty-One
Clementine

Clementine's jeans hung heavily on her hips as she trudged up the stairs to Lou's apartment. Her shoes left little puddles of water on each step, like bread-crumbs, should she need a path to escape. If she was welcome to stay past their evaporation, that was probably a sign that every-thing she'd worked to build with Lou over the past weeks hadn't been decimated by her delay.

What a day. No, she was well and truly a Bostonian now. What a *fucking* day.

This city had a knack for stealing her lifelines when she needed them most. First, her beloved Toyota, taken too soon from a highway McDonald's, and now her phone, lost to the sands of time slash stolen on the train. She knew rationally that she wasn't to blame for bad things happening. In fact, after convincing Lou Freakin' McCallister to purchase a canvas bag, the universe probably owed her some good karma. She was saving the environment *and* changing lives after all. But instead, that all-powerful bastard had disappeared her phone and then tried to drown her for good measure.

Knowing it wasn't her fault that she missed dinner was

210

doing absolutely nothing to dispel the guilt and misery. Or her hunger for that matter. What had she been thinking, leaving Lou? Of course everything had blown up the moment Lou let her into her life.

Clementine had learned by now that trust was Lou's trigger. Lou didn't depend on people to remain constant when things got hard. But Clementine *could* be constant. All she had to do was knock on the door and start again. Her hands were shaking, whether from nerves or a chill, she wasn't sure, but she lifted her trembling fist and made herself known.

When the door opened, Lou looked gorgeous the way she always looked gorgeous, effortlessly. She was in the jeans and a gray t-shirt she'd worn earlier, her bare feet on the hardwood floor of her apartment sang of comfort. But there was something else, too. Lou didn't look sad or upset, and for a split second, Clem wondered if her not showing up for dinner maybe wasn't the worst thing in the world.

Lou took a step back, holding the door open and Clem walked inside. She hovered on the rug by the door, trying to contain her new status as a water feature. She slipped off her shoes and the wet sound they made bordered on obscene.

Lou cackled and Clem's heart soared. "I thought you'd take the train, but it appears you decided to swim here instead."

"I am so sorry," Clem blurted, taking a step toward Lou and then freezing when her wet foot made contact with the hardwood floor. "I shouldn't have left, but I wanted to change into something nicer which I clearly didn't accomplish."

"You look nice to me," Lou said with a smirk.

Clementine glanced down at herself and yeah, 'nice' was *not* how she would describe her appearance. "I look like someone threw me into the ocean to see if I'm a witch."

"Well, *are* you?"

Was Lou messing with her? Surely teasing was a good sign

and not Lou indicating that she felt abandoned, right? "If I am, I'm a pretty miserable one. Maybe more like a re-enactor in Salem, going through the same motions of torture every day. I mean, I'm clearly not a witch if I couldn't even find my lost phone. I spent what felt like three years in the depths of the subway going to various lost and founds between downtown and my apartment. It was a labyrinth filled with riddles and misdirections offered in thick Boston accents.

"Oh." Lou's shoulders relaxed, a small smile tugging at her lips

"Is that... good news?" Clementine asked, trying to parse Lou's reaction.

"If you lost your phone, it makes sense why you didn't call and why you were so late and..." Lou trailed off as she looked Clem up and down.

"Why I didn't check my makeup before knocking?" Clem raised an eyebrow. "The *only* use for the front-facing camera. I never would have missed this Lou, or been so late. I kept holding out hope that I would find my phone if I just went one more stop and then one more, and then... you get it. All of my draft posts for the Howl accounts are on there, I didn't want to lose those and let you down. Let all of us down."

Lou stepped forward into her space and Clem's heart struck up a clattering pace in her chest. "Please take off your shirt so I can hug you?"

Clem let out a burst of laughter like a dam breaking. "Is that... a requirement for hugs?"

"You're soaked." Lou leaned back, placing her hands on Clementine's shoulders. "I don't want to ruin my shirt, but I need to touch you and know you're really here. I knew it wasn't about me, but it's also very hard when I'm feeling insecure to not think that *literally everything* is about me. I thought maybe you'd changed your mind."

The confession stunned Clementine. She was so used to Lou showing up in her armor of confidence and a sly smile. This raw vulnerability was like a geode being cracked open to reveal all its glittering secrets.

"Okay, for real, let's get you out of these clothes. I'll grab you something to wear." Lou took a step back.

Clem followed her. She reached out and ran a finger from Lou's collarbone, stopping just over her heart. More clothes were the last thing she needed. After that confession, she wanted no space between her and Lou. She wanted to hold her and whisper sweet things into her hair. But somehow that didn't seem quite like Lou's vibe and Clem needed to meet her where she was. So she made the next best move, which also happened to send a shiver of anticipation through her. The chill on her skin was replaced with the heat of desire.

"Or we could just leave them off... I mean your shirt is wet now, too..." Clem let her eyes linger on Lou's body until she was sure Lou could feel her gaze like a persistent touch.

Lou grinned and stepped forward until their lips were almost touching. "I'm not sure what's sexier, the thought of you in my clothes or the thought of you naked."

Clementine quirked an eyebrow. She wanted to maintain the gravity of the moment while also lightening the mood, like emotions were a dimmer light and she was adjusting them just enough. "Really, you have to think about this? Maybe I should just go." Clem took a step toward the door.

"No." Lou closed the last bit of distance between them, her mouth hovering over Clem's for the briefest moment before their lips met, an entire conversation in the solitary breath that passed between them. And then they were kissing like it was the oxygen they needed to keep going.

Lou's hands gripped Clem's hips as she pressed into her, clothes only a slight barrier to their desire. The sexiness paused

213

as Lou slowly eased Clem's jeans from her body. It is a simple and unfortunate truth of life that there's nothing sexy about removing wet denim. Lou growled her frustration. The noise shot desire through Clem. Once they were off Lou hit play, sliding a hand between Clem's thighs. She was ready to combust.

Clementine caught her wrist. "You're distracting me from my goal."

"Oh yeah?" Lou's brow furrowed. "And what *is* your goal?"

Clem reached forward and tugged on the hem of Lou's shirt until she lifted her arms and then stripped it off. Clementine's breath caught as she studied the soft, black satin of Lou's bra cupping her small breasts. Clementine had always liked to take her time unwrapping gifts, reveling in the anticipation of the slow reveal. "My goal is having you in bed. I mean, the front door looks nice, but I want to really see you."

Lou went to unhook her bra, but Clem shook her head. "Bed," was all she said.

Before she could utter another word, Lou lifted her. Clementine instinctively wrapped her legs around Lou's hips and god, the contact was exquisite. A month ago, after their hookup, she never could have imagined this moment. It wasn't frantic or fumbling. It was a slow dance of two people who wanted to enjoy each other.

If their first encounter had been a shot, downed in one to quicken the sensation of alcohol rushing in to numb, this night was a drink you sipped slowly, noting the undertones, celebrating the sharp bursts of flavor, honoring the history.

She buried her face against Lou's neck, kissing a path down from her ear to her shoulder before murmuring, "You're stronger than I thought."

Lou laughed, meeting Clem's gaze with twinkling blue eyes. "Please, you weigh the same as a case of scotch."

Yes, scotch. This night was a fine amber liquid. Aged to perfection by their month of dancing around one another.

"I wonder if I can list that weight on my driver's license."

"It is a universal measurement," Lou said as she walked them to the bedroom.

Clem's back hit the mattress when Lou let her go and she quickly looked about the space to take it in. The bedroom was nothing like she'd imagined it would be. Lou gave off the minimalist vibe of a mattress on the floor and blackout curtains. Instead, the walls were painted a moss green, except for the one with the window to the street, which was exposed brick. Below the window was a low bookcase filled with paperbacks that looked well-loved. It was so different from Clem's barren room. Her apartment felt like a place to live while Lou's was home. The room said that Lou was settled, committed, and she hoped that Lou might commit to her, too.

Clem sat up, leaning on her elbows so she could watch Lou remove her pants. Her black underwear was simple but sexy, the branding on the light elastic band drawing Clem's eyes to the jut of her hip bones. Lou was hard and feminine all at once. While there was nothing hard about Clem, just soft curves and understanding, she had never wished for a different body. But Lou's contrast only served to make her more breathtaking. New territory Clem was desperate to explore. "Come here," Clem bit back a smile as Lou settled onto the bed and crawled toward her. The sight made her stomach clench and she relaxed onto the bed, resting her head on a pillow.

Lou settled next to her and slid one hand over Clementine's stomach. "You feel incredible." Lou's hand grazed down between Clem's legs before halting.

"Oh no, I didn't realize your underwear got wet too."

"Well," Clem said, fighting back a blush. "The rain wasn't the only factor contributing to that outcome."

"Ah." Lou nodded. "Either way, it's probably time to get you out of them before you catch a chill, don't you think?"

All Clem could do was nod, a new wave of sensation settling in her core when Lou hooked her thumbs beneath the flimsy fabric. Her hands slowly teased the sensitive skin beneath Clem's underwear as she worked the garment over Clementine's hips.

"I wanted to do this so much that night we spent in Hart's Hollow."

Clem swallowed hard. "You did?"

"Mmhmm." Lou drew out the word, running a finger lazily through Clem's folds, dipping into her wetness before making her way back up to Clem's clit. Clementine squirmed beneath her. One touch and she felt ready to come. There was something so erotic about having Lou's full attention.

Lou circled her clit again, more slowly this time. "Ah, there," she said, making light strokes over the spot that made Clem's breath hitch and thoughts unravel.

She groaned. It felt incredible, and as badly as she wanted to come, she absolutely didn't want this to be over so soon. Clem gathered her strength and pushed up, flipping Lou onto her back.

Lou's eyes twinkled. "A woman who takes charge. I like that."

"You know I'm good at making things happen when I set my mind to it."

"Mmm," Lou moaned either in agreement or pleasure as Clem slid a leg between her thighs. She felt Lou's slick heat through the thin, black fabric separating them.

"These are cute, but I think they should go," Clem rasped as she pulled the fabric aside just enough to lightly run her finger through Lou's wetness.

Lou arched upward and Clem drew back just enough to

slide the fabric down Lou's legs. God, she was beautiful. As Clementine settled back down, her clit made contact with Lou's thigh. The whimper she made was quickly swallowed by Lou's own.

Clem set a slow rhythm as she rocked her hips against Lou. After a minute, Lou met her movements, her head falling back and blonde hair fanning over the white comforter.

Clem slid a hand between them, dipping into Lou's wetness again, then dancing her fingers to Lou's clit. Her hips jumped and Clem lightened her touch making a slow figure eight, the bottom half dipping down toward Lou's entrance. It was Clem's favorite way to touch herself. She found it was just the right amount of time between strong sensations to draw out her orgasm. And the way Lou was responding to it only increased her arousal.

Lou's hips rocked up insistently. "Please," she gasped before tilting her hips in what seemed like an attempt to roll them over.

Clementine withdrew her hand and grabbed Lou's wrists. Her touch was gentle but firm. It didn't stop Lou from pressing harder against Clem, seeking friction. "I know you're used to being in charge, but we've been working on you letting other people do things, right?"

Lou narrowed her eyes and groaned.

"Let's apply that principle here, too," she said, letting go of Lou's wrist and slowly bringing her hand back between their bodies. Lou's movements caused Clem to slide against her leg and it became harder and harder to concentrate on her slow and steady movements over Lou's clit.

As the rhythm of Lou's hips grew more frantic, so did Clem's touch, until her fingers skated over Lou with less precision than excitement. But that seemed to suit Lou just fine as she surged upward, her back arching and one hand tangling in Clementine's hair to pull their mouths together for a rough kiss.

"Inside," Lou gasped.

As soon as Clem slipped two fingers into Lou's delicious heat, she clenched around her. Lou's hand slid to the back of Clem's arm, pushing her deeper.

She came with their mouths still pressed together, her lips parting, tongue needy and insistent. All of Lou's muscles became taut and she wrenched her mouth away from Clem's to cry out. Clementine buried her face against Lou's shoulder, tamping down her own orgasm that threatened to crest as Lou continued to press into her before collapsing back against the mattress.

CLEMENTINE COULDN'T REMEMBER FALLING asleep. It was sometime after she'd lost track of how many orgasms she'd had and negotiated for mercy. But the grumbling of her stomach drew her from bed. She hadn't eaten since the lunch she'd had with Lou from a food cart in Boston Common. Lou was resting on her side, one arm tucked beneath her head. She looked too peaceful to wake, so Clem shook out a blanket that was crumpled on the floor at the foot of the bed and laid it over her sleeping form.

She felt a stab of guilt once she got to the kitchen and saw the single plate and glass on the table, the rest of the food still in the pan on the stove. That didn't stop her from opening drawers until she found a fork and speared two satisfying pieces of broccoli covered in teriyaki sauce. The best she'd ever had.

Footsteps in the hall stopped her mid-bite, and she turned to see a disheveled Lou ambling into the kitchen, underwear peeking out from beneath the low hem of her t-shirt with each step.

"I'm glad you're refueling," she said as she came up behind Clem and slid an arm around her waist.

"Yes, well, spending time with you seems to burn a lot of calories. First walking all over downtown, carrying bags of vegetables and then those bedroom gymnastics."

"I bet Alyssa also calls that 'Sweatin' to the 80s.'" Lou pressed a soft kiss to her neck.

Clem laughed. "You're probably right, but I don't want to know. Did I tell you I think she and Sam have something going on?"

Lou's eyes widened. "What? How?"

"Beats me." Clem shrugged. "Hey, do you know where the pineapple went? I'll cut some up for us."

"Yeah, it's over here." Lou walked to the other side of the kitchen and lifted the tote from where it sat on a chair. As she held it into the air, something vibrated inside it.

"Is that pineapple sentient?"

"Oh god," Lou said as she reached her arm into the bag. A moment later, she was clutching Clem's phone with wide eyes.

Clementine groaned, covering her face with her hands. "No fucking way. Please don't kill me for being such a space cadet. I've been told it grows on people. I could have sworn I had that when I left. God, I wasted all that time for nothing."

"I can't believe I didn't hear it vibrate when I messaged you."

Clem uncovered her face and looked at Lou. "Texts are on silent. They kept waking me up when I was trying to sleep through the morning after my shifts. There was nothing for you to hear. That vibration is probably something on socials. I turned those alerts on for the Howl accounts." She held out her hand, eager to see what the alert was. Earlier she'd posted about HowlQueen. They were only a few days out, so it was now or never if they wanted to draw a crowd big enough to save the bar.

Lou handed over the phone.

Clem's eyes went wide. No freaking way. The notification

on her screen overrode her elation at having her phone back and not needing to blow her meager savings on a new one. "Oh my god, Lou! Tanner Tavish shared my post."

"I don't know what any of that means." Lou placed the pineapple on the cutting board and pulled out a knife the size of a slice of pizza.

Clementine blew out an exasperated breath, strong enough to ruffle a few of her red curls. "Can you get on the internet, please? It's a hellhole, but it's home, you know?"

Lou reached over and tucked the unruly strands behind her ear, letting her hand linger on the side of Clem's face until she looked up from her phone. "I mean, sort of?"

"*Anyway,*" Clem said with an eye roll and a smile. "Tanner is a huge sapphic media personality. She's verified and has over 141,000 followers."

"That is a lot of people."

"Yes, thank you. She shared my post about HowlQueen and our mission to save the bar—the one with all the details. This could be huge for us."

Clem's phone lit up in her hand and she couldn't stop her grin. "It's my cousin, I'm going to reply real quick."

Jane: *Hey! Tanner Tavish just shared a post about the bar you work at. Uncle Denny said you're trying to save it? That's so cool! Astrid and I will actually be on the East Coast for the NYC Dyke March this weekend, so maybe we can stop by if the celestial dates match up.*

She chuckled. It had been way too long since she'd been out to Denver to see her cousin.

Lou gave her a curious look. "Jane thinks she might be able to come to HowlQueen. It seems a little unlikely, knowing her, but she and her partner Astrid will be in from

Denver for Pride in New York. It would be great if they could meet you. I mean, like it's not a big deal, it's just you're cool, they're cool, and—"

Lou leaned in and kissed her then. "If they're important to you, then, of course, I want to meet them. Write her back."

Clem: *You know you could just use a regular calendar too. The event is Saturday.*
Jane: *Sure, but that's way less fun. I'm so proud of you!!!*
Clem: *Thank you for getting what a big freakin' deal ™ this is! I tried to explain to Lou, and she asked who Tanner is.*

Clem bumped her hip against Lou's. "I spilled your secret about not knowing Tanner."

Lou wrapped an arm around Clem's waist, pulling her close. "I guess I'll just have to forgive you.

Jane: *Is that the cute blonde you brought to Hart's Hollow the other week? Sam said you two are obsessed with each other.*
Clem: *Wait, since when do you talk to Sam?*

"Am I the cute blonde?" Lou laughed.

"Do you see any other beautiful blondes around? Didn't think so."

Jane: *Clemmy, everyone talks to Sam. Even Astrid. I think James might have texted her once even.*
Clem: *Wow, okay. That's news to me. And yes, that's Lou.*
Jane: *Cool, I'm rooting for you two. Maybe see you soon if I can figure how Mars will align.*
Clem: *Literally not how that works. Love you.*
Jane: **loved your last message.*

Clem grinned at Lou, pulling her closer. "I think my cousin might come to HowlQueen."

"Really? That's great."

"I mean, she might not even be able to get *in the door*, now that the entire sapphic world knows about it."

"Very funny," Lou said, handing Clem the knife.

She stepped forward and tipped the pineapple onto its side, prepared for a beheading.

Right before she brought the knife down, Lou put a hand on her hip. "Why does your underwear say Wednesday?"

"Don't hate. *Day of the week* underwear is a classic sartorial choice. Plus, I had to restock quickly after my car was stolen.

"Okay, but that doesn't explain why you're wearing the wrong day."

"I'm not beholden to the myth of linear time, which is a destructive capitalist concept. Plus, I thought the little strawberries on this pair were cute."

"Well, they definitely go nicely with pineapple," Lou said, as she lowered her mouth to Clem's neck and bit down softly.

Chapter Twenty-Two
Lou

All too quickly, Pride had the city in its rainbow-glitter grip. Crosswalks between historic churches were decked out in ROY-G-BIV stripes, and there were so, so many sleeveless t-shirts.

The remaining days leading up to the event had been a whirlwind of last-minute arrangements after Rachel had proudly slapped a check from Founding Charter Bank onto the bar directly into a small puddle of beer.

When asked how she got the soulless behemoth of a financial institution to agree, Rachel had made a show of intertwining her hands behind her back and straightening her arms to stretch. Her shoulders flexed with the kind of definition that gave people body goals as she said, "I asked nicely."

Must have been pretty nice to get a check for three figures. Just barely three figures, but still. They'd used what they needed for supplies and prizes and put the rest into the Save Howl Fund.

Lou was terrified as she stood on the street in the pre-dawn light, waiting for the city to wake up. After work, she'd been too anxious to sleep because this was it, their big push to save the bar. By tonight, she'd know the fate of the place she loved most.

It was set to be their largest HowlQueen yet. The doors would open at ten that morning to serve the parade crowd, and things wouldn't stop until the last reveler left before dawn. She wanted more than anything to believe it would all work out, but she couldn't quite bring herself to. Still, knowing Clementine would be there by her side helped her weather the uncertainty.

Since their drowned and resuscitated date night, they'd been inseparable. Well, even more inseparable than before. Clem was upstairs now, naked beneath Lou's sheets and fast asleep. Part of Lou wanted to save Howl because she didn't want the magic of their relationship to end. Not that they were technically in a relationship, because Lou didn't do those. But whatever they were doing, she wanted it to last.

The first rays of light broke over the buildings and Lou couldn't deny it anymore—the day was here. She took one last look at the street before the parade chaos descended, and then she turned and went inside.

BACK UPSTAIRS, she woke Clementine up slowly, with kisses and soft touches that grew more eager once Clem pulled her close. It was a release and a comfort all at once to focus on Clem's body and her pleasure, a task Lou had a track record of accomplishing. If everything else fell apart today, she could still fall asleep with unruly red hair draped over her shoulder and this beautiful woman absolutely not snoring beside her.

Once she came, Clementine reached for Lou but she pulled away. She knew she wouldn't be able to focus enough to enjoy herself. "I've got too much on my mind."

"I know that," Clem mumbled. "Let me help."

Lou kissed her hard and fast before standing up and

extending her hand. "Join me in the shower so I can focus on you again." And she did. Twice.

THE SCENT of gin and tonics tanged the air as Lou wiped down the bartop for what felt like the thousandth time.

Clem had been buzzing around the bar all morning, snapping pictures to put on social media and it seemed to be working. When they opened their doors at ten, Howl was swiftly packed with customers, with a line forming on the street outside once they'd reached capacity.

Dana had put up some guardrails to form an area where people could have drinks and watch the parade crawl by. It was clear by ten-thirty when they came in to offload the cover charge money they'd collected so far, that they'd all way underestimated the turnout. Thank god.

The parade came and went in a steady stream of Janet Jackson and Taylor Swift, interspersed with projectiles of rainbow confetti and plastic bead necklaces. Lou stayed inside for most of it, okay with peeking her head out the door occasionally. It was nice to have a slight reprieve, even though the chaos of the crowd at the bar was doing wonders to take her mind off how badly she wanted this to work.

"Hey, someone's here to see you."

Lou hadn't noticed Clem come up beside her, and she reached for her immediately. She couldn't help herself. Even though she wasn't big on public displays, she wrapped her arm around Clementine's waist, needing the anchor to steady her nerves.

Clem stepped closer, sliding a hand into Lou's back pocket just as her gram came into view. She froze, torn between stepping away from Clem and not moving at all so as to not draw more attention. She pushed the fear aside and let herself relax into Clementine's touch. Sure, her grandma seeing them made it more real and increased the risk of it hurting worse if they split up. But nothing would feel as bad as pretending she didn't care. Clem had broken the part of her that was good at wielding distance like a defense.

"So good to see you two lovebirds." Her grandma smiled and held out a plate wrapped in tin foil. "I brought this for your event."

"Thanks, Gram, but it's not really the kind of thing with a table of snacks."

Clem leaned forward and lifted the foil enough to reveal the brownies underneath. "Aha. That's just because she doesn't want to share."

"Are those Gram's brownies?" Rachel called as she rushed by with a tray of drinks. "You better save me some."

"That girl is so sweet," Gram said. "You better share these, Louise. Clementine, can I trust you to tell me if she doesn't?"

Clem grimaced. "It's very hard to be put on the spot between two beautiful women, and actually—yup, I think I hear someone call my name."

Clem gave Lou's cheek a quick kiss and shot Eleanor a smile before rushing away to answer the imaginary summoning.

"Here, let's put these in the office," Lou said, motioning for her grandma to follow her.

She let her shoulders fall once they reached the open door. Here, away from the crowd and Clementine, her fear rushed back.

"You've got this, baby. And there's a little something in there to help out." Her grandma nodded to the plate.

"You better not be referencing weed this time either."

Eleanor shrugged. "I plead the fifth."

"In that case, I'll save them for after the show."

"Good idea. Try to just enjoy today, sweetheart. The die is already cast. You and darlin' Clementine have done all you can."

Lou furrowed her brows. This wasn't the first time someone had referred to Clem this way. It felt like an intimacy she wasn't part of, and that made her bristle. "How do you know to call her darlin' Clementine?"

"It's like the old song."

Lou tilted her head. There was a song? "I don't know it."

"I can't believe you don't remember your dad singing this to you, you loved this song." Her grandma hummed a few lines before singing in earnest about a miner forty-niner and his darlin' Clementine.

Tears pricked behind Lou's eyes and she tried to force them away, but the words pulled at the heartstrings like a seam ripper.

Eleanor stopped singing abruptly. "The song actually takes quite a turn from there and poor Clementine drowns while her lover, who can't swim, doesn't attempt to rescue her. But let's not focus on that today."

Lou's eyes went wide. If anything, she might be the one to drown today, but there wasn't a doubt in her mind that Clementine would jump in to save her.

Chapter Twenty-Three
Clementine

Alyssa glided in a little after noon on her roller skates, which seemed ill-advised, if expedient. They might need her speed with how busy they'd been so far. Behind Alyssa were two women in their eighties, also on skates, their arms linked together.

"Clemmy, I want you to meet June and Shirley. These babes are here to par-tay until they drop, or..." Alyssa paused, pulling her phone from her pocket, "for at least the next forty-five minutes until the van comes to take them back to Gray Gardens."

"Hi," Clem said brightly. The older women were so endearing, both looking at Alyssa like she was some kind of mystical creature. And, in some ways, she really was. Today, she was wearing iridescent hot shorts and a cropped t-shirt that said Born This Way, with a dragon hatching from an egg, breathing rainbow fire. Clementine would not be surprised to learn that she'd made it herself. Stores simply didn't create apparel perfect enough to capture Alyssa.

The afternoon zoomed by, all of the staff operating in a busy fugue state. Clementine spent most of her time taking portraits of people next to the purple neon wolf on the graffiti wall and then typing up quick statements about what Pride meant to them. Each post garnered more and more likes. The virtual tip jar she'd set up was practically overflowing by the time the sun went down.

Dana started holding people outside, and the crowd inside began to thin out as people went in search of dinner. Lou had agreed, reluctantly, to charge a small 'pay what you want' cover for the drag show.

Lou caught her eye from across the bar where Clem was coordinating the stage setup. She smiled tentatively, and Clem beamed back. Fake it until you make it. Or is it 'fake it once you make it'? Is everyone just always faking it? Should she write a new self-help book about how there is no secret, just people who have no fucking clue what they're doing? Maybe. Clem gave a few more instructions about the placement of the speakers and feather boas.

This was it, the night that would make or break the future of Howl, and Clementine was feeling good, feeling great, feeling not at all confident that this wasn't all a huge mistake.

Clem started at the presence next to her, absurdly close for someone who wasn't Lou.

"Are you going to eyefuck your girlfriend all night, or do you think you might serve a drink or two?"

"Happy Pride, Rachel. I didn't see you come back from your break."

"I'm surprised you overlooked my festive outfit."

Clem glanced down—Rachel was dressed all in black. The nearly imperceptible shiny writing on her t-shirt said, 'proud as fuck', so she *was* technically dressed up.

Clem was in a purple mini-dress. She'd had to borrow a pair of booty shorts from Alyssa just to ensure people didn't see more than they'd paid for. Howl was a lot of things, but the dancing didn't usually include the full monty.

Her phone alarm went off, signaling eight p.m., and she sent a quick text to Dana to open the doors. The stream of people that flowed in seemed endless, and Clem retreated behind the bar to help Rachel and Megan with the rush. Alyssa had volunteered to help Lou test the mic after it became apparent that she was inept with technology even when it didn't involve the internet.

They had a limited drinks menu tonight, Rachel's idea, which allowed them to mix pitchers in advance. When she'd presented the strategy after the community meeting, Clementine had been skeptical, but now that its brilliance was apparent, she wanted to kiss her, she was so relieved.

From across the crowded bar, Alyssa squealed loud enough to catch Clem's attention. It was like she'd spotted a spider but was happy about it.

Clementine craned her neck to see what Alyssa was so gleeful about. Jet black Betty Paige bangs caught her eye. It was odd how it reminded her so much of Sam when her friend was so far away. But wait, that black and white polka dot dress screamed Sam, and oh, shit. What was her best friend doing here? Elation swelled in her chest.

She was watching Sam so intently that Clementine hardly noticed the man lumbering around the bar. He was incongruous in a flannel shirt and faded jeans, tall and burly, and one-hundred percent her father. Clem nearly dropped the pitcher she was holding. At the last minute, Rachel swooped in and took it from her.

"Dad?" she called, trying to make it make sense. It couldn't be him. Why would he be here at all, let alone for Pride?

But 'flannel shirt in summer' screamed Denny Darby. So did the Maine Course hat he was wearing. If she had any coordination at all, she might have vaulted over the bar, but because she valued her pride and her ability to walk, Clementine speed-walked around the counter instead.

"Sam," she hissed, waving to get her friend's attention. "You brought my dad?"

"Isn't it great that we're both here? And it's good for the environment because we carpooled in his Airstream before he officially starts his road trip. Also, I'm going to need you to find me a ride back to Hart's Hollow, because he's just dropping me off."

"I thought he was joking about getting one of those."

"Definitely not. And it's so cool and sexy." Sam sighed dramatically. "Total chick magnet."

Clem glared. She loved Sam, but sometimes she didn't know what was wrong with her. Nothing related to her father should be classified as 'sexy' by her best friend. "Excuse me?"

"Oh relax, you baby. I mean it's got swagger. I want you to take some photos of me with it tomorrow. It gives off great retro American Road Trip vibes. Anyway, if you're concerned, I guess you better shut down your plans to strip tonight. Keep it PG. PG-13 max." Sam nodded to a picture on the wall where the bartenders were on the bar, mid-dance.

"That's dancing, not stripping."

"Potato, potato," Sam said with a shrug.

Clem shook her head but couldn't hold back her smile. It was so good to see Sam, even if it was unexpected and confusing. Having her best friend here made everything seem a little more possible. When Sam was around, magic happened. "You're supposed to pronounce the second 'potato' differently, you know."

"Why? They're the same thing. Just like you dancing on that bar is an erotic—"

"Oh hey, Mr. Darby!" Sam exclaimed as she turned and

231

threw an arm around Denny. "I found Clem."

Her father's arm fell over Clem's shoulders with the comforting weight of home. "Good to see you, kiddo. When Sam mentioned there would be a show tonight, I couldn't miss my chance to see it before hitting the road."

"How thoughtful of Sam," she said, narrowing her eyes at her friend.

"I sure thought so. Now, how about a drink before the show starts?" Denny's eyes sparkled in the light glinting off of the mirrorball.

"Excuse me," Sam cut in, "I see someone I know." She darted away, and a second later was engulfed in Alyssa's arms. Clem would definitely need to get to the bottom of that later.

She pulled a menu from the bar and handed it to her dad. He squinted for a moment before pulling out his phone, its screen flickering for a second before extinguishing.

"Dad." Clem brought a hand to her forehead in exasperation. "Why is your phone held together by duct tape?"

"It fell apart when I washed it. I guess it was in one of my pockets. You know, because you tell me never to go anywhere without it."

"Does it still make calls?"

"I'm not sure, I haven't tried it."

Clem furrowed her brow. "When did this happen?"

He shrugged like there was no possible way for him to have that information. "Last week, maybe?"

Guilt grasped Clem's heart and twisted it. Had it really been a week since she'd checked on her dad? She'd been so wrapped up in Lou and the bar that she'd forgotten to be present for the rest of her life.

"I'll have a..." his face screwed up until his eyes were so squinted they all but retreated into his head. "Starving Hysterical Naked?"

"Let me, Dad." Clem reached for the menu. "This one's on the house. And might I recommend the No Broken Hearts?"

"I'm fine, Clementine. You don't have to treat me."

"Your wallet is just a rubber band, Dad. Plus you should save your money for your road trip."

"Yeah, I washed *that* by mistake, too." Denny shrugged. "I guess it was in the same load as my phone."

Clem tried to keep the hurt from her voice. "If you need help with things, why didn't you call me? You know I'll drop everything for you."

"I know. That's the problem. You can't keep dropping everything for me. I want you to have a life of your own. I've been putting off something big because I didn't want you to be disappointed in me." Denny shuffled his feet before standing up a little straighter. "But I think it's for the best. I know how much you love the diner. We both have to let it go, Clem. I can't keep living in the past, chasing your mom's ghost. I—I'm ready for my own life too."

Clementine swallowed hard. They had been keeping each other locked in the past for too long. "I'm not disappointed in you. I just wish I'd understood sooner."

The words she spoke were true, she *was* happy for her dad. But it was also bittersweet—letting go of the diner that had meant so much to her mom. Knowing that she had been right to leave when she did.

Denny rested a hand on Clementine's shoulder.

She busied herself with grabbing his drink for him, not wanting him to see the tears filling her eyes. Clem cleared her throat as she handed over the glass. "Well cheers, to new beginnings."

"Cheers." Denny held up his drink. "So this event is like a fashion show?"

"Sure." Clem smiled. "Something like that. Now, drink up. Maybe down a couple of those before, let's say nine?"

AS THE NIGHT WORE ON, the bar reached its capacity and they had to turn people away. Her cousin Jane texted that she and Astrid wouldn't make it, and while Clem was disappointed, she also felt like another surprise guest might push her over the edge. She was at capacity, too. Their campaign had worked. Any money they'd spent on advertising HowlQueen and the cash prize was more than offset by the cover charge and the crowd in the bar, lined up to order drinks. Clem knew Lou didn't love charging a cover because they'd never done that before, but it made sense to offset the cost of the evening's production and Mimi Mosa, the drag queen MCing the event.

At nine on the dot, the main lights dimmed and the ones over the stage illuminated. Lou slowly walked to the mic. She'd agreed to kick the evening off, but even from across the room, it was clear that she wasn't relishing it. That was when an idea hit Clem. It was the kind of thought that was either genius or terrible, like ordering the fourth round of shots on a Tuesday night.

She turned to her dad. "You know, we're still short a few auctionees for the night."

"Don't you mean auction items?"

"Not at Howl, bub. Fancy getting up on that platform and strutting your stuff? I think you might start a bidding war."

Sam, who had materialized out of nowhere, smacked her dad's butt. "A stud like you could bring in thousands."

Clementine was caught between wanting to thank Sam for being on her side and wanting to murder her for touching her dad's butt.

"Girls." Denny sighed like he was about to deliver a sleep-over lecture. "I don't have anything to offer these people."

"Bi- and pan women exist, Mr. Darby." Sam's smile brimmed with devious delight at the turn the night was taking. "I hope you reel in someone great, Mr. Darby. I'm going to find Alyssa, I'll catch up with you two later!"

Her dad shook his head. "I'm already seeing someone."

"Brenda?" Clem asked.

He raised an eyebrow. "Is that a Q or an A?"

"Pretty sure that's my line, Dad."

"Fine, yes, Brenda, and I'm not sure she'd like me auctioning myself off to the highest bidder."

Interesting, so they *were* a thing. "Jealous type is she?"

He rolled his eyes but didn't bite

"Where is she tonight?"

"She's running the diner so I could go on the road trip and be here. And then we're meeting up in a week or so to hit the road together for a bit."

"Well, that's nice." It was hard to be mad at people when they were kind and good to your father, even if they did keep you in the dark about changing your family.

Clem was silent for so long that Denny cleared his throat.

"Fine, I've got another idea for what you can offer these fine people. It won't compromise your relationship, I promise. Let's get you over to the stage."

They waited off to the side for Lou to finish her opening remarks, which were mostly thanking people for coming while she nervously tapped her left foot. "Okay, and with that, let the auction begin."

Clem waved her arms to get Lou's attention. Lou handed over the mic a little too enthusiastically once Clem said she'd kick the bidding off.

She sauntered to the center of the stage, catching Sam's eye where she and Alyssa were cuddled together. Clem tried to siphon some of her confidence.

235

"Okay, you beautiful people! Welcome home! We're all Wayward Lovers here. Thanks for being here today to help us save this legendary space so it can welcome new generations for years to come!" Dana caught her eye from where they stood in the doorway, they gave her a slight nod. Clem took a deep breath because she knew what she had to do next, and that was embarrass herself completely. She pulled the microphone back from her mouth a bit, squeezed her eyes shut, and howled.

A chorus of howls rushed through the crowd, followed by a wolf whistle she knew to be Sam's. As the beautiful cacophony of the community continued, she motioned her dad up onto the stage. He looked about as comfortable as he had during a root canal, which she'd made the massive mistake of taking him to once.

"First up tonight is this fine specimen." Clementine gestured up and down her dad. His flannel shirt was only half tucked in and one of his boots was untied. *It just adds to the charm*, she told herself.

"Do you find yourself in need of a dad date? A fatherly festivity? Look no further! I know firsthand that this paternal figure gives excellent advice. He'll show up to your softball game and cheer you on! Or he'll take you to a Sox game and treat you to a hot dog and a soda. Have a big event coming up and want someone to show up with flowers and tell you he's proud of you? This right here is your guy! Let's start the bidding at twenty."

"One hundred," Sam yelled.

"Did I mention he grills a mean veggie burger with all the fixings?"

"Two-fifty," Rachel called out.

"Does he do weddings? A walk down the aisle?" A woman with pink hair near the front asked.

Her dad leaned in close and whispered, "definitely."

"He does," Clem confirmed. "And he'll even throw in a dance at the reception."

"Five hundred," the woman yelled.

"Five hundred. Do I hear five-fifty?" Even as she said it, Clem hoped no one outbid her. She deserved to be supported at her wedding and every day before and after. Everyone should get the kind of boundless encouragement she got from her dad. Especially Lou. She scanned the crowd for her face but didn't see her. Odd.

"Sold to the woman with the pink hair! And congratulations on your upcoming nuptials!"

Her dad leaned forward to speak into the mic. "Follow me to the bar and I'll get you that soda while we talk about your dreams for your big day."

The crowd went wild, and Clem waited for the elation to simmer down before returning the microphone to its stand. She was about to climb down the stage steps when a whistle stopped her in her tracks. She gazed out over the crowd, making eye contact with a woman who stood just behind Rachel.

"Wait, where do you think you're going? Come on, sweetheart, how much for you?" a slurred voice called out. "Come on, baby, take it off."

The next thing she knew, Rachel raised her arm at a ninety-degree angle and her fist made contact with the person's nose. The crowd was so silent that the crack echoed through the bar.

"Oops," Rachel said, smiling at Clem as she walked off the stage. Rachel had done a lot to show up for her people lately. She'd come through huge with the bank and she'd sworn she hadn't done anything illegal. And she'd been there to support Lou and the bar. Now even Clementine felt under her protection. She wasn't sure what to make of it, but what she did know was that it felt damn good to have someone like Rachel in her corner.

Clementine made her way back to the bar and spent the remainder of her night there filling glasses as Mimi Mosa led the drag show, crowning the HowlQueen just after one a.m. The winner was a drag king who went by Moe Money, who did a spectacular rendition of Pony by Genuine to beat Bananas Foster in the sudden death round. Bananas had picked an R. Kelly song, a massive mistake judging by the near-silent reception from the crowd.

After last call, she glanced out over the dance floor, spotting Sam and Alyssa closely entwined, just like the song Too Close was describing. They'd made it to the part of the evening where the music seemed to be exclusively chosen by Alyssa, judging by the extremely horny throwback vibe. Her dad had retired a few hours earlier, after his auctionee's wedding plans had been dutifully written on a cocktail napkin and tucked beneath the rubber band holding together his billfold.

When she looked back, she saw Lou retreating down the hallway toward the office. Clem glanced at Rachel who nodded for her to go. The bar was done serving for the night, so Rachel should be able to hold down the fort on her own as the remaining patrons cleared out.

LOU WAS SITTING behind the desk with her head in her hands when Clem entered the office. The plate of brownies from her gram sat untouched in front of her. She looked up as Clem crossed the room.

"What's wrong?" Clem asked when she reached her.

Lou looked at her computer and shook the mouse. As the screen lit up, Lou clicked a few times to open a spreadsheet. "I've been tallying all day on my phone, but I haven't calculated the final figure. I'm terrified. Before I do this, I just want to say that no matter what happens, this taught me that putting my trust in people is worth it. Even if I get leveled sometimes, I can always rise back up."

Clem cleared her throat. She didn't want to scare Lou off, not when they'd so recently found their way to each other. But everything she knew about Lou was pushing her to this moment. She needed Lou to know that no matter what happened next, she had Clementine's support. "I'm so proud of you, Lou, and the outcome of these numbers won't change that. I know it will be hard if it's not the result we hoped for, but I promise we'll get through it. You can count on the people who love you to lift you."

Lou blinked, all of her attention on Clem. "Love me?"

Clem gulped. And nodded.

Lou's hand stilled on the mouse and she turned to Clem. "I do, too. Love you, that is."

Clem gave her a reassuring smile. "Okay, moment of truth. Ready?"

"I am." Lou reached over and squeezed Clem's fingers, pulling her close. She hit a key with her free hand and a number that Clem couldn't see from her angle appeared on the screen. Lou's face fell and her whole body deflated.

"What's wrong?" Clem asked, even though she knew.

She was surprised when Lou collapsed into her arms instead of pulling away. When she spoke Lou's voice was muffled, her cheek pressed against Clem's chest. "We got so close, but even with your secret tip jar, we didn't make it. There's not enough time left for another Hail Mary. It's over."

Clem ran a hand through Lou's hair, trying to infuse the touch with all the comfort and support Lou deserved. "But you said we got close, right? So what about auctioning graffiti space on the wall? Or we could, I don't know, get more publicity? See if the bank will lower the amount they're asking you to put down."

Lou wrapped her arms around Clem's hips. "Babe, please stop. I appreciate how much you've done, but right now I think I just need to eat my feelings. Maybe I can open that bar in Hart's Hollow after all." Lou's smile looked a bit forced.

Clem rubbed gentle circles between Lou's shoulder blades. "You really did like it there."

With a crinkle, Lou lifted the foil from the plate and grabbed a brownie, shoving half of it into her mouth.

"I think I might join you in that endeavor if that's okay."

Lou nodded, her mouth too full to answer. But even under the spell of the magical brownies, she looked devastated and exhausted. In the last two minutes, their tireless efforts over the last few weeks had caught up with them. Clementine grabbed two more pieces, handing another to Lou. She accepted it silently.

As Clem took a bite, a white envelope poking out from the spot where she'd just taken the treats caught her eye. "What's this?"

"What's what?"

"There's an envelope under the brownies."

"Oh, it's probably just a note from my gram." Lou waved her hand. "She's sweet like that."

"Can we open it?"

Lou shrugged. "Sure."

Clem opened the envelope, leaving a chocolate trail on the seal. She eased out the folded paper. It felt thicker than a single sheet. She unfolded it, and a slip of pink paper fluttered to the desk.

Lou's eyes went wide. "No fucking way."

"What is it?" Clem glanced down and saw the check. But surely her eyes were bleary from exhaustion and conjuring up that extra zero. "Did your grandma just..."

"Give me a hundred thousand dollars?" Lou swallowed

audibly. "It would seem so."

"But how did she—"

"It doesn't matter." Lou sighed. "I can't take this money from her."

"Let me read the note. Maybe there's an explanation."

Lou nodded, her eyes locked intently on Clementine.

LOUISE,

This money is yours and I won't take no for an answer. I would have easily spent this on a care facility after my hip replacement, but you dropped everything to care for me because that's the kind of person you are. I am so proud of you. You deserve for all your dreams to come true and I feel blessed to contribute in some way to this one. Canoodle helped.

Love, Gram

P.S. Don't pretend you weren't already planning to take care of me in my later years. And if it helps you, you can think of this as an investment. You're the closest to a sure thing that I've ever known.

WHEN CLEM LOOKED UP ONCE she'd finished reading, Lou's eyes glittered with tears, like the sea on a sparkling day. They were silent for a long moment before Clementine spoke. "What are you going to do?"

"I'm going to do exactly what that perfect woman says. *We're* going to save Howl." A luminous smile broke across Lou's face.

Clementine leaned forward to kiss her, but just before their lips met, Lou raised her hand and smashed the rest of her brownie against Clem's mouth.

And then Clementine kissed her anyway.

241

Epilogue
Clementine

T he snow fell gently on the pavement outside, coating the city streets like powdered sugar on pancakes. Or at least that's what it made Clem think of. God, she missed having breakfast at Maine Course. She couldn't believe she wasn't home for Christmas Eve, but with people needing the day off, she and Lou were staying to cover shifts. Everyone needed someone to go to on Christmas, and Howl was that place for many who had nowhere else.

Lou had promised they would spend next Christmas in Hart's Hollow, and that alone felt like the only gift Clementine needed. A future with Lou.

While she missed her quaint little town, there were definite benefits to staying in the city, Clem thought as she snuck up behind Lou and wrapped her arms around her girlfriend's waist. *Girlfriend.* It had taken two months after HowlQueen for them to reach that word, which was scarier to Lou than one hundred *I love you's*.

Since buying the building in July, Lou had been slowly sprucing up the bar, clear-coating some of the more sentimental graffiti for preservation. The deep clean Clem had helped her with made the place feel lighter somehow, years of dust no longer lingering like a bad taste.

Nerves rumbled in Clem's chest as she thought about the gift she planned to give Lou tonight. While she hoped it was the perfect mix of casual and sentimental, she wasn't sure. But it was sort of a gift for Home of the Wayward Lovers as much as for Lou, so that seemed like a safe bet.

Lou leaned forward to grab a brownie off the plate Clem had put out on the bar earlier. She took a bite and chewed thoughtfully, almost like she was evaluating a wine instead of a chocolate treat. When she finished, she leaned back and planted a kiss on Clementine's cheek. "Babe, these are great. You got so close this time."

Clem sighed dramatically. "Damn, I'm going to crack that recipe one day or die trying." She'd had months to sequence Eleanor's ingredients, and she was running out of adjustments to make. She'd traded in her Top Chef viewing for baking shows. She was becoming suspicious that Gram's magic ingredient really was pot.

"If you bat your eyes enough at Gram, she might just give it to you. I get why she adores you, but sometimes it feels like I have competition."

"Is that right?" Clem mumbled, pressing a soft kiss against Lou's neck.

Lou's soft groan was cut short by someone at the bar clearing their throat. Right. Work.

Rachel and Alyssa stood in front of the polished counter. Both were wearing Santa hats, though Rachel had managed to find a black one, while Alyssa's was neon pink. They encapsulated her friends perfectly.

"I didn't think we'd see you two tonight!" Clem looked between them.

"My flight out is first thing in the morning." Alyssa

shrugged as she reached over the bar and grabbed an olive from the garnishes.

"And my parents are old," Rachel said. "They fell asleep right after dinner."

"That makes sense." Clem wondered where her dad and Brenda were right now. The last postcard she'd gotten was from Joshua Tree National Park. Ever since his phone had finally died in Texas, their primary communication had been the occasional postcard or payphone call, after Brenda had decided to ditch her cell in solidarity. Maybe it was because Clementine grew up with devices and constant connectivity, but the thought of not being able to look up directions or listen to any Taylor Swift song at will terrified her.

"So, are you two lovebirds just going to stand there, or can we get some drinks and do gifts?" Rachel asked, rounding the bar.

"*Gifts?*" Clem mouthed to Alyssa who shrugged.

"It would be a first from Rach, but you never know. Also, I can't drink much because I'm heading straight to the airport after this for my five a.m. flight to see my parents in Michigan."

"Ugh, that's brutal." Lou leaned her head on Clem's shoulder. "*After this*, I'm taking this one to bed."

"And what happens in bed?" Alyssa raised her eyebrows and laughed.

"I can tell you all about that." A voice from behind Alyssa said. "Also, I'll drive you to Logan, Lyss. I forgot your gift in my car, anyway."

Clem squealed and ran around the counter, pulling Sam into her arms. "You're here! How are you here?"

"I-95 South, mostly."

Clem rolled her eyes, but Sam's sass was part of what she loved about her. "That's not what I meant."

"I know. When you said you wouldn't be home for

Christmas since you had things to do in Boston and your dad was traveling, I decided to come to you. Alyssa helped me coordinate."

Alyssa smiled sheepishly. Clementine had gotten used to Alyssa and Sam talking, especially after realizing there was nothing she could do to stop it. Not that she particularly wanted to. Those two were drawn to each other in a way that was almost elemental. Like attracting like.

Sam let go of Clementine and pulled Alyssa into a hug. The only part of their whispered conversation that Clem overheard was Sam saying, "your eyeliner looks fucking amazing." Followed by Alyssa laughing.

By the time they pulled apart, Rachel was handing copper mugs full of mulled wine to all of them.

Rachel raised hers in a toast and they all fell silent. "To Howl," she said, "and to us."

"To the Wayward Lovers," Lou added, catching Clementine's eye. "And to this lovely woman with the fruity name, for being the glue holding everything together."

"Here, here," Sam chimed in as they all clinked their drinks together.

The wine was sweet and spicy on her tongue. The warmth of it radiated through her chest as she took another sip.

"Okay, now that I've quenched my thirst, I need to admit that I didn't get anyone presents." Rachel said with a laugh. "Besides my presence that is."

"You choosing to spend Christmas Eve with us of your own volition does feel pretty special," Lou said. "I don't think that's ever happened before."

"Yeah, well, I guess you've all grown on me. Even you, Lemontine."

Clem narrowed her eyes, but she couldn't hold onto her feigned annoyance. "I think you're okay, too, Rach."

"Okay, now that that's over, who wants some shots?" Rachel asked, turning away from Clem and Lou.

"Maybe in a bit for us," Lou said. She leaned in to whisper in Clementine's ear. "Come with me. I was going to wait until tomorrow, but I think I'd rather give you this gift now."

As they headed away from the bar, Rachel called out after them. "No problem, I'll just grab the most expensive tequila from the storeroom. Hope you two weren't planning to sneak off there."

Lou grabbed her hand as their friends' laughter echoed near the bar. "Maybe later." Lou winked at Clem.

"I have something for you, too." Clem's stomach somersaulted. Getting someone a first big gift was such a monumental step. She didn't want this to be a miss. Each present is an opportunity to convey to the other person, 'I see you, who you are matters to me.'

"Oh yeah?" Lou let go of Clem's hand. "Do you want to go grab it?"

Clem nodded toward the graffiti wall. "Meet back here in a few minutes?"

She took the stairs to Lou's apartment two at a time. The gift was small enough that she'd left it hidden in the Beets Me tote she knew Lou was absolutely never using. She skidded to a stop in the kitchen and grabbed the bag before rushing out again. She wanted to have her surprise installed before Lou made her way back.

Breathless, Clementine rushed down the stairs. There was no sign of Lou as she searched out the picture hook she'd surreptitiously hung earlier that day. It was just above the graffiti of a small house, simplistic as a kid's drawing, with Lou's name inside right where the door would be.

Clementine pulled the backless frame out of the tote bag and carefully hung it over the drawing.

She took a step back to examine her work. The black frame looked perfect, simple, and classic. She turned in time to see Lou's mouth fall open. *Damn.* She hadn't noticed her approaching. A red stocking with white fur trim was clutched to her girlfriend's chest. Should she have gotten Lou more things? That didn't seem right. With Lou, less was always more as long as the thought was there.

Clem took a step toward her, catching sight of the tears in Lou's eyes. "Are you disappointed? I know it's a simple gift, it's just—"

Lou put a finger against Clem's lips. "I love it, but it can't stay like that. Hold this?" Lou frowned, pushing the stocking into Clem's hands.

"Oh." Clem's heart sank all the way down to the scuffed floor.

MAYBE THE FRAME was wrong or...

Lou made her way to the wall, where she removed the frame and set it on the floor. Clem's heart broke just a little bit.

From the back pocket of her black jeans, Lou withdrew a sharpie. In stark black ink, she wrote '& Clementine' inside the house just below her own name.

Clem's breath hitched in her throat. She knew there were no guarantees, but framed graffiti of their names together seemed pretty close to a shot at forever.

Lou lowered the frame back into place and turned around, a proud smile on her face. "I've been meaning to do that." She recapped the sharpie and stuck it back into her pocket. "Okay, your turn."

Clem pulled open the stocking. It was light, nearly empty. The first thing she pulled out was a set of *day of the week* under-wear. The laugh bubbled up from deep inside her as she scanned the pack, her gaze snagging on the day with a strawberry print.

"You remembered."

Lou grinned at her, eyes crinkled at the edges. "Oh, that's a day I will never forget. Go on, there's something else in there."

Clem tucked the underwear under her arm and dug back into the stocking, swirling her hand around until she felt cool metal. She clutched it in her fingers and pulled it out. Dangling from a golden crescent moon key chain was a brass key. She raised an eyebrow at Lou. Excitement flared in her chest, but she pushed it down. They'd been taking things slow. Maybe the key was just for emergencies or—

"I was thinking that would make it a little easier when you move in. If that's something you want to do, I mean. Howl has been my home for so long, but now you're my home too. Something feels off when you're not here." Lou looked down at her feet. She seemed to be bracing herself for Clem's response.

Clem stepped forward and pulled Lou to her. "Yes. A thousand times yes. You and this wild bar are my home, too. Though I should probably wait to move in until this snow stops."

Lou laughed. "That's good because I still need to clear out an inch of drawer space for your two shirts."

"Hey!" Clem squeezed Lou's, sides making her squirm. "I own at least five shirts."

Lou pushed at her chest, breathless with laughter. "But how many of them are mine?"

"What's yours is mine, isn't it?"

"It sure is." Lou grinned, resting her forehead against Clem's. Both of them deliriously happy beneath the neon purple moon.

)(

Celebrate love with the **I Heart SapphFic Pride Collection**, eight standalone romances offering a taste of the very best modern sapphic fiction has to offer.
Be sure to subscribe to **I Heart SapphFic** to discover the latest in sapphic fiction every week! Because love is love, and everyone deserves a happily ever after.

IHeartSapphFic.com

Thank You!

Thank you for reading my book! The support of readers is what keeps me writing.

If you'd like to keep up with my releases and other news, you can sign up for my mailing list at www.lucybexley.com or follow me on twitter @bexley_lucy.

As an indie author reviews are critical to helping new readers discover my books. A review on Amazon and/or Goodreads is greatly appreciated, if you're so inclined!

Keep reading for a preview of Lucy's novel
***No Strings**.*

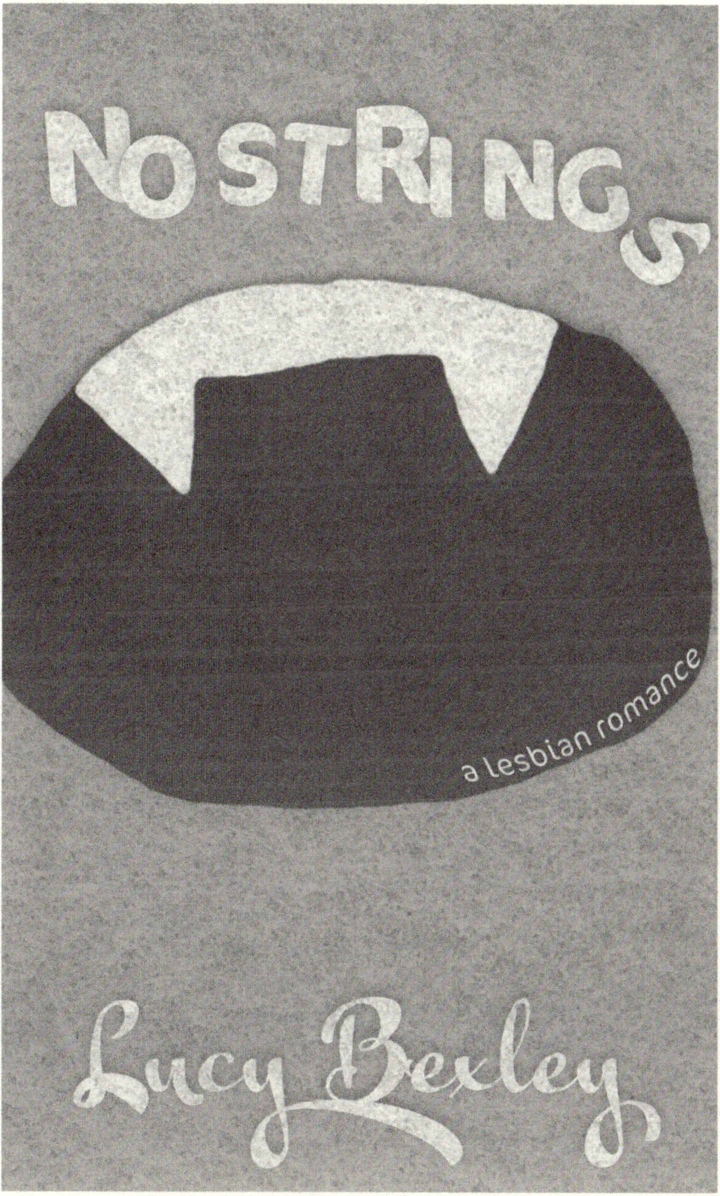
NO STRINGS
a lesbian romance
Lucy Bexley

Synopsis

Fun is the one thing **Elsie Webb** takes seriously. Though she'd be having a lot more of it if Haelstrom Media paid her enough to actually get out of debt. She's determined to hold out on contract negotiations for her kids' television show Fangley Heights until she gets what she deserves. There's only one problem, the head of the network just died and left her future more uncertain than ever.

Forty-eight hours and one funeral–that's all **Jones Haelstrom** has to get through before she can return to her life in LA that's as ordered and sparse as an IKEA showroom. When she steps in as CEO of her father's media company, Elsie Webb is her first problem to deal with. Elsie ends up challenging Jones in ways she never could have predicted, starting with an attraction neither can avoid.

As their attraction teeters on the edge of something more both agree to keep it casual. A no-strings agreement and disclosure to HR should be enough to keep things between Jones and Elsie from getting tangled, right?

Chapter One
Elsie

Was hitting someone with a puppet technically assault? Elsie's mind said yes, but her heart—and hopefully a jury—said no. She didn't want to risk hurting the star of the show, even if he was made of felt. Not to mention, that bundle of fabric and stuffing kept a roof over her head. Elsie grimaced. She didn't really think of Fangley like that —he was a more realized person than half of her colleagues.

The set of her show Fangley Heights was gearing up for a day of filming and Elsie was already nearing her limit.

"Stop trying to control the puppet. Relax. Let *it* control you."

Elsie cringed as Trey's hand came to rest on her shoulder like a small, hot pancake, lingering for a few scorching seconds before it slid off. Trey used his hypnotist's voice, something he'd learned from one of his afternoon acting workshops. Soft and wispy and boring as hell.

Elsie had to admit it was effective. Talking to Trey did make her want to pass out to escape any further interaction with him. His personality was a constant interruption. It was like he couldn't resist talking when she was trying to focus. Her entire job was to control puppets, and he was trying to make it into some kind of metaphorical, New Age thing instead of what it was: skillful manipulation. These puppets didn't even have strings.

As the nephew of the Haelstrom's second in charge, Trey was the network's golden boy even though Elsie carried the show and frankly, she was reaching her limit with being anyone's second choice. And okay, so maybe there was that one time she had insulted some 'important' sponsors by comparing their conversation to oyster crackers that have been in an old woman's purse since the Great Depression. So dry she was left choking on their dust. But still, people didn't give second chances anymore? Was it too late to stick a stipulation in her contract for next season that Trey's puppet, Smirch, would meet an untimely end? To date, giving Trey's puppet the worst possible name was her proudest accomplishment. Even if it was technically her roommate, Avery, who had come up with it during a particularly intense game of Jenga.

Elsie took a deep breath to keep from laughing at the memory of Avery knocking over the tower in exuberance when the name occurred to them. She checked her monitor as she raised her right arm over her head and above the small wall in front of her. One thing they don't tell you about puppeteering is, it makes your shoulders look great. Like seriously ripped. Well, mostly just the one shoulder, but still they should put that in the drama school brochure. Maybe she could contribute that tidbit so they'd stop asking her for money, which they absolutely knew she didn't have.

"I think if you just loosen your wrist, you could—"

Elsie sliced her gaze at Trey.

His warm whisper washed over her face and she shuddered. With her headset over her ears, she couldn't hear most of what he was saying, a small mercy, but the fact that she could see a bit of sweat on his forehead made his proximity vaguely threatening. What she'd like to do was control him. She'd donate him to Goodwill.

Elsie glanced back down at her monitor. Trey's fingers seared her skin as they wound around her wrist. His new gold watch jangled. She added 'demand a raise' to her running mental list of contract negotiation points. Elsie had a good feeling that all she had to do to get all the stipulations she wanted was to hold out for a few more days. The network would cave, she just knew it.

She took a deep breath and lowered her headset. "Are you trying to derail my entire process?"

"You just looked like you needed my help keeping this little guy steady." Trey reached up to touch Fangley. *Nobody* touched Elsie's puppet. She flicked her wrist so Fangley's hand smacked Trey's forehead before he had the chance. He blinked at her but made no move to call the authorities. So hitting someone annoying with a puppet technically wasn't assault, just as she'd suspected.

Rebecca, the showrunner, poked her head through the studio door and called Trey over. Elsie felt the tension drain out of her. Even Fangley's shoulders relaxed.

Elsie used the momentary peace to ready herself for the scene they were filming that afternoon, the one where Fangley and his cat sidekick, Ratatouille, put on way too much makeup in an attempt to fit in. The beautiful thing about the show was that its connection to reality could be tenuous as long as the bits were engaging. For example, why would a blue-tinted young vampire like Fangley and his Maine Coon sidekick think doing a full clown face of makeup would make them *less* conspicuous? Either way, she was looking forward to the arrival of Gabby, Ratatouille's handler.

The Fangley universe worked on a perfect kind of logic: very little of it.

Fangley Heights was in its third year of production. Most days Elsie couldn't believe her luck. She had picked essentially the most unemployable major, despite her father's desire for her to do something respectable. What he really meant was something with a high earning potential. Her father saw money as a down payment toward happiness, but he always forgot about the mortgage. Elsie had found no correlation between respectability and the size of her bank account. Quite the opposite, actually. Besides, she literally couldn't do math or handle bills. Even calculating tips was beyond her. On the other hand, the idea of saving people made something catch in her chest. So business and medicine were out. Her father wanted her to be employable. She wanted to be happy. But on *Fangley Heights*, most days she was both. Now if only everyone she'd ever met would stop making weird jokes about her being a puppeteer. At the very least bad jokes should be original.

But there wouldn't be a job, puppeteer or otherwise, if she couldn't get next season's agreement worked out. With each contractless day she barreled closer to an uncertain future.

She'd pushed her luck in negotiations, but why shouldn't she be better compensated? Fangley was her intellectual property, even if Haelstrom Media owned the trademark. Though it felt hard to say where everything would land with that in light of Hunter Haelstrom's recent passing. That little vamp went all the way back to a web series she'd done to kill the time she should have spent memorizing Hamlet in grad school. A little something productive to assuage her guilt over wasting time.

Her classmates tried to dismiss children's television as fluff, but this wasn't Punch and Judy hour. *Fangley Heights* had depth. It had whimsy with slightly charred edges. It only barely made sense. It was a show about an orphan vampire being fostered by a family in Brooklyn—a true American story. When Haelstrom Media had reached out to her just before graduation, she couldn't believe her luck. Elsie had felt so sure signing that contract would be her golden ticket, but she was young and naive. She didn't understand sub-clauses and percentages or that one paragraph they always threw in that stipulated media appearance requirements.

Maybe they'd learned their lesson after her season one sponsor disaster. She wished now she'd read that contract, committed every line to memory. Been asked to do a series of complicated crosswords before signing it. But she hadn't, because this was back when she still trusted people to do the right thing. She thought she'd pay off her loans, buy an apartment, and stop worrying about getting by. And yet, they were wrapping up season three and she was still sharing a place with Avery. Treating themselves meant the fancy two-for-one egg roll special.

Elsie was struggling, even though her character was a cultural icon to kids everywhere who were still learning to tie their shoelaces. Fangley was a celebrity. If a puppet could be a celeb. What was she saying? *Of course* a puppet could be famous. Oscar the Grouch? Rizzo? Iconic. Plus, as a nine-year-old vampire desperate to fit in, Fangley was relatable. For the pun-filled *Make-Over-Done* episode, Elsie had spent a solid week working with their local designer and props team on *Drag Fangley*, as she'd been thinking of him. He looked almost frightening this way, just this side of familiar, like a woman in a face-mask. A ghoul you could trust.

Elsie studied Fangley and wondered if she should have let the costume department and designers just craft a mask for him. They had made some latex prototypes to mimic a cold cream and blush treatment, but they all looked too much like meringue, the cold cream mask crested in waves. And when

Elsie had done a run-through of the scenes with Fangley and the mask, none of his expressions had been visible. Which upped the creep factor considerably past the tolerance of their kindergarten focus group.

The creation of a new Fangley had set them back several weeks and Rebecca warned they were approaching a meeting-with-the-boss level of being behind schedule. All of that was up-in-the-air now with the new boss still being uncertain. But Elsie had a good feeling about today. The "makeup" could be layered on individually to the new version of Fangley; she had the blush and eyelashes lined up on a table behind the wall of the set. Everything was ready to stick on Fangley's ghastly face. They'd be taking a Mr. Potato Head approach. There was probably a merchandising opportunity here, not that she was giving those ideas away to Haelstrom Media for free anymore. Elsie was still waiting to see any income from her point zero five percent share of sales from trademarked Fangley merchandise.

Elsie set about her pre-rehearsal routine. The choreography of puppets was intense. Like synchronized swimming, or one of those two-piece horse costumes. Reliably, Elsie was the ass of their outfit. In this week's episode, Amanda was playing Fangley's next-door neighbor and Trey was playing Fangley's nemesis, the elementary school's suspicious science teacher. A perfect role because it was easy for Elsie and Fangley to get into the mindset of hating him.

Elsie racked her body over the foam roller, extending her back and listening to it creak and pop as she raised her arms over her head. They had an area off to the side of the set for the explicit purpose of working out the kinks that came with contorting their bodies into puppeteering postures. Sometimes it took hours after a shoot for the stiffness in Elsie's torso to fade to tolerable. She brought her hands to the ground, bracing into a wheel shape. There was a whiff of the medieval about modern-day self-care; facial peels, cooking yourself in the sun, stretching your body over a cylinder until it gave way with a series of satisfying cracks. Torture therapy.

Elsie stood slowly, like she was being raised to standing. She punched in her code and freed Fangley from his case. The puppets sitting in a row in their glass enclosures, like little lockers, reminded Elsie of babies in a hospital nursery. Tempting to snatch but constantly monitored.

Elsie set Fangley on the fake stone wall as she considered his outfit. In an increasingly routine bout of interference, the network had insisted on Fangley wearing his black cape even though that made no sense if he was trying to fit in. Everyone knew Fangley preferred to only wear his cape at home, it was a comfort item, like a blanket. But there was concern from 'certain sectors of the market' that kids were forgetting that Fangley was a vampire because the show was doing too good a job of humanizing him. Even though vampires are human, technically. Though in this case, everyone's a puppet.

The door to the fake brownstone creaked open, and out stepped Trey. His conversation with Rebecca must have been brief for him to already be back on set; Elsie hadn't realized they'd finished talking already. So much for her break.

Now she was left to wonder how long Trey had been there, silently observing her? Add that to the list of things it was better to never know. Maybe the network should be more concerned about humanizing Trey.

He hopped down the stairs from the front door to the stage and clicked his heels. In her head, Elsie watched a fantasy of him slipping on a banana peel. Ah, the power of imagination.

"So are we going to do this scene, Els? I've got a good feeling about this afternoon."

"I always come to work, Trey."

"As long as you don't throw a fit about outfits again." He

reached for Elsie's shoulder but pulled his hand back as though her arm had been replaced with a bear trap. So, he had the ability to read body language after all.

"Having an opinion isn't throwing a fit. Are you going to throw a fit about your lines?" Trey's secondary character, Myrtle, was slated to be roped in by Fangley to help fix his makeup disaster in time for the spelling bee.

"No self-respecting ten-year-old girl would go along with Fangley's makeover plan."

"As someone who was once a ten-year-old girl, I can confirm that they're usually not very self-respecting."

Elsie breathed a sigh of relief as the director walked onto the set. The official signal that filming was about to start. Only Trey could be less annoying playing an evil puppet named Smirch than as himself.

THEY WERE deep into filming the second scene, the one with Trey's character, when he tripped over Elsie's not-at-all outstretched leg and they had to pause for the day. As they broke and the crew brought Trey ice, Rebecca waved Elsie over to the production control room.

This would be a good opportunity to get Rebecca's advice on her contract woes. Though the way her forehead was doing a Shar-Pei impression gave Elsie pause. Maybe she could see if the props department still had some of that cold cream from *Drag Fangley* on hand.

"So, I've got some bad news." Rebecca gave her a tight smile.

"Okay." *Shit.* "Is everything alright with Fangley?"

"Yes, of course. He's a puppet." Rebecca looked at Elsie like she was ridiculous for caring about the vampire that was literally keeping them both in a job. Millions of people cared about

Fangley. He even had his own fan club: The Fangers. Not a name she would have chosen, but the fanbase of five-year-olds were not to be swayed.

"I just got word from the network, and well, you're aware that Hunter Haelstrom passed away last week, right?"

"Yes, it's very unfortunate." Elsie nodded. It was one of those things that was sad in the *royal we* sense but not necessarily upsetting to her personally.

Rebecca shrugged. "He was in his 80s and never once looked me in the eye."

"Okay, so marginally sad. I assume some people are very upset. I didn't really know him, aside from the name on my check. Do you have any idea who's taking over? Have you heard anything?"

"I'm pretty sure the will named his widow. I've only met her once, at the Christmas party two years ago, but I got the sense she wasn't a fan of the work we do here on the Heights. Did you meet her there?"

"Oh, I think I was sick that day." Elsie shrugged. She probably had been sick—sick of absolutely everything going on at work. "Do you think she'll change the show? I mean, she wouldn't, right? The numbers are good and growing each year, but I don't trust Stu for a second not to try to oust us."

Rebecca raised her hands. "I don't have any information. I know these things aren't always logical. We should take every opportunity to make sure she knows how amazing this show is. And I think it's in our best interest to get this season wrapped this week even if it means spending a few nights together. I don't want Stu to see even the tiniest window to give this show to Trey."

"I don't mind pulling all-nighters, but you know I have a no-overnights-with-Trey policy." Elsie shuddered. "Besides, who will get Trey an air cast? He might even lose the leg."

"I've never met anyone who applies soccer foul performances to real life. Once I saw him get a paper cut and fall to the ground asking for stitches."

Elsie caught the gleam in Rebecca's eye. She almost never let loose on Trey. Rebecca was in her 50s and the consummate professional. At work, anyway. Rebecca at Chewy's, the bar down the street, was a delightful person to spend time hating things with.

Elsie wiped a tear of laughter from her eye and took a deep breath. She loved mean Rebecca. Was there anything more soul-nourishing than shit talk? "I'm so sad I missed that. Next time keep the camera running. We can add it to his showreel. Maybe get him some more dramatic roles."

"Noted." Rebecca's face sobered. "I think it's critical for everyone to sign and lock in their contracts. Please tell me you're not still dragging your feet on yours." Rebecca looked at Elsie like she was going to explain why she wasn't mad, just disappointed.

Elsie grimaced.

"I mean it about your contract, Elsie. You need to sign."

"Signing it is me saying it's okay to treat me this way. To underpay me while making a killing off of my ideas." Elsie's last contract draft had been an offer so laughably low that she'd used it to sop up her spilled Lucky Charms milk.

She had *created* the show, and yet every year it felt like she was begging them to pay her enough to buy fresh vegetables. The fact that an apple in Manhattan went for ten dollars was beside the point. Then again, wasn't some money better than no money at all? That's what Avery would tell her. *Just keep us in bubble bath and bubble tea, babe.* Maybe if the show went up a little and met her halfway she could consider maybe, possibly, signing her name on the dotted line. Which was always a solid line, actually.

"I know you wanted to hold out for more money, and I think they're ready to meet you at..." Rebecca glanced at her iPad. "Seven percent below your ask. I'd take it if I were you."

All wavering drained from Elsie. *Seven percent BELOW her ask?* Were they absolutely fucking with her? Last week it was five percent. She planted her feet. Absolutely fuck that. "That's a worse offer than before. How much below Trey's ask are you advising him to take?"

"Even if I had all the details, *which I don't*, you know I can't discuss the specifics of other people's contracts." Rebecca's eyes flitted to the monitor in the control room that showed Trey sitting on the floor holding ice on his ankle and scrolling through his phone.

"Right, because telling me how much I'm being screwed would be grossly unfair to you and the network." Elsie turned to leave. She had an overwhelming desire for this day to end.

Rebecca caught her arm. "Look, just think about it, okay? This show matters so much to all of us. I don't want to see your dream crumble."

But Elsie *had* thought about it. Fangley Heights was her baby. The only thing she'd ever invested herself in fully. But if she could love something she created this much, who was to say she couldn't do it again? She thought about the notebook on her desk, full of half-finished sketches and jokes that brought tears to her eyes. That had always been her barometer for good ideas—what reaction they sparked in her. If she didn't find her own jokes funny, why would anyone else?

Elsie pushed open the door. "Trust me, Rebecca, this is far from my only dream." The door clattered behind her. If drama school had taught her anything, it was the power of a dramatic exit.

Chapter Two
Jones

Jones was late. Her mother, Birdie, loved to say that she herself had never been late a day in her life, because there's no such thing as being late when you run the show, though Jones had a distinct memory of waiting until dusk for Birdie to pick her up after school. Watching the parking lot next to the playground empty until it was just her and Carl, the janitor. (Yes, as a child she'd spent enough time with the school janitor to be on a first-name basis.) Those were the days that Birdie claimed school simply ended earlier than expected.

Jones had inherited a lot of things, but her mother's brazen disregard for others wasn't among them. Jones was late because she didn't want any part of where she was headed. That, and she was currently responsible for another very small human who walked in slow motion. And it was probably even more important for her to be on time now that she was the one in charge of her father's company, however temporarily. She needed to give the impression that it might be permanent, otherwise no one would take her seriously.

After the funeral, Jones' stepmother had booked herself a few days at the spa. It felt so weird to Jones to call someone eleven years younger her stepmother. When Charity asked for time to herself, Jones had wanted to be annoyed, but she understood that Charity was facing a life much different from the one she'd had a week ago. If Birdie had taught her anything, it was that mothers didn't have to be selfless. Sometimes the very act of being selfish, knowing what you needed and taking it, was the thing that made us better to those we care about. So Jones had said she'd stay with her father's child. Well, his other child. Her brother—she needed to get used to saying that. Even if it was just until Charity got back from her mud baths and mourning. Only three days to go, or closer to two depending on what time Charity got back on Saturday for Bentley's birthday. And then Jones could go back to her life. Back to only caring for herself. She'd pick up right where she left off, reviewing the new thousand-dollar snail serum in every A-lister's virtual cart. She could feel the hydrating benefits already.

The city sky gave a roll of thunder. Though it could have been a building being demolished. Both equally common occurrences. Actually, the city probably had more demolition dust storms than actual storms.

Jones glanced down to check on Bentley to make sure she'd remembered his rain jacket but he was gone. Children are like assassins, most dangerous when they're silent. She stopped in the middle of the sidewalk. Other pedestrians on West 42nd streamed around her; one gentleman cross-checked her and knocked her bag to the ground. Apparently Mr. Hockey Moves had places to be, but he could have looked a little less smug about it. Jones shook it off. It wasn't like she was a tourist, even if she technically hadn't lived here in close to two decades. She retrieved her bag then widened her stance to withstand further attempts to trample her as she spun around slowly and scanned her surroundings.

Jones had been in charge for three days and she'd already lost her brother. She'd never realized panic was a thing she could taste—it sat like battery acid in the back of her throat.

She was looking for a small child dressed like an executive on his yacht. Chinos, boat shoes, one of those little belts with the whales on it—or was it lobsters? Either way, some sort of sea dweller she'd never mess with. One might think this look to be distinctive, but in Midtown it was yuppie camo. When it came to dressing him, she'd done the best with the options available to her. It wasn't just their thirty-seven-year age gap that was making this weird. At over forty, Jones had decided long ago that kids were not in her future. And now, everyone from the cashier at the bodega where she bought milk for her coffee that morning, to the owner of the florist for her father's memorial kept referring to Bentley as her son. Most times, she didn't have the energy to explain the intricacies of their modern family. It was, in a word, a mindfuck.

Jones spotted his tiny figure dressed in an absurdly expensive Day-Glo sweater crouched on the sidewalk half a block back. She released a sharp exhale of relief. What was he—oh god he was picking up a piece of gum. Kids had immune systems of Teflon, right? Or at least city kids did. Honestly, for something Bentley could pick up off of a street in Manhattan, gum was pretty tame and unlikely to be lethal.

She walked back into the rushing stream of oncoming pedestrians and squatted down next to him. "Hey, buddy, can you stay with me?"

He looked up at her with the same slate blue eyes as her own, and it was then that she noticed he was chewing on something. Crunching, really, the sound as one with the jackhammer one avenue over. They really would be putting her immune system theory to the test.

Why would anyone leave a child in her care? Even if she had agreed, a few days was a few days too long.

Jones held out her hand for her brother's, but instead of reaching for it he leaned forward and spit into it. Gum, hard as a flattened penny landed in her palm. This was one for the books. Jones Haelstrom, kneeling on a city street with a palmful of spit and fossilized gum. She threw it into the oncoming traffic like a grenade.

What would Birdie have to say about this? *It's New York, if you're not eccentric there, you're not alive.*

Eccentric and in need of a shower. Oh, right, and really fucking late for this meeting with Haelstrom Media's lawyers.

Jones looked down at her knees. She was in the dress she'd worn to the funeral a few days before. For some reason, she'd expected to go back home to California shortly after the burial, before whatever this new interminable situation was. But what else could she do except offer to stay when Charity said she planned to leave Bentley with his nanny? *You could have gone straight to JFK and boarded a flight home,* Birdie's voice in her head supplied helpfully. Jones had agreed to stay, and now she was stuck like gum to the sidewalk, getting walked all over, while Charity was mummifying herself in a mixture of kelp and clay.

Jones scraped her palm on the concrete and stood.

She grabbed Bentley's hand and tried very hard not to think about why it was sticky.

THE BUILDING'S lobby had a mausoleum quality, all smooth white stone and echoes of ghosts. The double-height ceiling stretched upward, drawing her eye to a banner that hung above the gold elevators. It was a tapestry portrait, faded in the sun, so that the man's tie was now a magenta, but she'd know those icy eyes anywhere. Her father stared back at her like some sort of larger-than-life communist propaganda. Welcoming. Humbling. Deeply unsettling.

He had always considered himself above others.

The security guard glanced at her ID and waved her through. His generic black suit and the clear wire dangling along his neck like an errant curl, brought to mind a secret service agent. Well, even if the security was lax, he at least seemed prepared for secret comms about lunch deliveries. *The Eagle's chicken caesar wrap has landed.*

She knotted her free hand around the strap of her bag. On her other side, Bentley swayed repeatedly against her leg, knocking her off balance in her heels. How could three days create a year's worth of exhaustion? And why the hell was she wearing heels? Right, because she'd only brought one other pair of shoes, and they were her favorite slip-ons, which she loved too much to put them through the marble and meetings and misery of this day. Plus, without her father around, there was no one to get a rise out of by dressing down like she had when she'd interned for him in college.

For the first time in her life, Jones had under-packed. The call that her father had passed came in the middle of the night, and she'd thrown a few things in a carry-on. She figured she'd buy something somber in New York and take the first return flight she could find after a reasonably respectful amount of time. Say, twelve hours after his funeral. She'd definitely planned to be back for work on Monday. And, well, it was *a Monday*. And this was technically work. Only instead of returning to the silly little lifeforce-draining lifestyle articles her editor gave her about green juices purifying the soul, she was in a cold Manhattan lobby re-wearing her funeral clothes. Not that Jones would turn down a super fruit soul cleanse herself about now, such was the weakness of her resolve in that moment.

The elevator doors slid shut, and Jones met her own gaze in the mirrored surface. The doors had a slightly wavy effect, like a carnival funhouse where no one exits feeling good about themselves. It was like she was gazing at her future self, and that self was...exhausted. And oddly puffy. If she didn't find a place in New York that sold vegetables instead of bagels, she wouldn't survive the week.

Bentley wriggled his hand free and smashed a few extra buttons. *Perfect.*

They'd be taking the scenic route.

What was a few more minutes? When you're late you're late. And Bentley pressing buttons meant he wasn't eating street gum. Maybe she was starting to understand parents who were chill amid the chaos. She leaned back against the wall, taking some pressure off her feet. These heels were the devil's vise.

Bentley's reflection loomed. He was a captain of chaos, a titan of terror. He could pass for a boy CEO of a startup, heading to a meeting with an angel investor. Jones wished she'd thought to dress down as a power move. His look said *money matters to me but impressing you doesn't,* and frankly, Jones would be trying to channel that energy for the next hour of her life. She *hoped* this meeting didn't take more than an hour. She still needed to figure out dinner, and Bentley kept rejecting her salad options. Even the ones with exciting things like sunflower seeds or blueberries. Kids were impossible.

)O(

THE STUDIO WAS STILL BRIGHT, even though it was mostly deserted. A few people lingered near a small set, including a woman wearing a headset and arranging a jumble of stuffed animals.

Behind her, a throat cleared. Every muscle in Jones' neck locked.

"Ms. Haelstrom?"

A man with an egg-shaped head and a wreath of hair extended his hand. When he moved, his head gleamed brightly in the lights. "Stu Winkle, I'm not sure if you remember me. Do you still go by Joanie?"

Jones freed her hand from Bentley's and placed it in Stu's. He very nearly stifled his grimace as she transferred a bit of stickiness. Oh yes, she definitely remembered this guy. When she was a kid, he once offered her candy that was so warm from his pocket, the thought of it still made her gag. By the time she'd interned here during her senior year, his offers had been a lot more suggestive, though equally gross. Still, as much as she might find him distasteful, she couldn't just ignore her father's right-hand man, at least not while he was partially in charge of Haelstrom Media.

"Of course, Stu, good to see you still making people uncomfortable in the workplace. You can call me Jones." He kept shaking her hand until she pulled it from his grasp. Another maneuver she'd borrowed from Bentley.

Stu laughed like he was in on some joke between them. "Come on now, I was just being welcoming."

Jones ignored him. After her years of dealing with Stu and not wanting to annoy her dad, it felt nice to finally speak her mind. She squatted down. "Bentley, how about you go over there and play with the toys?"

Bentley took off running, his little boat shoes squeaking on the floor. Stu reached out a hand as though to pull the boy back.

Jones shot Stu an amused look. "Sorry, I probably should have asked first. Is that okay? I mean I could always bring him to the meeting."

Stu's face sobered at the mention of Bentley in the board-room. "Oh no, this is perfect. Fangley Heights babysits kids after school every day. It's their bread and butter. I'll just fire off a quick text, and someone will be here to watch him in just a minute."

She followed Stu to the door, but when he held it open with half his body blocking it, she stayed back. Jones wasn't exactly large, but she was an adult and there was no way her hips were getting through that space without him "accidentally" brushing against her. No thank you. The silence stretched as they both waited for the other to break and move first. Jones nodded at him, and after another moment he pushed the door wide and shuffled through. She'd hold her own door with two broken arms to avoid the feeling she was getting from him. Jones had gotten enough slime on her from the gum incident already. And she'd had enough actual contact on their walk from the train to last her a lifetime. Only the F train could make her miss the 405. At least in LA, accidental contact looked like being rear-ended.

Jones followed Stu through the labyrinth of hallways, her nervous energy ricocheting in her chest like a lightning bug trapped in a jar. Everything looked so different from when she'd interned here all those years ago, Haelstrom Media had moved up in the world both in terms of cultural cache and by two whole floors in this building. She fought the impulse to run and instead slowed to let herself fall a few paces behind. Her eyes scanned the gleaming white floors. She expected to see a trail of slimy footprints in the shape of his loafers, but they just let out a pitiful little dog toy squeak. If only she knew where she was going, she could excuse herself and find a restroom or a quiet corner to take a few deep breaths and center herself. She did a quick safety check for an exit sign and locked eyes with a woman who was watching them with an amused expression on her face.

The woman's gaze drifted over Jones appraisingly. Jones felt the heat of her green eyes like the sun on her skin. So maybe not amused. *But interested?*

Jones looked down at her weird funeral clothes. Okay, interest was unlikely. Maybe she was just sizing Jones up as the new boss. Jones straightened to her best boss height, which was just her real height, but more serious.

Jones watched as the woman raked her fingers through her shoulder-length brown hair, sweeping it to one side so that her curls shot out erratically. It was wavy in an uneven way that reminded Jones of finally letting her hair down at the end of the night. Sweet relief. The freedom of no one left to impress.

Though, if Jones was being honest, the woman had an air of not wanting to impress at all. It was *nice*. And the complete opposite of how she currently felt. So much of her life was people trying to win her over because of her last name and the reputation that came along with it. But this woman had her arms crossed, and she was openly staring. It was straight up subway etiquette. Her ripped coveralls weren't artful, but well worn, almost like the holes hadn't been there when she bought them. How novel. She had them unzipped to the waist with the arms knotted around her midriff, like she'd stopped midway through undressing. Coveralls should not be sexy. Everything about the woman was starting to feel deeply unfair to Jones. Her t-shirt had a weird pattern, black and purple and green. It reminded Jones of a bowling alley. An establishment she'd been invited to exactly once, and she'd promptly sprained her wrist. After that, Birdie had instituted a strict no sports birthday party and bat mitzvah rule, which was fine by her.

Was the OshKosh B'gosh woman on the crew for one of the shows? That would explain the giant hammer she was dragging behind her. It looked impossibly heavy. Jones wasn't a gym person and had no real concept of weight, beyond the fact that her groceries were always too heavy to carry, which was why she got them delivered.

Stu had kept walking, content to let this woman struggle. How irresponsible. Well, that was a potential workplace injury risk Jones wasn't willing to take the liability for. Not on her first day as interim CEO. Plus, if she offered her help, maybe she could do the impossible and make a friend here, instead of just meeting with weird leering men in bespoke suits.

"Can I help you with that?" Jones stepped toward the woman, before she realized she'd made up her mind. Anything to avoid a lawsuit.

"With what?"

"That, um, hammer? I don't want you to get hurt." That's right. Jones was calm, logical. She had everything under control.

The woman's voice tipped into laughter. "Sure," she said, her eyes flashing and she flicked her wrist.

Shit. Not even an hour in and she was going to need a hospital. She'd never caught anything in her life, and she definitely wasn't going to start with a hammer. Jones ducked and braced for impact. The hammer glanced off her shoulder, and she waited for the pain to come; for her bones to become dust upon impact. Apparently, there would be a lawsuit after all.

And then the hammer bounced. Because Jones, the most gullible woman alive, was so out of her element that she thought the studio would have a mammoth tool lying around instead of some foam prop.

The other woman gave her a sheepish grin. The green in her

eyes bloomed. "Oh, shit, sorry. I thought you'd try to catch it. Not...whatever that was." She gestured vaguely up and down Jones' body.

Jones would not blush. She was in charge today. "Why would I try to catch a hammer? It looks like the ones used to drive stakes on a railroad."

The woman shrugged. "I wasn't around when the first railroads were built. But this is television, baby. Nothing here is real."

She'd delivered that last line with an honest-to-God wink. People who could pull off winking had entirely too much power.

Jones felt rage and embarrassment fighting for prominence. And something else just beneath the surface, something that felt a lot like attraction. Since when was a woman throwing something at her a turn-on? *Say something. Anything.* Jones searched her brain for something quippy. "But *I'm* real." *Ugh, not that.*

Green eyes looked her up and down again before the woman took a step back, then another. "Good to know. Thanks for offering to help. And sorry for hitting on you, you know... with the hammer."

The woman sent Jones a smirk that she felt low in her stomach. Jones was still watching her incredulously as she started walking and crashed full force into the squishy wall of Stu's body. *This could not be her life.*

"Your father never mentioned you were the chivalrous Haelstrom." A crocodile grin split Stu's face. Jones wanted to throw him back into the swamp.

"I'm surprised he mentioned me at all. But sure, I like to lend a hand when I can."

Something rustled behind them and Jones turned to look. She couldn't help it. The woman was pulling her hair back up into a messy bun, which, in turn, was causing her shirt to ride up and show—

"Yes, I can see that. Or a shoulder, in this case. Do you need some ice for that embarrassment?"

Jones fought back the sunburn feeling rising on her cheeks. She only wanted ice if it was a glacier drifting slowly out to sea with her on it. "Are you ready?"

"If you're sure you don't need medical attention, then I'm glad you're still interested in doing business today, since that's why you're here. Right this way." Stu was looking at her like he knew her, which she didn't. He didn't know a single thing.

"Who was that?" She demanded, forcing some authority into her voice. She needed to get this day back on track, now.

"Oh, no one really. Just Elsie, she works on Fangley Heights, that kids show."

"Doesn't that show have the fourth highest ratings on the network?"

"You should know better than to believe everything you read on the internet, Jones. If you wanted the data, you should have asked me for it. Besides, the show could be even more successful without Elsie Webb."

He held the door to the conference room open for her. Never trust a man who holds a door in such a way that you need to brush past him to enter. Stu had perfected that art. Had he learned nothing from his earlier attempt in the studio? Jones grabbed the door handle from him and pulled it so far open its hinges creaked. *There, enough room for everyone.* As she entered the room, she glanced down the polished table to the owlish lawyer sitting at the end. The space was a portrait of everything she'd never wanted. None of this should be her problem. Not the clothes, or the kid, or the embarrassment still flooding her veins from the hallway incident. Her father hadn't trusted her with anything since she'd bombed her internship. Though it wasn't really her fault that she'd refused to take coffee and lunch orders. Her father had accused Jones of being too much Birdie's daughter. Not willing to do what it took to succeed, just looking for a handout. But she wasn't, not really. She just didn't feel much like his daughter either.

Stu pulled out a chair with a dramatic bow, like it was some kind of gallant offering. Jones pulled out the next one over and sat down. This wasn't some restaurant without prices on the menu. He was not going to be in control of this for much longer.

"Sorry to call you in today, Ms. Haelstrom. If these contracts could have waited, believe me, we would have let them." The man extended his hand toward Jones. His grip was bruising. Like he didn't know the difference between a handshake and arm wrestling. "Chuck Westley. I'm your lawyer, well, the network's, professionally speaking."

Chuck and Stu, unreal. "Sure, nice to meet you. Jones is fine."

"So Joanie, like Chuck here was saying, we've gotta hammer out these contracts. No pun intended. The longer the negotiations drag on, the more tempted the talent will be to ask for more. You wouldn't believe how greedy they are. And believe me, we're already giving them plenty. It's children's television for God's sake and these people are confusing it with art."

"Again, it's Jones. Like I mentioned earlier, I did some research last night. It seems like the Children's Entertainment sector is where we make the majority of our money. Especially through merchandising."

"Like *I* said earlier, you can't believe everything you read on the internet." Stu smirked.

Jones sat up straighter. "Okay, so which part of that was incorrect?"

"None of it, I just meant generally speaking. But sure. It's easy to sell puppets and plush toys to five-year-olds. That's hardly an accomplishment." Stu's eyes shone black. A shark in the water. "I was telling you earlier that the show could be more successful. Your father and I were in early talks about a spinoff without Fangley's character. It would focus on Smirch, Trey's character, he's very popular."

Jones hummed noncommittally as she pulled a notebook from her bag and quickly sketched the path they'd taken through the halls. Stu might have escorted her in, but she'd be seeing herself out.

"I think we have a real opportunity here, Trey could be a star, but instead he's stuck listening to Elsie. We're wasting a lot of potential on Fangley Heights."

"Huh. Noted." Jones gave him a close-lipped smile and pulled forward the stack of contracts Chuck had slid toward her. No part of her wanted to review legalese. But who did? Contracts and terms and conditions, you only read them if you had to. And even then, she only skimmed before clicking accept. "So what exactly do you need from me?"

"Just a cursory review so you can sign off on the terms listed. This is really just following protocol. We've been hammering out these details for weeks. Think of yourself as a rubber stamp. Just a name on the line." The lawyer smiled warmly.

"O-kay," she said slowly, fanning through the top pages of the stack like they were a flip book about to reveal their stop-motion secret to her. "I'm not sure why I'd want to think of myself like that. Anything I should know about this contract for Elsie Webb with the red flag on it?"

"Well, Elsie's a bit of a handful. She got us in some hot water at a charity event last year where she refused to confirm Fangley's orientation," Chuck said.

"She got questions about the orientation of a vampire

puppet? A child vampire puppet?" Jones was failing to see how Elsie was to blame in this example.

"I don't think it's unreasonable that people want to know what messages their children are getting," Stu said, his voice getting louder with each successive syllable. "But she made a joke of it. Once Elsie makes up her mind about something, there's nothing that can sway her. Everything becomes a moral issue for her. That night she asked the host why so many adults at the gala were sexually interested in puppets. And then later she apologized for kink shaming and recommended Furry conventions to those interested."

Jones held in a laugh, squinting through the glee that story made her feel. She would have paid good money to have been at that event. "And that bothered you all?"

"Of course it did. She lost us a lot of money, but we haven't figured out a way to do Fangley Heights without her. Anyway, we've had some back and forth on her contract negotiations, but I don't think we'll be getting much more pushback." Chuck pushed his glasses up his nose and flashed a look toward Stu.

Well, that sounded ominous. Stu's obvious push for his nephew Trey was a red flag but unsurprising. In this town flattery and nepotism got you everywhere. But something else felt off about this pressure to sign, too, something lurking beneath the surface of these negotiations. She needed an out with a little time to think, and for once she had one in the form of a probably still sticky little brother. "You know what? I left Bentley hanging out down there, and I don't feel great about that. How about I take these with me and review them tonight?"

"Well, like I said, Joanie—"

Jones cleared her throat and Stu paused as she leveled him with a glare.

"Ahem—Ms. Haelstrom, there's not much for you to

review. I've signed off on these terms, and Chuck made them airtight. You giving the okay is just a formality." Stu removed a pen from his pocket and pushed it toward Jones. She slid it back with a single finger. It was unpleasantly warm.

Jones glanced at her map, committing it to memory before snapping her notebook closed. "But a required formality, right? As the current CEO?"

"Interim, but yes. That's technically correct." Chuck nodded.

"Well, the world hinges on technicalities, doesn't it?" Jones lifted the contracts and shuffled them into a neat pile with a few taps on the conference table. The sound was louder than she'd expected, and the nervous look that passed between Chuck and Stu sent a little jolt of power through her. Maybe being temporary CEO of her father's company would have some perks after all. "Okay then. Have your assistant reach out tomorrow, and we can arrange a time for someone to pick these up. I'll leave any changes or clarifications in the margins."

Stu smiled wanly. "Just to be clear, Jones, we really don't have time for changes. Your father felt fine about these. We need to have them wrapped up before Monday, or we'll be in a very precarious position, bargaining wise."

"Well, let's hope no changes are needed then, since I'm not my father and I don't see his signature on these." She dug her heels into the carpet and pushed back from the table, sliding the contracts into her oversized leather purse.

Stu stood quickly, knocking over the bottle of water she hadn't given him a chance to open. "I'll show you out."

"That's not necessary. Just two lefts and a right?" Jones turned and raised her eyebrows at Chuck for confirmation. If she had to look at Stu's slimy face again, she'd need to shower in industrial-strength cleaner.

"You learned your way around pretty fast." Chuck smiled at her, but it was more like a grimace.

"I'm surprised my father never mentioned I'm a quick study. Well then, I'm sure we'll be in touch." She pulled the door closed behind her, wishing she still had that giant hammer to swing.

)O(

If you enjoyed this sample, you can continue reading *No Strings* right here!

About the Author

Lucy Bexley writes romcoms where queer women trip over things and fall... in love with each other. Her stories balance laughter and love with real-world struggles such as anxiety and addiction. Lucy lives in Boston with her partner, pets, and several cases of seltzer. She's the author of six sapphic romances including Must Love Silence and No Strings. When she's not writing jokes in a Word doc, she's writing them on Twitter.

https://www.lucybexley.com

89669950R00173